The Soul Searcher
A Middle Aged Adventure
by
Kathy Whitney Barr

Chapter 1

Libby O'Malley planned to go on a low carb diet again, but instead she took a hard right turn into the first 7-11 she saw. This was unfortunate since she had already worked her way up to a size 16W (W as in Women's not Wide). She was pushed over the edge by a comment on the radio. Normally, she would have laughed, but this was the end of very long, very hard day.

First, Libby was returning from taking her youngest son, her baby, to freshman orientation and was going home to a very empty nest. The college administrators assured her that leaving said youngest son, Brendan, three thousand miles away in California was a great idea. However, because he was eighteen and obviously an adult, they couldn't tell him what to do, and she wouldn't get any information from them about him. Nevertheless, tuition bills would be sent regularly. The dean's parting words were, "All right, parents, start your engines." Which sounded to Libby a lot like, "Don't let the screen door hit you in the backside on the way out."

Second, when she walked out of the Philadelphia airport she felt like someone slapped her in the face with a dirty, wet dishrag. It was just another hot, humid night on the East Coast, but it was exactly the same weather as the day she and Brendan flew out from PHL, spurring him to say, "Why would anybody live here if they didn't have to?"

Finally, fifteen minutes into the hour's drive from the airport to Libby's house in the Pine Barrens, a so-called expert on NPR said, "Let's face it, after a woman reaches menopause and is out of her childbearing years, Nature is ready to toss her like an old shoe."

"You pompous twit," Libby exploded and wrenched the radio knob so hard it came off in her hand. And the walls came tumbling down.

Talking to God might have helped, but Libby was annoyed with Him just then. Talking to her priest, a friend or her dog may have worked. Nature might even have saved her if it had been daytime or at least a clear night. Too bad it was one o'clock in the morning and overcast so none of these rescues were available. She was a people person, nature girl caught alone in the overcast night, and she was on California time so it was hours before she would sleep.

At 7-11, Libby bought everything and anything – all the junk food her heart desired as well as eggs, milk and bread. When she got home, she put the real food in the refrigerator. Grabbing a spoon, she lugged the rest of it into the family room and sat in front of the TV. This type of eating required background entertainment. She spooned triple chocolate fudge ice cream onto a large chocolate chip cookie. She pressed another cookie on top making the first of many customized ice cream sandwiches. When the bag of cookies was empty, she went into the kitchen during a commercial to get a tall glass and an iced tea spoon. She then moved onto root beer and chocolate ice cream floats. By three o'clock in the morning the ice cream carton was empty and she felt sick.

Libby abandoned everything on the coffee table. After a stop in the bathroom, she went to bed. She drew her knees up to her stomach to relieve some of the pressure. "What a nincompoop you are, Libby. Tomorrow we go back to being a grown-up." After a monumental burp, she felt slightly better. Crashing from a long day and a sugar high, she fell asleep.

Libby woke at noon, still on California time, so it felt like nine o'clock in the morning. She was jet lagged and queasy. Chamomile tea was all she could stomach. Mug in hand, she stopped short at the threshold of the front room. Empty Amazon boxes, shopping bags, shoe boxes and clothes that didn't make the final cut of Brendan's wardrobe for college lay scattered all over. The scene reminded her of coming home with her firstborn, Matthew.

Returning from the birthing center, everything looked the same as the previous morning when she and Frank had left - a cup of tea on the table, shoes in the hallway and the notebook, into which they had written the timing of contractions, rested on the arm of Frank's chair. It was deceptively the same, yet their whole lives had changed overnight.

This time, Libby came home alone, no baby, no Frank. If Frank were here, this empty nest thing wouldn't be so bad. Frank, may he rest in peace, was one reason she wasn't talking to God just yet. God had decided Frank deserved his heavenly reward three years ago at the age of fifty-four. Libby's mourning was a work in progress. Sometimes she got ahead of the sorrow and the guilt, but then something like this would happen and put her back into the midst of them again. She knew she needed to hold onto God like the lifeline that He was, but sometimes she got obstinate. It didn't hurt anybody but herself. "I need Victor," she said.

Libby made a U-turn and walked away from the front room. She got carrots from the kitchen and went out the back door. Carrie Bannon, her next-door neighbor, had Victor. Libby walked the quarter-mile long trail through the woods to Carrie's house. As the barn came into view, Libby heard whinnying. Three horses ran up to the corral fence. Libby fed each of them carrots. "You're so beautiful," she said, stroking velvety muzzles and patting strong necks.

A ball of orange fur streaked toward Libby. It was her little, red Pomeranian that looked like a fox. He jumped into her arms. "Hello, Victor! Did you miss me, dog friend?" she inquired rubbing his belly and kissing his nose. She put the dog down, because after him, a little girl arrived. "Hi, Miss Wibby," she said.

Libby picked her up and swung her around, "Hello, Kylie. How's my girl?" Kylie shrieked and laughed.

Bringing up the rear, was Kylie's mother, Carrie. "Welcome home, Libby," Carrie said giving Libby a hug. "I'll make some tea and you can tell me how it went at USC?"

"Perfect," said Libby, carrying Kylie on her hip.

Inside, as Carrie put the kettle on, Libby started her story.

"Brendan was definitely anxious. He was irritable during the flight and in the hotel, but when we got on campus, he was more himself. The students, who helped the freshmen move in, were great. They carried most of Brendan's stuff up for us. We were unpacking when this tall, twenty-something guy walked into the dorm room carrying a suitcase. His face was gaunt, his ears had multiple piercings and he had a short Mohawk haircut. 'You, Brian?', he asked. Brendan says, 'I'm *Brendan.*' 'Whatever,' the guy says."

"Oh, wow," Carrie said with a nervous laugh.

"Yeah, so the guy sticks out his hand and says, 'I'm Golden Eagle.' Brendan looks surprised, but I shake the young man's hand and say, 'I'm Mrs. O'Malley. It's good to meet you.' Then Brendan says, 'I took the bed near the window, hope that's okay with you,' and the he guy says, 'I don't give a crap, where he sleeps.'"

"Oh my God!" said Carrie.

"Yeah, I almost wet my pants. I thought he was talking to me about Brendan. Then a teenaged boy comes in the room carrying a laundry basket full of stuff and says, 'Hi, Brendan, how ya doin'? I guess you met my cousin already.' Then 'Golden Eagle' breaks into a big grin. It took a minute for me to get it. They'd punked us!"

"You're kidding! What's the roommate's real name?"

"Dave."

"Dave? Dave Golden Eagle?"

"No, no. Dave Mills, but he is Native American on his mother's side. He and his mother and sister live with his grandmother on a Lakota reservation in North Dakota. After that, we all had a big laugh and everything was fine."

Carrie ferried the tea, three mugs, plates and some muffins over to the table. "Do you want to have a tea party with us, Kylie?"

"Yes, please," Kylie answered from Libby's lap.

"Have some muffins, Libby," said Carrie.

"No, thanks, I've got to get back on Atkins. Brendan finally put pictures from his graduation up on Facebook. I look more like an offensive lineman than he does. So far, he's got the pictures with me in them tucked away in an album, where the whole world can't see them. I told him I want him to keep them there, but it feels like blackmail waiting to happen."

"You look fine, Libby," Carrie said.

"That's very sweet of you, but this summer, there were graduation parties or college send-offs almost every weekend. I meant to do more power walking. I never found the time, but I always found the cake." Libby took a sip of tea. "Brendan was teasing me about my chubby cheeks. He said, 'I may have a gut, Mom, but I can hide it under my clothes. You can't hide your face.' My sons are too honest for my own good."

Libby bounced Kylie in her knee, "You would never say something like that to your mommy would you, Kylie?"

"Mommy is the prettiest," said Kylie.

"That's right," Libby said giving the girl a hug. "Oh, Carrie, I know these years are so busy, but try to enjoy them." Libby thought back to her little boys' dimpled hands, downy arms and easy hugs and kisses. "Matt is twenty-four, Will is twenty-two and Brendan is eighteen. They're all grown-up. I can't believe it went by so fast." Libby buried her nose in Kylie's dark brown curls so Carrie wouldn't see her tearing up. Libby didn't want to give any hint of the sadness that just drove her from her own home

"You're my mother mentor, Libby, you know I mind what you say," said Carrie.

"Oh, Carrie, you're already doing so much better than I did at this stage. You're so calm and patient," Libby said, giving Carrie's hand a squeeze. "I should get home. Brendan left a mess to be dealt with. Thank you for taking care of Victor while I was gone."

"I'm getting the best of that deal," Carrie said. "Are you ready to take care of the horses again, while I take Ray up to the VA hospital next week?"

"I'm looking forward to it. I'm planning to take Baldy out for a trail ride." Libby paused, then continued with concern in her voice, "How's your hubby feeling?"

"He has his good days and bad days. The chemo really takes it out of him. They'll do a scan in a month or so to see how it's working."

"Where is he?"

"At work, he says it keeps his mind busy and it pays the bills," Carrie said with a shrug.

"One thing he doesn't need to worry about is the horses. They'll be fine. Do you need help with them while you're home? I could easily come over."

"No, not yet, Libby."

"Okay then, I'll see you in a few days," Libby said with hugs and kisses all around.

Libby and Victor walked home. Every day was a good day for Victor. When she walked with him in public his foxy good looks - pointed nose, erect ears, bushy tail and red glossy coat - and friendly demeanor created a charisma few people could resist. It was like being out with a celebrity. People ooh'ed and ahh'ed over him and asked if they could pet him, which Victor took as his rightful due. But when he and Libby were alone, she was his queen and he, her loyal subject. Now in the woods, he lifted his nose in the air. His nostrils quivered and he ran ahead stopping to sniff the ground to gather the daily news. He saw a squirrel, which he barked at and chased up a tree. Victor waited proudly for Libby to catch up and see his conquest. His long tail curled over his back showing its white underside and waved like a pompom.

"What a fierce beast you are!" Libby complimented him.

They passed through the orchard, Libby wanted to see what had changed in the five days she'd been gone. Caring for fruit trees was work. They had to be sprayed for insects and diseases, pruned, fertilized three times a year and watered, watered, watered. The satisfaction Libby got from them made it all worthwhile. She watched over the trees throughout the seasons with parental pride and childlike wonder, and nothing was quite as good as ripe fruit picked from your own trees. Years ago when the boys were young, they climbed the mature trees, played hide-and-seek and tag in the orchard, caught lightening bugs and ate lots fruit.

Libby checked the apples first. They were formed and ripening. "You are coming along beautifully," she said, gently touching clusters of Golden Delicious and Winesap apples that weighed down their branches. "After the first frost, you'll be perfect."

The peaches, figs and plums had already produced a good harvest. Over the summer Libby made jars of preserves for family and friends.

Libby then passed by the cherry trees. The sight of them pricked her heart. "Poor, poor things," she said touching the bare twigs that were all that was left of four cherry trees. This was her biggest horticultural fiasco. Three years ago, the autumn after Frank died, Libby planted two Bing Cherry trees and two Black Tartarians for cross-pollinating. The first spring, they were too young and produced a few flowers, but no cherries. The next season, she got one cherry between the four trees. This spring, the cherry trees leafed and blossomed, but a week later they were dead, not dormant, but dead, and she had no idea why. They seemed cursed, but she still couldn't bring herself to cut them down. She took out her pocket knife and cut some sample twigs to send to the county agriculture agent for testing.

Libby walked up to the back of the house and turned on the sprinklers for the apple trees. With a hose attached to a second faucet, she watered the rock garden and flower beds in the backyard and the vegetable garden on the south side of the house. She walked around to the front yard, opened the tap for that hose, and gave the shaded flower beds near the house a drink. Banks of pink and white impatiens were broken up by green and white variegated hostas. Along the driveway closest to the house, backed by tall, pale fountain grasses, three thick rows of lavender, one each of short pink, medium white and tall purple varieties gave the impression of an approach to a magical cottage in the woods. The scent alone was calming and could cure a headache.

Libby got a pair of garden shears and collected a summer bouquet. She cut white roses with creamy pink centers, blue hydrangeas, pink zinnias, purple lavender and fern fronds. She arranged them in a white pitcher put on the kitchen table. She delighted in the magical way the faint pink roses and bright pink zinnias complemented the pale purple and blue hues of the hydrangeas and lavender.

A cool breeze blew in from the East. Libby saw her opportunity to get the lawn done. She got the mower out and checked the oil and gas. She pulled on the starter cord, but the darn thing wouldn't rewind. "Sugar, honey, iced tea!" she pseudo-cussed, and went inside and looked up on YouTube how to repair it. She got a socket wrench and went out to the 'patient'. She opened the housing, untangled the cord and reset the spring. "What a pain in the patoot," she complained, but she was pleased with herself for fixing it. The engine turned over.

She pushed the mower along in concentric ovals, and then pulled it up the stairs to the upper terrace. Despite the drop in temperature, she was perspiring, and she wiped her face with the bottom of her t-shirt. It felt good to exert her strength. "It's not perfect, but it'll do," she said aloud after she'd finished and surveyed her work.

Libby's stomach growled, working had made her feel righteously hungry. She went to the patio and lit the gas barbecue. Cooking for one didn't seem so bad if it was outside on the grill. She treated herself to a well marbled steak, green and yellow squash and tomatoes from the garden. The primal, make you weak at the knees, smell of cooked meat was in the air and the strip of fat lining the beef was its epicenter. At the table on the screened-in back porch, she cut off a nub of fat and put it in her mouth. The salty crispiness melted on her tongue, firing thousands of taste buds. She bit through the crunchy outside into the buttery soft and sweet inside. Mmm, low carbing had its moments. "Oh God, this is good," she said by way of grace. Victor lay under the table waiting, and Libby cut up a few small pieces of meat and put them down for him on a plate. He wolfed them down immediately.

After eating, Libby headed inside to do the dishes by hand. She couldn't imagine dirtying enough dishes in a week to make it worthwhile to run the dishwasher, so she used it as a big dish drainer. Finally, she went into the living room and turned on the TV. There was an old *Law and Order* rerun.

"Ahhhh," she sighed as she lay down on the hunter green leather couch. Victor jumped up on the third cushion and sprawled across her feet. In addition to the TV, she turned on her laptop, and went back and forth between games of Word Whomp and Boggle. But even the combination of TV and computer didn't keep her mind occupied. She wondered if she was killing her attention span with all the screen time. She turned both off and decided to read for a while.

At ten o'clock, Libby got up to get a flashlight and a sweater, and Victor ran to the door for their nightly constitutional.

He leapt up and down and pivoted around in tight circles while she tried to fasten his harness over his back and shoulders.

"Sit!" she commanded. "Do we have to do this every time we go out? Hmm? I don't trust you not to run out to the road, so I guess we do."

She wrestled him into a sitting position and pinned him between her feet before she finally prevailed. He yanked on the leash with his teeth. Her sons told her from their experience they knew she could swing him around in the air by his teeth and he wouldn't let go. She didn't try it, although the mental picture tempted her. Victor was ecstatic and pulled her toward the front door. She opened it and he jumped up on the screen door. She opened that and he tumbled out onto the front porch. He panted and lunged on the leash.

"I am glad you only weigh fourteen pounds, Victor, or I'd be flat on the ground by now." Along the walkway and the driveway, he literally ran circles around her. She passed the leash from hand to hand around herself so he didn't wrap her legs up in it.

"This is the best part of the day isn't it, Boy? Though, I'm afraid you're going to wear yourself out before we get to where I can let you run."

Victor calmed down enough to prance straight ahead. He led the way through the trees into the meadow. He stopped to enjoy smells around trees, under bushes and in the grass. After a few false starts of two or three circles he finally picked a spot, circled about eight times and did his duty. Libby cleaned up after him with a plastic bag and unhooked the leash, Victor took off like a rocket around the meadow. She looked up at the night sky and saw Venus hanging brightly below the crescent moon. Orion's Belt and the Seven Sisters were visible, too. Libby breathed in the cool, fresh air and felt a bit of peace. "Let's go in, Victor," she called awhile later. He put his paws on her knee and she gave him a good scratch behind the ears and reattached his leash. Having run his excitement off, he walked along side her to the porch. Inside, she took off his harness and leash and put them on the floor in the corner by the front door and hung her sweater on the closet doorknob.

Libby then went through the downstairs rooms turning off lights. "Come on, Victor, time for bed." She went up the stairs as he hopped from step to step behind her. She went into her bedroom, while he curled up on the rag rug in the hallway outside her door. After a shower, Libby was ready for bed and to make amends. She knelt down beside her bed to say her prayers.

"In the name of the Father, the Son and the Holy Spirit. Amen," she said crossing herself. "All right, dear Lord, I know I've been acting like a spoiled brat. I'm sorry. Though, You have to take some responsibility, too, you know. The night sweats, hot flashes and raging hormones are not making this any easier. In my opinion, this whole menopause design is flawed. It's even worse than the hard parts of being pregnant, and at least with pregnancy you get a baby to balance it out in the end.

"Here is my gripe. I played by the rules. I got married, I had three children and, yet, here I am alone. I don't like it and I don't think it's fair. We've been over your taking Frank away too early. I still don't agree with You on that, but I'm not in a position to argue. Same with the kids leaving the nest, but do the boys all have to go so far away? I know Frank started it with, 'They should go to the best school they can get into.' He was a good provider with savings and all that life insurance, sometimes I think he must have known he was going to die young. It's the distance that's the problem. It's not supposed to be about me, but it's hard not to take it personally that Brendan went as far away as he could while still being in the continental United States.

"Okay, those are my grievances. I know I need Your help and I trust that You will help me through this life change. I love being a mom. I know 'you're a mother for life', but I feel like I've been laid off or I'm more of an outside consultant. I need something worthwhile to fill the days in between. I'm only fifty-two. Only You know how long it will be before the boys get married and I get some grand babies, so I can't just wait around for that. I lined up some stuff to get me up and out in the morning. Show me Your will for me and give me the grace to do it when I see it.

"So, are we good now?" she asked glancing upward and waiting a moment.

"Okay then, thank You for the blessings of this day - good weather, good food, the beauty of the Earth, the lawnmower working, eventually, and my friends and family."

She paused for a moment searching for what she had forgotten. "Oh, yes, and for dear, old Victor."

She continued. "Please watch over the boys, dear God. Thanks for getting Brendan safely off to school. Please help him to find good friends, learn good things and to be good. Help Matt in his new job and new place in New York. Watch over Will out in South Bend in his studies, choosing a career and his choice of girlfriends.

"Have mercy on Frank's soul and all our friends and relatives who have died. Keep each of us close to you so we can all be together with You someday. Have mercy on the souls in purgatory, especially those who have no one to pray for them. Forgive them their sins and bring them into heaven with you. Please comfort those who are sick in body, mind or soul, especially Ray. Heal them and help them and their families to feel Your love for them. Amen." She crossed herself and pushed down on the mattress to get up. Her bum knee was acting up again.

Libby pulled down her coverlet and top sheet. She slipped between the fresh sheets, slightly stiff from drying on the clothes line, and the coolness gave her goose bumps. She felt a thrill as she snuggled down into the bedclothes and let out a squeak. "It's so coooold!" It was delightful to be cold for a few moments knowing she would soon be warm and cozy.Then she laughed at herself for being so easily amused.

Chapter 2

Libby's reason for getting out of bed Thursday morning was to teach a computer class at the library and by eight-thirty, it was time to leave. She picked up her purse and pawed through it looking for her car keys. They weren't there. They weren't hung up on the hook by the door.

"Blast it all, where are my keys?" she groaned. If Frank were here, he would know where they were. Before he would tell her though, he'd ask why she didn't just put them in the same place every time and perhaps tell her she was harder to train than the dog.

"Think! Think!" Libby commanded herself. "I didn't drive anywhere yesterday. The night before I bought food. I came in from the car carrying the bags. I put them down on the counter." She looked on the counter, underneath the mail. Not there. "Oh fudge, I'm going to be late." She hated being late. "Before I got a spoon, I put the milk in the fridge. The key ring was probably still on my little finger." She opened the refrigerator and saw her big shamrock key ring behind the milk.

Libby blew out a breath that ruffled the curls on her forehead. "Thank goodness!" She grabbed the keys and ran for the door. So did Victor. "Sorry, Victor, you're not going anywhere." She opened the door a crack. He was barking full out, causing his feet to bounce off of the floor just a tad. "I'll be back for lunch," she said as she pivoted 180 degrees around in the doorway so she could face him. She stepped backward out the door on one foot, with her other foot she gently pushed him back inside and quickly closed the door, all done in one fluid movement, it was the choreography of the ballet of her life with Victor.

The wooden trellis over the front walk was covered in "Heavenly Blue" morning glories backlit by the morning sun. "Your blue drives me wild," Libby whispered passionately to them as she rushed past the blossoms and buzzing bees. She drove the van down the curving country road, going her usual seven miles over the speed limit. The six-mile drive into town went through some of the sweetest countryside around, with sugar maples and oaks arched over the two lane road. It had been weeks since the road crew mowed the shoulder of the road. Orange day lilies, white Queen Anne's Lace and blue corn flowers flourished on the roadside in a late summer frenzy. She drove with her windows down to catch to sent of honeysuckle on the moist air. As driving was her preferred time for saying her morning prayers, she began.

"Thank you, dear Lord, for seeing me safely through the night and for giving me this new day. I offer you everything I think and say and do today. Please help me with Your grace to think, say and do things that are pleasing to You. I'm heading over to the library right now and I'm going to need some help with Mrs. Palmeri. If there's anything else special you want me to do today, Lord, I'm listening." She paused to listen for a message. "Why is it that You never talk to me? Some people say you talk to them all the time. Just sayin'." She sighed and said, "Amen."

Libby stuck her left arm out the window and let it ride up and down on the waves of the passing air and belted out the words to *Oh, What a Beautiful Mornin'*, the show tune that she and Frank danced to at their wedding.

At Mizpah Free Library, Libby headed for the far corner of the parking lot. "I am still young and healthy. We'll leave those up-close spots for the golden oldies." She walked briskly to the front door and saw Sue Blakely at the Main Desk. Sue, was a part-time librarian, the mother of six children and Libby's best friend. They had met in a local Catholic mothers' group when their eldest sons were toddlers. Each of Libby's sons had one matching in age in the Blakely family. Over the years, the two women logged thousands of miles and hours carpooling to school, Boy Scouts, sports, parties and anything else six boys could get involved in. Libby and Sue were closer than sisters; they thought of themselves as soul sisters.

"The Senior bus called; they're running late," Sue said.

"Halleluia, I was afraid I'd be late," said Libby.

Sue gave Libby a hug. "You're in 'professional mom mode' I see. You look great."

"Thank you," said Libby with a little bow. "This pant suit said right on the tag, 'Makes you look ten pounds thinner instantly'."

"That lapis blue really goes with your winter coloring. As Frank used to say, 'Libby's got the whole Snow White thing going on'. So how are you and the empty nest doing, Sweetie?"

"It's so strange to be the only human being in the house and not expecting anyone anytime soon. I'm thankful for Victor." Libby said with a smile, "And it does have its upside. I read for a couple of hours last night."

"Really? What are you reading?" asked Sue.

"War and Peace."

"Oh, something light, I see."

"You know me, I'm still making up for all I haven't read, being a science type in college," Libby said with a shrug. "I'll tell you, though, some of these old classics are like soap operas. Andre is in love with Natasha, but then he dumps her because she almost elopes with that jerk Anatol. She stills loves Andre and wishes she could apologize to him. He gets wounded in the war and just happens to end up on her doorstep in desperate need of TLC. She tries to nurse him back to health and he finally wakes up just in time to accept her apology before he dies."

"That was an interesting summary of one of the great love scenes in literary history," said Sue with a chuckle.

"It was great, really, but I do think I should read something happier right now."

"Probably," said Sue, "with everyone out of the house, I can't even imagine."

"I thought I was ready for this, Sue. I picked up extra volunteer work to take some time off of my hands, but the nights are already boring and lonely. With nobody left in school I lost most of my social life - no football games, Moms' Nights out, PTA fund raisers or anything."

"Maybe you could switch some of your volunteer hours to night time or have you thought any more about getting a job?"

"I still don't want to make any big commitments right away. Frank and I both wanted me to be able to stay home with the boys and he worked so hard to make it possible. I want to be able to drop everything and go if they need me."

"Meanwhile," Sue added, "you're sort of in limbo."

"I need to talk to Fr. Larry some more about this."

"Good old Fr. Larry, how is he doing?"

"He's doing me a lot of good. I'd be out of my mind by now without him."

"He's been your soul doctor for almost twenty years now, right?"

"He prefers the title, 'Spiritual Director'. He's been there for me ever since you and I started going to the Mothers' Mass."

"What a great bunch of women," Sue said. "I probably wouldn't have had the last three of my kids if it wasn't for them. Dear Becky! I figured if she could have 10 kids and keep it together, I could have five, and then I got the two girls for the price of one."

"Sharing war stories and tricks of the trade sure helped," said Libby.

"Father Larry kept my mind from going to mush with his homilies and spiritual reading assignments," Sue said. "He never lost his train of thought no matter how many kids were there or how much noise they made. Of course, he did turn his hearing aid off during Mass. Then at the end, he'd compliment the kids for being so quiet!"

Libby laughed at the memory. "When I first saw that hearing aid I figured going to Confession with him was going to be great, he'd never even hear me. That was back when I used to think of Confession as a carwash. After I confessed with him three or four times, he said, 'I see your still having trouble with that. What we can do about it?' He not only heard me, but remembered what I said weeks earlier!"

"He did have a good memory," agreed Sue.

"He still does," Libby said. "Many a time I've avoided doing something wrong, just because I couldn't bear the thought of telling that dear old man I'd done it again. I think that's half the good of having a spiritual adviser. That and having someone to deliver messages from God when He doesn't want to communicate directly."

"Still not talking to you, huh?" Sue said with a laugh.

Libby shook her head. "Meanwhile, how are things at your house? How's my goddaughter?"

"She and her sister are growing boobs and getting mean," Sue said rolling her eyes. "I thought boys were tough as teenagers, but they're going to seem like a walk in the park compared to the girls. Maybe I should start going to Confession with Fr. Larry again."

"He would love that and then my soul sister and I would have the same soul doctor."

Sue laughed and glanced at the front door. "Looks like the senior bus is here."

Libby nodded. "There's Mrs. Palmeri; I'd better go."

"See me later before you leave, Lib," said Sue.

An elderly woman dressed in black pushed a walker through the handicapped entrance.

"*Buon giorno, Signora Palmeri. Come stai?*" said Libby

"*Buon giorno, Signora O'Malley. Eh, mezza, mezza,*" Mrs. Palmeri replied with a shrug. She lifted her hand from the walker tipping it from side to side like a scale measuring her satisfaction with life.

"Let's sit over here," Libby said leading the way to the computers. "Have you practiced what we went over in your lesson last time?"

"I try it, but nothing happens."

"How far did you get?"

"I turn it on good. I put in my name and the secret word, but nothing happens."

"Does it say you put in the wrong name or password?"

"It don't say anything. It sit there. I sit there. I push the button and nothing. Then the whole thing, she is black. I do it again. *Niente.* I want to throw it out the window, but it is a present from my grandkids so …"

Libby helped Mrs. Palmeri into a chair and sat next to her. "Let's try it here from scratch with the library username and password. Okay, you turn it on."

Slowly Mrs. Palmeri's reached around to the back of the monitor and pressed on the toggle switch. The computer screen lit up; the cursor blinked in the username space. She doggedly typed 'library' with her arthritic index fingers. She maneuvered the cursor down to the password space with the down arrow.

"Is Galileo, yes?"

"You have a good memory," said Libby.

"He is *paisan*," said Mrs. Palmeri. "Now I poke this thing."

"Right, you click the mouse."

"Is disgusting touching *un roditore*."

Libby laughed, "Let's think of it as cute, little, white mouse."

"Aghh, you mean like a rat with the red eyes?"

"Let's not think about it at all."

"Fine, I poke the mouse." They waited. Nothing happened.

"We wait long enough and the whole thing go black, like at my house."

"Hmm," mused Libby, "we're not getting an error message. Poke it, I mean, click it again." Mrs. Palmeri clicked again. Nothing.

"Let me try it," suggested Libby. She took the mouse. Click, click. The Windows music and screen came on.

"That's not fair," cried Mrs. Palmeri.

"It's all right, Mrs. Palmeri, these things can be temperamental."

"Is a stupid machine!"

"Yes, it is. Let's try again from the beginning," said Libby. She closed out of the opening page and logged out. "Put in the user name and password. Then click."

Mrs. Palmeri did what Libby said to do, but again nothing happened.

"I think I've got it, Mrs. Palmeri, after the password you have to click the mouse twice. Okay? So, click, click."

Mrs. Palmeri slowly clicked once and more slowly clicked again. "Click … click," she said for added effect. Still nothing. "I give up."

"I think you're not doing it fast enough," said Libby. "Try it again. Click, click."

Click. ... Click.

"Still not fast enough."

Crossing her arms, Mrs. Palmeri said, "That as fast as I go."

"Wait," said Libby, "try this. Keep the cursor in the password box and push the 'Enter' button."

"You want one or two?"

"Just one should do it, I think."

Mrs. Palmeri pushed the 'Enter' button. She and Libby didn't breathe for moment. After a few seconds the monitor winked to the main screen and played its chord.

"We win! We win!" said Mrs. Palmeri. She jumped up an inch from her seat and plopped down again. She hugged Libby and patted her cheek. "You a good girl!"

The two women got online, surfed the web and brushed up on emailing. After the forty-five-minute session was over, Mrs. Palmeri pushed herself out of her chair with her walker to meet the senior citizens' van that would take her to the county nutrition center to play cards and have lunch.

"Mrs. Palmeri," Libby asked, "could you come for lessons in the evening?"

"The old people's wagon don't run after dark."

"Oh, of course, I'm sorry. Never mind."

"Eh, maybe I get Luciano to drive me."

"Please ask him. If he can, Mrs. Palmeri, call the library and let me know."

"You a nice girl, Libby O'Malley."

"Thank you, Mrs. Palmeri. I hope you have a good day."

"Today is fried chicken and rice at the Seniors. Is not so good."

Libby stopped to see Sue again before she left. "What's up?" Libby asked.

"I saved the YMCA fall course schedule for you." Sue pushed the booklet across the desk. "Maybe some kind of exercise class at night would be good for you."

Libby looked at the classes. "Last time I went to an aerobics class I started limping before the week was out. My knees couldn't take the jumping."

"How about water aerobics or swimming?" Sue asked.

"I don't like indoor pools that much. On top of that, changing, showering, washing my hair and all, it just takes too much time."

"Libby, I thought we were looking for ways to use up some extra time."

Libby shrugged. "I don't like getting wet on a cold night and summer's over."

"How about a dance class? You love music and dancing."

"Dancing is for couples. I'm not ready for that."

"Libby, I don't think you're the type of person who was meant to be alone."

"Sue, I'm looking for a social life not a love life."

"Fine, let's see what they have for social life in here." Sue flipped a few pages. "This is perfect. Folk Dancing! It's line dancing with no partners."

"You may have something there. May I see that?" Libby asked. "Tuesday nights seven to eight thirty. It starts next week and I can just walk in. All right, Susan, I'll give it a try. Thank you. I know I can be a pain in the backside."

"You certainly can be," Sue said smiling. "You promise you'll go to the folk dancing class?"

"Cross my heart," Libby said.

Chapter 3

Libby was up to her elbows in raw ground beef making meatloaf for Ray and Carrie Bannon when the phone rang. It was Brendan. Libby grabbed a paper towel to put between her messy hand and the receiver. It was his first call home since he moved into his dorm.

"Hi, honey, how are you!" Libby said.

"I'm good," said Brendan.

Libby winced, but resisted correcting his grammar. "I'm so happy to hear your voice. Tell me all about your classes, your dorm ..."

"My classes are fine, except for Calculus. The guy who's teaching it is from Jamaica or Haiti or something and I can't understand half of what he says."

"Maybe you could drop his course and look for another section," she suggested.

"No other Calc sections fit. First year engineering courses are practically cut in stone. Things at the dorm are okay. We had a Frosh O party with a cool climbing wall."

"They made you wear a helmet, right?"

"Yes, Mom," he sing-songed.

"Brendan could you wait just a second while I wash my hands. I'm making meatloaf."

"I'm almost to class, Mom. I'm just calling to ask you one thing. A friend is having a kind of Mary Kay party online. She sells it to make money for college. She's asking everyone to invite friends and family to go. Could you do me a solid and check it out?"

"I don't use much makeup."

"Lainie says there's skin care stuff, too. I'm going to get some moisturizer for guys."

"This Lainie must be some friend for you to do that."

"She says that the sun is stronger in California and the air is dryer than what I am used to so I should get something with sunscreen. Plus, since you and I agreed it wouldn't be worth flying home for such a short break, she said she'd ask her parents if I can go to their house for Thanksgiving. She lives a few hours north of here."

"I'd be grateful for that. So, where can I see a picture of this young lady?"

"Gee, Mom, that's kind of shallow, but you can probably find something on her business website. I'll send you the link. Thanks, Mom. Gotta go."

"Goodbye, Brendan. I love you."

"Love you, too, Mom. Bye."

The paper towel and the raw meat had dried onto on Libby's hand. She went to the sink to clean up. "He sounded happy. That's good," she said out loud to herself and to Victor, if he was listening. "I can't wait to see who this Lainie girl is."

Brendan sent the promised link after dinner, Libby clicked on it immediately. The home page was very pink. She went to the "About Me" tab. A photo of Lainie popped up. She was dressed fashionably but modestly, and was a natural beauty with flawless skin. Lainie's bio said she was a Commended National Merit Scholar. "Hmm, smart and pretty," Libby mumbled. Lainie also volunteered with the Special Olympics and wanted a career working with autistic children. Libby liked this girl's style.

"She's quite a girl. I wonder if she's Catholic." Libby forced herself to take a breath. "Whoa, whoa, hold your horses, Libby. We're not arranging a marriage here, Brendan's just making a new friend. A friend he's willing to wear moisturizer for and who might be taking him home to meet Mommy and Daddy at Thanksgiving." She shook her head and smiled and clicked on the skin care tab.

"Let's see. 'Wrinkle Eraser Night Time Serum', I could use that. 'Youth Renewal Day Time Cream with SPF 15'. Well, that covers all 24 hours. And how about a 'Special Rejuvenating Cucumber Cleansing Masque'?"

"Ouch, that's almost eighty dollars!" Libby said after shipping and handling was added at checkout. "If it delivers all it promises, it'll be worth it." Thinking of her son far away and his new friend, that was a girl, she clicked the "Order Now" button.

Chapter 4

Friday morning was the start of Libby's stint as a volunteer tutor and mentor at her children's old school. She had volunteered often when her own children attended school, but she hadn't stepped foot in Mizpah Middle School in seven years. As the boys moved through elementary, middle and high school she moved along as a volunteer – playground monitor, library helper, coach for spelling bees, science olympiads and speech contests, chaperone for class trips, dances and whatever else came up.

Libby was also the homeroom mother for one of the boys' classes each year, she even had "Homeroom Mother Software". Her friends laughed, but the software was great as it had flyer, letter and spreadsheet functions for everything from assigning snacks for parties, collecting money for class trips, teachers' gifts and fundraisers, to getting volunteers for the PTA fashion show and soliciting donations for the annual auction.

This time Libby, was here as a community volunteer not as somebody's mom, none of the students would know her, and several teachers had changed as well, but the school office staff was the same. The school secretary was a petite, blonde woman, who still looked like a teenager from behind.

"Hi, Angela, I'm here for mentoring."

Angela turned around. "Oh, Libby, I haven't seen you in ages. How are you?"

"Adjusting to an empty nest. How are you doing?"

"I'll be getting there soon," said Angela, "and I'm not looking forward to it. Is it as bad as some people say?"

"It's pretty fresh right now, and I feel like I'm in a haze. I'll let you know how it's going in a few weeks." Libby signed the guest log and asked. "So, who am I working with?"

"You have Jesse Pine. He's a sixth grader. You said you could tutor in math, right? He needs helps with decimals."

"Don't we all?" Libby said.

"You're probably right," said Angela with a laugh. "An aide will bring him to room 117."

Libby walked down the hall noticing cheery bulletin boards announcing the beginning of a new year. The smell of floor wax, tacos, crayons and construction paper welcomed her back to happy times. She loved working with school kids. When her sons were in first and second grade and she came to school, they would grin and say, "That's my mom." In third and fourth, they would give small waves, hands half hidden at their waist or behind their backs. By time they got to their all boys high school it was, "I'll meet you in the parking lot after school."

Libby got to Room 117 and pulled two school desks together. She wanted to make the situation cozier than the usual teacher-student interaction. She could afford to be this kid's friend; she wasn't responsible for the total development of his character just a little remedial math and language arts. At 10:30 sharp a young woman walked in with a boy, "Hello, Mrs. O'Malley, this is Jesse. Jesse, this is your new mentor, Mrs. O'Malley."

"Hello, Jesse, it's good to meet you," said Libby.

The boy looked down at his shoes. When the aide left, the boy looked up from under long dark bangs, "I don't need no mentor."

"Tell me why you don't need a mentor."

"I don't need to know any of the crap they teach here. When I grow up, I'm gonna be a drug lord or a pimp."

Dear child of God, Libby thought, *you have been watching too much TV and we are both so lucky I am not the apoplectic woman I used to be.* She eyed his baggy shorts and T-shirt and said, "I see. Well, if you're dressing for the job you want, I would say you look more like a drug dealer today."

Jesse smiled despite himself, then went back to trying to look tough.

Libby continued, "And, if you are going to be a drug lord, you'll need to learn math. Otherwise, your customers or your thugs may cheat you."

"I'll cap 'em if they do."

25

"Ah, but, you won't know if they're cheating you if you can't figure out how much money they owe you to begin with. Do you know how many pounds are in a kilogram?"

"A what?" asked the boy.

"A kilogram. Aren't drugs measured in grams and kilograms? You know kee-lohs."

"Oh, kee-lohs," Jessie said trying to sound like an authority. "Yeah lady, they measure the stuff in kee-lohs."

"So how many pounds are in a kee-loh?"

"I D K."

"Excuse me?" said Libby.

"I - don't - know," said Jesse still not looking at Libby.

"Then I'll tell you. There are two point two pounds in a kilogram," Libby said. "So if you have ten kilos of cocaine how many pounds would that be?"

"A lot." Jesse smirked.

"But how much exactly?" Libby walked over to the white board and wrote, "10 x 2.2 pounds =" . "Let's see what you've got," she said. Her nose stung from the pungent smell of the dry marker, as she held it out to him.

"Lady, either you crazy or you tight," he said taking the marker.

"You may call me Mrs. O, if you like."

"Mrs. O," he said weighing the name. "I'm down with that," then together they reviewed decimals for the next half hour.

That evening, Libby lay on her green leather sofa with Victor lying on her stomach. She was reading *Under the Wide and Starry Sky,* an historical novel about Robert Lewis Stevenson and his American lover and later wife, Fanny.

"Get up, Victor. I can't sit here any more," Libby said and pushed him off. "This is the first time I've missed the opening game of a St. Joe's football season in how many years? Let's see, Matt is twenty-two and he started high school when he was fourteen. Eight years ago, all five of us went to our first game."

Libby went out into the fenced-in back yard and Victor followed. She breathed in the mild air and looked up at the clear sky. "It's a perfect night for a game. I thought about going, Victor,

I really did, but it was an away game and I didn't feel like driving an hour each way, besides who knows who'd be there? Watching kids you know play and sitting with their parents is what makes it fun. Maybe I'll go to the next home game, at least I'll recognize some of last year's underclassmen and there'll probably be a few parents I know in the stands."

She walked off her latest bout of empty nest blues for a while, when she was feeling better she said, "Let's go back in, dog."

Chapter 5

"*Hava nagila, have two nagila, have three nagila, they're very small,*" Libby felt giddy dressing for the first folk dance class and mad up silly words to the folk song. She found her long, multicolor, flared skirt and a white peasant top in a closet in the back bedroom. She arrived right on time.

At seven o'clock, an older man with a wispy comb over called the class to attention.

"Good evening, everyone. My name is Herb Bessey and I am your instructor for the ballroom dance class."

Libby moved toward the door to exit. "Miss, are you leaving already?" Herb asked.

"Oh, I'm sorry," Libby said, "I made a mistake. I thought this was the folk dancing class. Can you tell me where that class is meeting?"

Everyone looked from Libby to Herb. "This is the right place, but the wrong night," he said, "They meet on Thursday nights." He walked toward her closing the gap between them, so they could speak more quietly. "Since you are already here, why don't you join us?"

"I've already taken ballroom dance lessons," Libby demurred.

"All the better. What's your name?"

"Libby."

"Libby," Herb said confidentially, "my wife usually helps me teach this class. She demonstrates the steps with me and dances the man's part with the extra ladies, but she's busy this session. I'd really appreciate it if you would stay and help me out. You wouldn't need to pay any fees, because you'd be my assistant. What d'you say?"

Libby sighed, but agreed, "Of course, I'd be glad to help." She never could turn down a request for help and besides he'd called her 'Miss'.

"Wonderful! You won't be sorry. It'll be fun," Herb said with a wink.

"Okay, everyone," Herb announced, "this is Libby my new assistant." People chuckled and a few applauded. Libby blushed as Herb introduced her.

"Let's get started with the Foxtrot," Herb continued. "Everybody get into a circle single file. We'll walk out the basic steps in time to the music and then we'll put it together with partners."

He stepped into the center of the circle. "We can Foxtrot to any music with four-four time. The two basic series of steps are 'Slow, slow, quick, quick' and 'slow, quick, quick'. The slow steps are longer and take two beats. The quick ones are shorter and get only one beat. Men start on the left foot and women on the right foot. Slooow, slooow, quick, quick." He showed the length and timing of the steps. "Libby, does this look familiar?"

Libby nodded.

"You come inside the circle and I'll put on the music." Herb turned up an instrumental version of *Haven't Met You Yet*.

"Let's count the rhythm first. One, two, three, four. One, two, three, four. Libby, start on your left foot. And one, two, three, four."

"Good!" said Herb. "Okay, now everyone."

After a few fitful starts, all the students were moving. Later, Herb and Libby demonstrated the proper dance position and the steps done as a couple. Herb had people partner up, and as there were always more women than men at these classes, he and Libby danced the man's part with women without partners.

There was stepping on toes and nervous laughter, but the rest of the hour flew by, until Herb announced, "That's it for tonight, folks. You all did very well. Thank you for coming."

The class gave Herb a round of applause. Taking Libby's hand, he said, "And for my God-sent assistant, Libby." The class applauded again.

As people began leaving, Herb asked, "Will you come back next week, Libby?"

Libby was surprised to hear herself say, "Sure, Herb, that was fun and good exercise, too. I'll sleep well tonight."

Chapter 6

Wednesday morning, Libby got up early to take care of the Bannon's horses. The family was traveling overnight for Ray's cancer treatment during which Callie and Kylie would stay in lodging subsidized by a veterans' group.

The Bannons had two of their own horses. Baldy, a seven-year-old American Paint gelding with blue eyes and big patches of black on his white coat, was Libby's favorite. Skelly was the senior citizen of the barn at seventeen years old. He was all black with a white star on his forehead and age had added white hairs around his muzzle. Both horses were trained for Western style riding and were good trail horses. The third horse, Zoe, was a boarder. She was a flighty, four-year-old palomino mare and an English show horse specializing in jumping in Hunter Classes. Her owner was a girl on a college equestrian team, and Zoe was to have gone back to college with her rider last week. Unfortunately, a horse at the campus barn developed Equine Herpes, and the school quarantined the barn, so Zoe had to stay home for now.

The horses nickered when Libby opened the barn door. Three heads with pricked up ears pivoted in her direction over the stall gates. "Good morning, sweeties," she called and breathed in the delightful odor of horses, hay, manure and cedar chips. The horses thumped their hooves in anticipation.

"Hi, Baldy," Libby said as she reached up to pat him on the neck. He bobbed his head and pushed her shoulder with his nose. "Morning, Skelly." She rubbed his soft upper lip. "How are you doing, Zoe?" She reached up to pat the young mare, who threw her head back and pranced sideways in the stall.

"Okay, okay. No small talk, just food," Libby soothed. She gave each of them half their daily rations of ten pounds of hay and ten pounds of mixed oat, corn and molasses feed. Libby took the five-gallon water buckets out of each stall and dumped what little water was left in them into the corral. She hosed buckets clean, put them back in the stalls and filled them with fresh water. She then left the outside doors connecting the stalls to the corral open so the horses could get some air and exercise while she ran a few errands in town.

When Libby returned in the afternoon, she cleaned out the stalls with a pitchfork. Done with the work, she brought out Baldy's saddle, blanket, bridle and brush to get him ready to ride. She could tell Ray hadn't felt up to riding this week, because the length of the stirrups hadn't been changed since the last time she rode. After the horse was saddled, she tied on a saddle pack with snacks and water. Using the middle rail of the fence like a ballet barre, she swung her heel up and stretched her hamstring and calf muscles. Afterward, she climbed on the rail, stepped up on the stirrup and swung her right leg over Baldy's back. It was a cheat, but she had to forget her pride and use her head when her knee acted up. She rode Baldy over to the training ring and put him through his paces. She had him walk and jog to warm up, then at a slow canter she steered him through figure eights. They practiced some fancy pivots, rollbacks and spins then she gently tugged the reins and said, "Woah." One thousand pounds of muscle and bone stopped on a dime. Libby smiled with satisfaction.

"That was perfect, Baldy." She patted him firmly on the neck, "I wish I could have trained my horse, Honeycomb, as well as Ray trained you." Awed anew by the relationship between horse and rider, she added, "I still don't see why you let us ride you at all."

Behind the ring was the forest with an old deer trail that cut between pines, maples and oaks. Libby took Baldy out on an easy trail ride to cool him down, and now it was time for Baldy to play therapist just as Honeycomb had when Libby was a teenager.

Libby spoke out loud in a conversational tone, "On top of everything else that's been going on, Baldy, I've got the end of the summer blues worse than ever. I'm nostalgic for those days when the kids and I stayed all afternoon at the lake. Matt and Will doing cannonballs off the dock to see who could make the biggest splash. Brendan stomping around in a puddle he'd dug for his army men to play in. Me drying them off with towels off the clothesline, stiff and smelling like sunshine. Eating ham and cheese sandwiches on Kaiser rolls and juicy Jersey peaches. The big boys waiting an hour to go back in the water lying on that old army blanket. Brendan snuggling in my lap in the lounge chair. All three drowsing while I read them *Treasure Island*. And that time they gave Frank the 'black spot' while he was cooking hamburgers on the barbecue." She laughed at the memory.

Baldy had one ear cocked back and the other forward, so Libby knew he was listening. "At the same time, I feel like there is something that I should be doing now, but I don't know what it is. So, I end up sighing a lot and feeling anxious."

The dappled shade made impressionistic patterns on the ground and Baldy's neck. His head bobbed like a metronome. Libby fell in with his steady gait, rocking side to side in the saddle. She held the reins loosely, closed her eyes and breathed in the smells of pine and humus from decades of decaying leaves and needles. Baldy stopped and Libby opened her eyes in time to see a male cardinal fly out of the underbrush.

"He's a beauty isn't he, Baldy. Maybe I'll take up birdwatching for a few years. I'll travel to South America and Australia."

Baldy snorted.

"You're right, I don't know if I'd like traveling alone. I could go on a group tour, but I wouldn't want to go with a bunch of retired couples. It's so awkward, being the odd woman out." Baldy twitched a fly off his ear and she shooed one off his neck. She became pensive, "I wish I'd made more girlfriends. Most of the women I know are occupied with their families and work. Maybe I could find a tour just for women and meet new friends."

Half-an-hour later they arrived at their destination. Libby slid down off of Baldy's back less than gracefully. Sitting in the saddle for that long made her stiff. She walked him over to the cedar pond, where the water looked like iced tea. Near the shore, the sunlight filtered through to the sandy bottom making shadows of swimming minnows She removed Baldy's bit so he could drink and graze, and she pulled a bottle of water and an apple from the saddle pack for herself.

The water felt good going down her throat. She bit into the shiny red and green McIntosh; drops of juice burst into her mouth. That first bite was intoxicatingly sweet and tart. "Mmmm," she sighed and walked along the shore.

White flowers bloomed on the lily pads giving off a damp bouquet. Bees methodically collected nectar and pollen from the low, woodland flowers. A pair of iridescent dragonflies hovered and darted in a courtship dance. "Time to make hay, or in your case dragonflies, while the sun shines," Libby remarked. It was a lazy afternoon for her, but there was anticipation in the air. The days were growing shorter and nature had deadlines to keep.

Libby lay down on a mossy patch and put her hands behind her head. Through the hole the pond made in the tree canopy, there was a perfect blue sky. She couldn't help but smile while seeing that color. She stared at the sky and occasional cloud for a long time. She wanted to soak up this color so she could have it whenever she needed it to feel happy again. Finally, she realized the sun was getting low. She went to Baldy and put her arms around his neck leaned into his chest with her cheek pressed against him. He stood with his head over her shoulder. She breathed in the smell of horse. "Thank you, Baldy, I needed this."

It was time to go back and do the evening feeding and go to the first choir practice of the year. She felt good having things that needed doing.

After showering and having dinner with Victor, Libby drove to St. Francis Church for choir. She got there early so she could make a visit to the Blessed Sacrament. In the sanctuary, the red tabernacle candle and votives were the only light as she genuflected with a firm grip on the back of a pew and pulled herself back up. She sat and looked at the tabernacle. "I was in the neighborhood and thought I'd drop by," she said. She didn't feel a need to say anything more. She looked at Him and He looked at her. She felt an infusion of quiet joy. After a few minutes she stood up, nodded and went downstairs to the music room.

The choir members were catching up on each other's summer doings when Derek, the young director, called them to order. "Ladies and gentlemen, let's get started." People grouped themselves by voice parts. Binders with sheet music were passed out. Derek led them through vocal warm up exercises up and down scales. "Let's start with the Randall Thompson's *Alleluia*," he said. "New people, just look over the music and listen to your part for now." He played through the opening bar of each of the four parts. "Everybody from the top."

'*Alleluia*' was the only word in the whole song. The music of the hymn was layered part on part in a round. The rhythm surged and ebbed. As harmonies formed, the vibrations inside Libby resonated with the waves of sound from the organ and other choir members. The chords made the hairs on her neck stand up. It was like a meeting of heaven and earth.

Chapter 7

Mrs. Palmeri moved her computer lesson to seven-thirty on Thursday night. By eight fifteen she and Libby had progressed to searching archives of Italian newspapers. At the end of the session, Libby accompanied the elderly woman and her walker toward the front of the library.

"There's Luciano now," said Mrs. Palmeri. Libby saw a handsome man in his late thirties come through the left set of double doors. He had dark, wavy hair brushed back from his forehead and a ruddy complexion. She took in the strong, straight nose, square chin and dark eyes. *A sculptor would have a field day with that face*, she thought. *He's tall and broad shouldered like a bulked-up Hugh Jackman. He sure doesn't take after his mother. Well, maybe the eyebrows.*

Mrs. Palmeri called across the vestibule, "Luciano, this is *Senora* O'Malley, the one I am telling you about. She is a widow, like me. She has three big sons. Smart boys. Good boys. The littlest one, he go away to school. She is all alone in a big house in the woods. She sings in the choir at our church."

Mrs. Palmeri had done her homework. Libby's cheeks were on fire; she stared down at the little woman wondering how to stop her broadcast.

"Lucio," Mrs. Palmeri said sternly, "come here."

When Libby looked up, a shorter, rounder man in his fifties approached her from the double doors on the right. He removed his golf cap from his head revealing a neat fringe of salt and pepper hair around his bald pate. He walked toward her and held his hand out. "Mama has told me such good things about you."

Out of the corner of her eye, Libby saw the younger man walk past them taking in the scene with an amused smile on his face. He had dimples like Hugh Jackman, too.

Libby moved her full attention back to Luciano. "It's a pleasure to meet you, Mr. Palmeri," she said shaking his hand.

"Lucio, he never marry," interrupted his mother. "He has a nice house and a nice car. A good job. A stone cutter. He is an artist with stone."

"How interesting," replied Libby.

"Thank you so much for teaching Mama to use the computer," said Luciano shyly. "She likes it a lot."

"Your mother is an extraordinary woman," Libby said. "Not many people of her generation would put the effort she does into learning a new technology."

"She is motivated," said Lucio.

"Yes, I heard her grandchildren gave her a computer as a gift. I think she wants to make them proud of her by learning to use it."

"She asked for a computer for her birthday."

"Really?"

"Yes, she wants to read the news from the town where she was born."

"We were just working on finding Italian language newspapers online."

"She wants to keep track of the obituaries."

"That's a little sad, but many of our seniors read the obituaries to make sure they don't miss the passing of old friends."

Mrs. Palmeri, who had been uncharacteristically silent, piped up, "I want to see if any dead S-O-B owes the family money, so we get our money back!" Libby stifled a gasp. "The library is full of useful information. I have to go now; I have another student. It was a pleasure meet you, Luciano. Good night, Mrs. Palmeri."

Mrs. Palmeri gestured impatiently toward Lucio.

"Oh, yes, I hope to see you again, Mrs. O'Malley," he said bowing slightly. Libby nodded awkwardly, not knowing how to respond to this obvious set up.

Libby made her way back to the Reference Desk. The torso of a tall man blocked her view of Sue, who was Librarian-In-Charge tonight, but Libby heard Sue's voice.

"Here's Mrs. O'Malley, now."

The man turned. He didn't see Sue waggle her eyebrows Groucho Marx style at Libby. "This is Mr. Baynard, you're next appointment."

Libby looked up into the face of the man she had mistaken for Luciano Palmeri.

"Ah, Mrs. O'Malley, I've heard so much about you," Mr. Baynard said.   "It seems everyone has," Libby replied knowing the heat hadn't left her face yet. *Oh Lord, please don't let this turn into a hot flash,* she pleaded silently. "Delighted to meet you, Mr. Baynard," she said extending her hand. His hand was large and warm. He held her hand and her gaze. His eyes were grey with distinct yellow rings around the pupils. White lines radiated through the irises like fireworks to the black outer rim.

"Follow me over to our computer center," Libby said. She felt self-conscious knowing the man was looking at her from behind. *Well, of course he's looking at you,* she scolded herself silently, *you told him to follow you.* She hoped his eyes were on her head. She had gotten her hair done recently, so at least that was in good shape. *This is ridiculous,* she thought wending her way through tables and desks to the back of the library, *I am too old for this foolishness and he's too young.*

They reached a table with two chairs and a computer.

"May I?" Mr. Baynard asked pulling out a chair for her. "Do you mind if I remove my jacket?" he asked. He wore a charcoal grey pinstriped suit with a gold and red tie. His jacket fit him perfectly, broad at the shoulders and narrowing at the waist and hips.

"No, of course not, please make yourself comfortable," she replied.

Mr. Baynard removed his suit jacket, folded it and placed it on a chair next to them. His dress shirt revealed that there wasn't much padding in the shoulders of his jacket. His trousers – she couldn't just call them pants - had no belt loops. He wore suspenders, the kind that attached to buttons on the inside of the waistband. He seated himself and positioned his chair to face her.

"I don't get many men, I mean, I don't get many young men ... for, um, for computer tutoring," Libby stuttered. She was desperately trying to keep her train of thought as a bead of perspiration slid down the small of her back. Mr. Baynard smiled but said nothing.

"What do you want to learn about computers?" she asked.

"I am seriously out of synch with the times," he said. "I know almost nothing about them."

"That is remarkable. You are one of the only men your age, that doesn't use a computer for hours each day, and the others are probably *bona fide* hermits."

"Up to now I haven't had the time or need to learn," he replied, "I depended on people who worked for me to do my e-work, but I've changed jobs and now here I am with time and the need."

Libby shook her head in wonder, "In that case, we'll start from the beginning." She regained her poise as she faced the computer and began her spiel. "Let me show you how to turn the computer on."

Mr. Baynard talked little, listened attentively and watched closely. He learned the basics of the machine, getting online and separating the wheat from the chaff in simple searches during their forty-five minute session.

"You covered a great deal in one session, Mr. Baynard."

"You're a good teacher, Mrs. O'Malley."

"Thank you."

Mr. Baynard stood and pulled Libby's chair out for her. She picked up her purse. He retrieved his jacket and put it over his arm. "May I make an appointment for another class?"

"Sure," said Libby, "let's check the schedule.

She went to the Information Desk's computer to access the class schedule. "For your next class did you want night or day, Mr. Baynard?"

"Night."

"Mr. Larimer has an opening on Monday at seven-thirty."

"Later would be better. When will you be available next, Mrs. O'Malley?"

"Not until next Thursday at eight-fifteen again. I only volunteer one night a week."

"I'm not in a hurry. I've waited this long, I can wait until next Thursday."

"Okay then, same time next week," Libby confirmed.

"Very good," he said

The lights blinked off and on. They looked around. He was the last patron left.

"The library is closing," Baynard noted as he put on his jacket. "May I walk you out to your car?"

"That's not necessary," she said. "This is a safe, little town, Mr. Baynard."

"I would feel better if I did. It's dark and the library is nearly empty. The parking lot will be deserted," he said.

Libby remembered that she parked at the far end of the parking lot near the hedges and trees. "Well, if it would make you feel better."

"It would."

As they walked out of the front door, he offered her his arm. "Well, Mr. Baynard, now I feel like an old lady being helped across the street by a Boy Scout."

He chuckled as she put her hand on his forearm.

"I haven't noticed you around before, Mr. Baynard. Are you new to the area?" Libby asked.

"I've been here for a few months now," said Mr. Baynard, "but I don't get into town much during business hours. I work late and travel a bit, and I don't have a wife or children to get me into community activities. It's women who keep society civilized." He paused, "Where are you parked?"

"Over in the far corner under the trees," said Libby.

"Now, I'm really glad I walked out with you, and coincidentally, I'm parked nearby." He gestured toward the long, black pickup truck with a windowless utility cap parked a few spaces down from her van.

"I think I've seen your pickup before."

"Really?"

"Yes, you don't see many pickups like that, no offense, but it looks like a hearse on steroids. I saw it with out-of-state tags somewhere around here." She snapped her fingers, "Now I remember, I saw it parked out on the road near my house. Did you look at a house for sale on Good Hope Road? A while back?"

"Yes, I did. I don't remember the property, but I liked the name of the street," he said.

"That's remarkable. It's right across the street from where I live. We would have been neighbors."

Just then, the parking lot lights flickered off. "Oh!" Libby said, "The county and their austerity plans, I can't see a thing." Suddenly, Mr. Baynard scooped her up in his arms. As her body went parallel to the ground, the sensation of falling caused Libby to throw her arms around his neck, at the same time she cried out, "What are you doing?"

"You were about to step into a pothole," he said. "I was afraid you'd twist your ankle."

"I think I know the one you mean, I've never been out here in the dark. How did you ever see it?"

"I've got pretty good night vision," he said.

"I'd say it was extraordinary. You must eat carrots by the bushel or something," she said.

"Or something," he said.

"It's been a while since I been I've been swept off my feet, but you can put me down now," she said, embarrassed that they were still holding onto each other and amazed that he could pick her up so easily. She wasn't a petite woman. The last time Frank had picked her up was to throw her into a lake right after they were married. Afterwards, he told her he'd thrown his back out, and that was twenty-five years and three babies ago.

Mr. Baynard carefully set her on her feet and said bashfully, "I'm sorry for being so forward, I just acted instinctively."

"That's okay, I'd rather be surprised than have a badly sprained ankle."

When they reached her car, he asked, "May I have your keys?" She looked puzzled.

He said, "My father taught me always to open a door for a lady."

"Oh," said Libby. She fumbled in her purse for her keys praying she wouldn't be reduced to dumping everything out on the hood of her car to find them. She was relieved when she plucked them from the bottom of her purse and handed them over. Mr. Baynard unlocked the car door, opened it and handed her into the driver's seat.

"Thank you, again," she said.

"It was my pleasure, Ma'am," he said giving her a Boy Scout salute before handing her the keys and closing the door.

Libby laughed at his antics. She was surprised at how happy it made her that he laughed at her Boy Scout joke and joined in on it. After ten years of raising teenagers, she lost count of the times she was told she was 'not funny' or 'not cool'. She learned to have a thick skin about such remarks, but she missed being thought of as witty. One of the things she enjoyed most about Frank was that he laughed at her jokes.

Chapter 8

Libby was surprised to find herself at a Hollywood party. She was even more surprised to find Hugh Jackman smiling at her across the room. She thought that maybe he was looking at someone behind her. She turned around, but she was in a corner by herself. Hugh tried to make his way over to her, but women kept stopping him to get his autograph. Finally, he reached her. "I've been wanting to get close to you all night," he whispered in her ear. He put his arms around her and lowered his mouth to hers. His kisses were tender at first and then more urgent. She was about to tell him what a great kisser he was, but he started to get sloppy. He licked her lips and her cheeks.

Libby's eyes flew open as Victor licked her face again. "Shoot, Victor, you woke me up from a good dream." She held Victor's head and gave him a kiss on the snout, "It's not a sin if you dream it. I'll take that as a little gift from above, God knows there probably won't be sex in my future anywhere but my dreams." Victor cocked his head at her. "Don't look at me like that," she said "you were neutered before we adopted you."

Libby looked past Victor to her alarm clock. "Let me think, it's hard to keep track of what day it is. It's like being on a permanent vacation. Okay, today is Friday, September 14, so I have my second tutoring session with Jesse. We'd better get you out for a run and both of us some breakfast."

A few hours later when Libby met Jesse again in Room 117, he didn't look any happier to see her than the last time.

"Hi, Jesse, how are you doing this week?" she said brightly.

"Hi Jesse, how you doing this week?" he mimicked.

Libby ignored his rudeness. "It says in your folder that you did well on the math test you took a couple of days ago. What did you think of it?

"It was fine."

"The lesson plan says we can do some reading aloud. How about you read two pages and I'll read the next two?" she said holding a paperback book up. "That's what I used to do with my sons."

"I ain't your son and you ain't my mother."

"That's God's honest truth, Jesse."

"Why do you come here?" demanded Jesse, "Did you read in a book somewhere that poor kids need rich people like you to make 'em smart and stop 'em from being criminals or something?"

"Why am I here? That's a fair question. My youngest son just left for college, and now I'm home all by myself except for my dog. I am lonely and bored so I decided to come here so I would have someplace to go and something to do on Friday mornings."

"Ain't you married? You're Mrs. O'Malley. Where's Mr. O'Malley?"

"My husband died a few years ago."

"Hunh," he grunted. "What's that book you got?"

"The Indian in the Cupboard."

"That's not some stupid Harry Potter book, is it?"

"No, it came way before Harry Potter. You want to try it and see what you think?"

"Okay, I guess."

Back at home, Libby stopped at the roadside mailbox at the entrance to her driveway to pick up her mail. Her order from Lainie was there. After dinner, she finished the historic romance novel she was reading. It was set in Ireland in the 1820s.

"Well, Victor, they pulled that one out of the fire at the last minute. For two hundred fifty pages Moira and Padric have had one misunderstanding after another. Then in the very last paragraph she tells him she's loved him all along and he says, "Then marry me and let's go home, darlin'."

Libby reread the best parts again, their first meeting, what attracted them to each other, their first kiss and other shenanigans. She especially liked the shenanigans. She gave Victor a nudge,

"Get up, dog. My leg is falling asleep." Victor jumped off of the couch, and she got up to get him supper, theorizing as she worked.

"What gets me, Victor, is most of these romances stop just after the wedding. The implication is they live happily ever after. What they don't tell you is that all that heart pounding, dry mouthed, starry-eyed passion has been scientifically proven to have a shelf life of about two years. It's also been proven the majority of married women who read romances novels are less satisfied with their marriages. Reality just can't live up to the hype. Believe me, if you have a man and a woman with strong personalities, you are going to have power struggles for the next twenty years, at least. That's what Frank and I did. But I guess, there's no danger in reading these things for me anymore. I have no marriage to be dissatisfied with."

Done with feeding Victor and cleaning up the kitchen, Libby wondered what to do for the rest of the time before bed. She brightened up, "I know, Victor, let's have a girly night with those new beauty products I got in the mail." She got the package and sat on the sofa to open it, while Victor jumped up on the sofa and put his head on her lap. She opened the box and read the booklet of directions. "This is quite a ritual," she told him getting ready to get up again, "upsy-daisy, Victor, I've got to go upstairs to do this."

Libby went up to the bathroom, "Okay, now I'm supposed to take a close look in a magnifying mirror to determine the condition of my T-zone." She dug into the bottom drawer of the vanity, pulled out the round mirror Frank used to adjust his contact lens and flipped it over to the magnifying side. Her oversized pores, tiny broken blood vessels around her nose and the laugh lines making triple parentheses around her mouth jumped into high relief.

"Good grief," Libby said putting down the mirror. She shoved the mirror back into the drawer. "Let's just assume that I need help all over."

Libby splashed on warm water, massaged in cleanser, rinsed and swabbed on toner with cotton balls. *"Apply masque to freshly cleansed skin and wait for twenty minutes,"* she read. She smoothed the thick, green emulsion over her face leaving circles of white skin around her eyes giving her the appearance of a big, green owl. She decided to go downstairs to watch CNN for the twenty minutes. When Victor caught sight of her in the hall, he barked up a storm.

Chapter 9

Libby laid several dresses out on her bed and was having a hard time deciding which one to wear to ballroom dance class. She finally went with the emerald green one with an Empire waist. The crisscross neckline accentuated her assets, while the a-line skirt disguised her negatives. She went all out with pantyhose and a pair of two-inch heeled sandals. When she opened the front door, Victor made his usual mad dash for it. The heeled sandals kept Libby from moving quickly enough to block his exit. He bolted out the door and was yapping and making excited circles on the walk way.

"Victor, get back in here," Libby said in her sternest voice, which rarely worked and it didn't this time either. She clapped her hands and pretended to head back into the house. "Time to go in," she called. Victor usually fell for this ruse, and he might have done so this time, but a squirrel caught his eye and he chased after it. The two animals raced through the woods lining the driveway.

"Dang it, Victor, you are going to make me late." Libby walked down the drive as quickly as she could in that blasted footwear. Victor yelped. Tires screeched.

"Oh no, oh no, oh no!" Libby cried. She kicked off her shoes and ran. A red sports car was stopped on the road. The driver got out of his car, and saw her coming out of the driveway.

"Is that your dog?" the young man called out.

Libby could only nod.

"I'm so sorry. He ran right out in front of me."

A small heap of orange fur lay in the middle of the road. Tears blurred Libby's vision. She knelt down by Victor's side, and saw his back legs twitch. There was only a trickle of blood coming from his nose. She stroked his fur, but there was no reaction. Another car came down the road behind the red card and stopped.

"Is he badly hurt?" asked the driver.

Victor's eyes were open and staring.

"He's dead," Libby said quietly.

"I'm really sorry," the young man said gently, coming to her side.

"It's not your fault. He shouldn't have been out by the road," she said dully.

"Is there anything I can do?" the man asked.

"No, I'll take him." Libby slid her hands between Victor and the asphalt. His head lolled grotesquely toward the ground as she lifted him and walked toward the house. The young man hung his head, got back into his car and drove away as did the driver behind him.

Libby placed Victor on the sofa. She looked up Herb's number on her cell and dialed.

"Hello, Herb? This is Libby O'Malley. I'm sorry, but I can't come tonight."

"Is something the matter?" Herb asked.

"A dear friend of mine just died and I have ..." her voice broke. She just had to hold herself together for one more minute, "I have some things I need to do. I have to go."

Libby hung up the phone and sat on the sofa next to Victor. She stroked his head.
"Oh, Victor, why?" She buried her face in his fur. An inhuman sound came out of her. She sobbed like a child for a long while.

Libby jumped when she heard a knock at the door. She wiped her eyes and nose on the backs of her hands. Who could it possibly be? It was nighttime; there were no lights on in the house. She got up and turned on a lamp. "Who is it?" she called as she went to the door.

"It's David Baynard, Mrs. O'Malley."

Libby was stunned, but opened the front door and stared at him through the screen door. "Mr. Baynard? What are you doing here?"

"Herb Bessey told me that a friend of yours died."

"Herb? Why would he call you?"

"He didn't call me. He told me at dance class."

"But you're not in the class."

"I was going to join it tonight."

"Did Herb tell everyone why I wasn't there?"

"No, he just said you weren't coming tonight. Privately, I asked him why and he told me. He said you sounded distraught. May I come in?"

Libby was bewildered. How did he know where she lived? Oh, yes, she told him he had looked at a house across the road from her. Now, he was joining her dance class? This was so weird. There was a part of her that didn't think she should let him in, but her good manners kicked in automatically. "Oh, uh, yes. I'm sorry."

"I just came by to see if there was anything I could do," Mr. Baynard continued as he came in the door.

Mr. Baynard followed Libby into the living room, where Victor was. She gestured towards the sofa, "This is Victor, who was my very dear friend." She held back a sob, but tears came down her cheeks again.

"Oh, what a shame," Mr. Baynard said looking down at the little dog.

"I don't know where my manners are," Libby sniffled, "would you like some tea?"

"No, but I think you could use some," he said. "Sit and I'll get you some."

"No, no," she said," that wouldn't be right."

"I insist. I assure you, I can find my way around a kitchen well enough to boil water."

Libby heard the water run, cabinet doors open and close and a mug clink on the counter.

"You have quite a collection of tea here," he said. "What kind would you like?"

"I don't know," she said.

"Perhaps some Tension Tamer would be best," he said.

Libby sat beside Victor with her hand on his side. Mr. Baynard came in with a mug of hot tea and set it on the coffee table. "Tell me what happened to Victor."

Libby told him the story.

"I'm so sorry, Mrs. O'Malley." He put his hand over hers,"He is a beautiful animal."

"He was good company. He could sit here with me, doing nothing and be happy." She smiled wistfully, "He just loved life."

"That is the best any living being can do," said Mr. Baynard as he handed her his handkerchief.

"Thank you," Libby said and dabbed at her eyes and nose. "He was so good natured. I don't think his goodness could ever be tainted. What really breaks my heart is that this is it for him. Now, he'll go into the ground and rot. It seems so unfair for a little mortal soul as vivacious and sweet as he was."

They sat quietly for bit.

"What do you want to do with his body?" Mr. Baynard asked.

"I want to keep him here at home." Libby stroked Victor's ears. "I know this must seem like such an overreaction to you. I'm sorry."

"There is nothing to be sorry about," Mr. Baynard said. "You didn't ask me to come. I came because I wanted to see if you needed help. If you show me where you want to put him, I'll dig a grave for him."

Libby got a shovel from the porch and led Mr. Baynard to the back yard. "This was Victor's little kingdom," she said. "Let's put him in the corner near the ivy. Maybe later I'll plant a tree over his grave." She blotted her eyes again with the handkerchief.

David took the shovel from her hand. "Ow," she said, shaking her hand in pain, "I must have gotten a splinter from the handle."

"I'm so sorry," Mr. Baynard said putting down the shovel. He took her hand and ran his finger over the pad of her palm. Libby felt it snag on the sliver of wood. He looked closely at her hand, squeezed gently around the splinter and pulled it out. A drop of blood welled up, and he put his mouth over it and kissed it.

"Mr. Baynard, that is a foolish thing to do," she said incredulously. "How do you know I don't have AIDS or hepatitis or some other thing."

"Nonsense, not you, Mrs. O'Malley, and neither do I. Anyway, doesn't it feel better?" he asked.

"Well, yes it does," she said, "but still."

Mr. Baynard put his hand on her arm. "Go in and wrap Victor in something. I'll take care of this."

Libby went inside to the linen closet and let her fingers play along the towels and sheets until the soft touch of flannel caught her attention. She pulled out a flat, single sheet, its sailboat design was muted with time and wear. It would make a good shroud for Victor. She took the sheet to the living room and put it on the sofa next to Victor, and picked him up as she had so many times before, but the response of his wriggling muscles was gone. She supported his head so it wouldn't hang down and sat with him on her lap as they had done thousands of nights together. Out of habit she massaged his deformed right, front foot. Someone had stepped on it when he was tiny leaving him with only two and a half toes, although that never slowed him down. Holding him close, she rocked him back and forth.

Mr. Baynard found her like this. "Everything is ready outside," he said softly.

Libby didn't respond.

"Do you want to wait?" he asked.

"It won't do any good," she answered.

"Would you like me to do it?" He motioned toward the sheet opened on the couch.

"No, I have to do it." Libby turned with Victor in her arms. Gently, she arranged him on bottom third of the sheet, her hands trembling as she folded the short end over him, tucked it under and folded the sides over him. Picking him up again, she wrapped the rest of the sheet around him. She wondered at how small he was, he was bigger in life.

Mr. Baynard placed his hand under Libby's elbow, helped her up and led her to the back door. There was a narrow but deep hole in the corner.

"Mr. Baynard," Libby started to say.

"Please call me, David."

"David, would you hold him for a moment?"

David took the flannel bundle. Awkwardly, Libby got down on her knees at the edge of the hole. She reached up for Victor and David placed him in her hands. She reached down into the hole until she felt the damp clay on the backs of her hands and placed Victor there. David took her hands and helped her to her feet.

"I hate to leave him there," Libby said. She suddenly had a terrible thought. "He's definitely dead, right? He won't wake up and be buried alive, will he?" She felt that she should open the sheet and check one more time, just to be absolutely sure.

David gently put his arm around her. "No, he's gone."

She lean her forehead against his shoulder and cried. Tears slid down her face and onto his shirt. He soothed her like a child.,"Shhh," he whispered patting her back.

Finally, she straightened up and took a deep breath, "I'm ready now."

"You don't have to stay for this part. Go in, and I'll join you in a few minutes."

"Thank you," Libby turned and went inside. Later she heard David put the shovel away. He came into the kitchen and washed his hands.

"How are you, Mrs. O'Malley?" he asked.

"Libby," she offered. She was sitting at the table. Her eyes were red and swollen as was her nose, "I am very tired."

"Do you think you will be able to sleep?"

"I don't see how I could keep my eyes open much longer."

"I'll go then," he said. She got up to see him to the door.

At the door, David turned and put his hands on her shoulders. "I'll call tomorrow evening to see how you're doing."

"I don't know how to thank you. I don't think I could have done this alone."

"I'm glad I could help."

Libby closed the door and went to the kitchen. She washed Victor's bowls out for the last time and put them up on a high shelf in the broom closet. She took his pillow and put it in the washer. Upstairs as she changed into a nightgown, she noticed that her dress had some blood and dirt on it, so, she washed it out in the sink, scrubbing the stains with soap and an old toothbrush. She hung it up over the bath tub, climbed into bed and fell into a deep sleep until she heard knocking at the door.

It was still dark outside, but she couldn't find her clock to see what time it was. The knocking persisted. She put on a white eyelet robe and grey felt clogs and ran down the steps.

"Who is it?" she called through the door.

"It's David, Libby. I came by to see how you're doing."

Libby opened the wooden door. For the second time she talked to him through the screen door. "David? What time is it?"

"Well, from the position of the stars I'd say it's not too late." He looked at her robe and said, "I'm sorry were you already in bed?"

"No, I just woke up. Did I sleep the whole day away?"

"If you were still in bed from last night, yes."

"I guess so."

"May I come in?"

"I don't mean to be rude, especially after you've been so kind to me, but I don't think it looks right for me to be alone with you in my house especially in my nightgown."

"Then put something on and come outside. If you've been in bed all day, you really ought to take a walk and get some fresh air."

Libby went into the laundry room and exchanged her nightgown for a sun dress. She came out on the front porch to join David.

"Turn out the lights," he said, "I have something to show you."

She turned out the porch and living room lights.

"It's the end of the Perseids meteor showers." He held out his hand to her to guide her down the steps and led her to the open field on the side of the house. It was a clear night and the stars were bright. Out of the corner of her eye she caught movement of light.

"There's one!" David pointed over her shoulder. "They're coming from the Northeast."

The meteors came at a rate of at least two or three per minute. Most cut little chords across the invisible circle of the Earth's atmosphere, but occasionally one would streak diagonally through the middle of the sky.

"Come over here and lie down. You can see the whole sky," said David.

Libby saw a dark rectangle in the grass next to the wall of her garden shed. It was a blanket. "You sure came prepared," she said with misgivings.

"It's only a blanket," David smiled and sat down. He patted the space beside him. "Come, sit down."

Libby sat on the corner of the blanket farthest from him.

"It's better if you lie down, you can see everything without straining your neck," David said and then followed his own advice.

Libby lay down and looked up at the panoramic view. How long had it been since she had lain out under the clear night sky? Probably not since Brendan was in grammar school, probably to watch for shooting stars, then, too. Another one streaked across the sky. Faint breezes blew through the trees and grass as grasshoppers and crickets chirped. Those sounds were drowned out by the low roar of a fireball, after which the sky continued its soundless fireworks.

"This is heavenly," Libby sighed.

"Are you ready to go in yet?" asked David.

"No, just a few more minutes."

"Good," said David. He rolled toward her and raised himself up on his elbow. She looked at him. He lowered his lips to hers and kissed her lightly. He put his hand under her head and kissed her mouth again. She said nothing. She didn't want to think of words to say. She wanted to feel his kisses move along her jaw to her neck and back up behind her ear. Deep inside her something fluttered and her heart shifted into overdrive. She turned toward him, put her arms around his neck and breathed in his scent. He smelled good, not like soap or cologne, but like beeswax candles, clean with a hint of sweetness. She took a deep draught. He kissed her more deeply. Involuntarily the muscles in her back arched and she was pushing herself toward him. Suddenly she opened her eyes with a gasp. She had her pillow in a strangle hold and her mouth was still kissing back. "Wowzers," she whispered as she woke up completely. Her eyes were sore, her nose was stuffy and she had a headache. She remembered that she had been crying. She remembered that Victor was dead.

Chapter 10

In the bathroom, Libby found her dress dry and stainless. Looking in the mirror she saw her face looked the way it felt – puffy and warm. She washed and dressed mechanically, dreading going downstairs.

Victor was woven into her life. Just yesterday, he sat waiting for her at the bottom of the stairs, then stretched and kowtowed to his mistress. She bade him rise and taking his head in her hands, kissed him on the nose. He licked her toes, tickling her ankles with his soft, red fur.

She laughed and asked, "Do you want to go out the back?" His claws clicked like a tap dancer as he ran ahead to the back porch door. She caught up and opened the door to let him out. He didn't wait to get outside, but lifted his leg before he got off the porch. "Blast it all, Victor!" she said, running out and shooing him into the yard.

Now, she laughed and cried at the memory. She walked out the back door to see Victor's grave. The overturned soil had dried to a dull, tan patch amidst the greens of the grass and ivy. Back inside the house, she saw Victor's red leash hanging on the closet doorknob and remembered the frantic, happy wrestling matches they went through.

"God, I am so tired of losing the ones I love," Libby said clenching her fists. "What is going on? Why Victor? What difference could it make to You if he stayed with me?"

The house seemed empty. Her chest felt empty. She didn't want to do anything. Nothing she could do would make things better.

Libby didn't want to have to face people she knew and pretend everything was all right, so she planned to stay home. She hoped music therapy might help. Thinking of the saddest songs she knew, she started singing an old blues standard.

"I hate to see that evening sun go down
I hate to see that evening sun go down
Cause my baby, he's done left this town

If I am feelin' tomorrow, like I am feelin' today
If I am feelin' Tomorrow, like I am feelin' today
I'll pack up my truck and make my get-a-way"

Singing didn't help; Libby's spirit was still sore. Her grief manifested itself in restlessness, anxiety and turbulence. She wanted to break something or hurt someone. She had to get out, go somewhere no one she knew would find her. Not bothering to eat breakfast, she grabbed a red beach towel, her bathing suit, purse and car keys. She stalked outside, threw her stuff into the van and got in. Slamming into reverse, she wound the van around in a tight circle in the driveway throwing up dust and gravel. Once she got to the road, she peeled out and the tires screeched. The effect would have been better in a pickup truck or a sports car instead of a mini-van, but that was all she had. She headed East toward the ocean.

Libby did not stick to her usual seven-miles-over-the-speed-limit rule. It was early and the road was clear, so she tromped the gas pedal hoping with speed she could outrun her hurt. She wanted to go far and fast. Farm fields and scrub forests flew by. She had to hit the brakes for a stop sign or a sharp curve here and there, but she didn't have to think about her route. She drove by gut instinct to a place she knew well. In little more than an hour she reached Ocean City. It was a weekday and with the summer season over the place was nearly deserted. She parked right next to the boardwalk where most stands were already battened down. Down on the beach abandoned life guard stands and boats were pulled high up on the sand waiting for the weekend shift.

Libby saw a sign stating it was illegal to change clothes in a vehicle. "Too darn bad, a lot of things that aren't supposed to happen, happen anyway," she said and got into the back of her van where she was hidden by the tinted windows. After she was in her bathing suit, she walked up the wooden ramp and down the stairs to the sugar-white sand. The sand was warm between her flip flops and the soles of her feet. She dropped the bundle of her towel, clothes and keys down on the hard packed sand near the water, and with her hands on her hips surveyed the ocean.

It was wild with big rolling waves, up to three at a time slamming on to the shore. Water sprayed high off of the edge of the rock jetty that ran fifty feet out into the surf. In the back of her mind she remembered hearing a hurricane was forming off the Carolina coast. The forecast said it would blow out to sea before hitting New Jersey. The air on the beach was calm, but somewhere out there, hundred-mile-an-hour winds churned the sea and pushed it North into this beach inlet. She walked into the ocean and took a sharp breath at the first touch of cold, foamy water. She got used to it and went out further where waves rushed in at knee height. The water pulled out again, sucking sand from under her feet. She was up to her ankles in wet sand when the next wave came. The immensity of the ocean always awed her and with the added power of the storm it lured her deeper. She pushed through the crashing water, lifting her arms over her head and turning sideways to present a narrower area for the hard slap of the waves. When she got out past the breakers, she lay back and floated on the great humped backs of the waves. Her chest muscles relaxed as she was pushed toward the sky and then dropped into the trough between waves. The water felt like silk flowing around her legs.

Libby had not looked back to the beach for a long time, turning over onto her stomach she saw the little, red dot that was her towel. The waves had pulled her far out; she needed get closer to shore. She was a decent swimmer, but swimming in the ocean could be tricky. She had broken the cardinal rules - she was at an unguarded beach, swimming alone.

This was not smart, Libby, she chastised herself. She took powerful strokes and kicked hard, but got nowhere. When she turned her head to take a breath, a little wave on top of a wave hit her in the face. Salt water got into her mouth and eyes. She choked and spit. Her eyes stung so she couldn't see, and she still couldn't touch the bottom. Icy fear surged through her, emanating from her belly out to her hands and feet and head. Unable to stop herself, she panicked. Her arms and legs flailed on their own. She went completely under and was turned over by the next big wave. She wasn't sure which way was up.

Mentally giving herself a stern shake, she shouted inside her head, *You are not going to drown and leave your sons orphans, because you had a temper tantrum.*

She opened her eye a crack underwater to see which way daylight was and pulled herself to the surface, gasping and coughing.

Help me, Lord. Help me, Lord. Libby prayed repeatedly. She calmed down and floated on her back for a moment resting and thinking, *I'm moving away from the shore even though the tide is still coming in. Could be a riptide.*

She searched her mind for what she knew about riptides. They were very powerful, and she was in big trouble. Something from the Boy Scout swimming merit badge book came to mind, "Riptides are not wide. The victim should swim parallel to the shore until he is out of it."

Libby swam to the right, doing a side stroke and scissor kick. That required less energy and let her keep an eye on the shore so she could see if she was making any headway. She got close to the jetty, which was good and bad. Good - she wasn't being pulled further out. Bad - she was getting too close to the huge boulders. Carefully, she rode a wave toward shore. She only took it in a little ways, but now she could stand with her head above water.

She was staring at the jetty trying to determine, without her glasses, how close she was to the submerged rocks, when a big breaker came up behind her. She got caught in its motion and was dragged forward and under. Luckily, she hit the sand in shallow water instead of a rock, however, the little wind she had left was knocked out of her. Another wave roared in and her body was rasped along the broken shells on the bottom. She got up on her hands and knees, sand gritting between her teeth, but she couldn't get on her feet fast enough before the next wave knocked her flat again and dragged her back out. When the third wave pushed her further up on the sand, she was finally able to crawl the rest of the way out of the water's grip. She collapsed on the dry sand. She thought about how close she had come to dying, and started to shake. It took moment to focus on the sand and the two small tan feet in front of her.

"Mrs. O, is that you? Are you okay? We thought you were a goner. My aunt called 911."

Libby rolled over on her side and was amazed to see Jesse's worried face. Gasping, she managed to sputter, "Tell her ... I don't need 911 ... anymore."

"Okay." Jesse shouted at the top of his lungs, "Hey, Aunt Jackie, she don't need 911 no more!"

Libby sat up hunched over on the sand. Her chest hurt, when she took a deep breath. She coughed and she took shallow breaths. A young woman in a black bikini and metallic sandals came running. Jesse said to her, "It is my teacher, Mrs. O! Can you believe it?"

"You mean that feisty one you were telling us about?" Aunt Jackie asked. To Libby she said, "You don't look so good. You're all red and scratched up."

"Yeah," said Jesse, "you're a mess. Your hair is stickin' up on one side and your eyes are bloodshot."

Jesse's aunt gave him a nudge and shook her head. "What were you doing out so far? Are you okay? Do you need help?"

Libby shook her head, intending to answer the last question. Instead she hoarsely asked her own question. "Did you see a red towel?"

"That was yours? I saw it way back there," Jesse said pointing down the beach. "Do you want me to get it for you?"

"Yes, ... please," said Libby. As Jesse and his aunt turned to go she added, "Be careful, my keys are in there."

Libby sat on the hard packed sand with her legs straight out in front of her facing the water. Not able to stand up yet, she turned over onto her hands and knees and crawled a little further from the surf. The hiss of the waves coming in and retreating sounded like the breathing of a giant beast. She stayed parallel to the ocean so she could keep an eye on it. When Jesse returned, he helped her put the towel out on the sand. She rolled over on the towel and lay down. Shading her eyes from the sun with her hand she said, "Thank you."

"We're gonna get ice cream. Do you want to come?" Jesse asked.

"That's kind of you to ask, but I think I'm just going to rest here for a while."

"You're sure?" asked Jessie's aunt.

"Yes, and again thank you both so much."

"Okay, then, Mrs. O. I'll see you on Friday," said Jesse.

As he and his aunt turned to leave, Libby said, "I just realized, today is a school day. What are you doing here, Jesse?"

"My aunt said I needed a mental health day. How about you, Mrs. O?"

"I needed a mental health day, too."

Libby realized her mood had improved, she didn't feel depressed or restless. Scaring the hell out of herself was, apparently, good for getting rid of the blues. She closed her eyes and listened to the pounding waves. Now and then she turned her head and cracked an eyelid to make sure she was still a safe distance from the fury. She mumbled a prayer, "Thank you, God, for saving me and for sending Jesse to help." Looking out at the sea again she mused, *Here is this enormous bowl of water and I'm sitting right on the lip of it. One good slosh and this whole beach would be wiped out. Lord, please keep the sea where it belongs and me out of it.*

Libby fell asleep and awoke to the shrill tweets of sandpipers. She opened her eyes and watched the little birds and their comical, stiff-legged run. They looked like a fast-forwarded old home movie. She looked around her and decided it was time to get up and go home. She was sticky from salt rime and sandy all over, and when she sat up, she felt dizzy and headachy. She looked at her legs. They were sunburned as well as scraped. "Great, I forgot sunscreen along with every other sensible thing today."

Slowly, Libby got up and walked back to her car. Having had the stuffing knocked out of her, she wasn't moved to break the law again and change out of her suit in the car. As she pulled her blouse over her bathing suit, the skin on her shoulders felt hot and tight and she desperately needed to use the bathroom. Her first stop on the way home was Mickey D's. In the bathroom one glance in the mirror told her hair was a disaster and she hadn't 'tanned' evenly. There was a white splotch over one eye where her bangs had blocked the sun. Her hair was so stiff and knotted, it hurt too much to pull a comb through it. Making a bee line out to her car, she pulled on an old ball cap and went through the drive thru. Parking at the far end of the lot, she devoured a Big Mac. After that and a large cup of hot tea she felt much better. Sitting there in her car, she thought about what had almost happened today.

"I did everything wrong and almost got killed today. So what should I learn from this? I always tell you, Father, that you have to be very direct. I don't get subtle messages. I'm better off with the sledgehammer approach. Today was probably a sledgehammer moment, but I still don't know what it's telling me to do."

At home, Libby felt the dull ache of Victor's absence. She went upstairs and took a shower, but no water temperature was comfortable. Warm burned the sunburn and cool gave her the shivers. Eventually, she dressed in a nightgown, took a pain reliever and went to bed with wet hair. When she woke up it was dark outside and she felt groggy, sore and sad. She put on her robe and went downstairs. It was only seven thirty, so she had hours to kill before she could fall sleep again.

"I should have stuck with the music therapy," Libby said to no one. She flipped through her music file. Finally, she found what she needed, *Dies Irae (Day of Wrath)*. For 800 years it had been part of the Mass of the Dead. From her boys she knew the haunting Gregorian chant melody had been used in the soundtracks of *Star Wars, Mad Max: Fury Road* and *The Matrix* to convey loss and destruction. Now it was Libby's soundtrack.

Libby chanted the Latin words, while the English translation ran through her mind.

> *"Day of wrath and doom impending*
> *David's word and Sibyl's blending*
> *Heaven and Earth in ashes ending ...*
> *... The mighty trumpet's wondrous tone*
> *Shall rend each tomb's sepulchral stone*
> *And summon all before the throne ...*

A knock at the door stopped Libby short. "Who is it?" she called through the wooden door.

"It's David, Libby. I came to see how you're doing."

Libby remembered her dream. The hairs on the back of her neck stood up. "I wasn't expecting anyone," she said. She opened the main door but kept the screen door between them.

"Don't you remember, I said last night that I would call on you?" David asked.

"Oh, I thought you meant on the phone."

"I'm sorry if I'm disturbing you. I wanted to make sure you were all right."

"I had a rather wild day."

He motioned toward her bathrobe, "Were you getting ready for bed?"

She looked down at herself. "No, I just got up from a long nap."

"Why don't you change and come out for a walk?" David suggested. "It's a lovely evening. You could probably use some fresh air."

Libby's body shook as she headed to the laundry room. Was she diving headlong into dream *deja vu*? She found undergarments, a maxi skirt and a pink, cotton sweater. She winced as she pulled the clothing on over her sunburn. She wished she could go upstairs and get some aloe, but it would be rude to keep David waiting. She returned to the front door and slipped on sandals she'd left in the hall.

"That was quick," David remarked. "You look lovely." He held his hand out to her to guide her down the steps. "You're shivering," he said. "Would you like my jacket?" He didn't wait for an answer. He took off his jacket and placed his over her shoulders. He took her hand, pulled her arm through his and placed his warm hand over her fingers.

"It's not really cold, it just the dampness," Libby said. "Do you think we'll see any of the Perseids tonight?"

David looked down at her and said, "I'd be surprised. They usually peak around mid-August. I'm afraid we're a few weeks too late."

"Of course, I guess I lost track of time." Libby felt relieved and giddy. She laughed as they walked over the lawn.

"What is it?" David asked.

"The blades of grass are tickling my toes. Wait!" Libby stopped, closed her eyes and sniffed lightly. "Do you smell the honeysuckle?" She took a deep breath, "Mmm. It is so sweet, I can taste it."

"Yum," he said, "that is good."

She laughed again and gave him a poke with her elbow.

"There may not be any falling stars, but it's a good night for stargazing," David said looking straight up.

"There's the Big Dipper, the Little Dipper and the North Star and over there is Orion's Belt." Libby said pointing from right to left.

"Let's see what else we can find," David said, "west of Orion should be the Seven Sisters that he perpetually pursues. There." He pointed. "They are part of Taurus, which is not quite as visible tonight, but there is Queen Cassiopeia and her daughter Andromeda."

"Very good!" cheered Libby.

Libby and David walked arm in arm. A breeze caused a flurry of small mimosa leaves to fall heralding the beginning of autumn. Libby sighed wistfully.

David quoted,

"Margaret, are you grieving
Over golden grove unleaving?"

Libby recited the next couplet,

"It is the blight that man was born for
It is Margaret that you mourn for."

"Dear old Gerard Manley Hopkins always hits it out of the ball park." Libby mimed a batter swinging for the bleachers.

"I only remember a few lines here and there," said David, "ones that have meant something to me. I bet you like this one:

And for all this, nature is never spent;
There lives the dearest freshness deep down things"

"That is one of my favorites," Libby said. "I think it's saying when life lands on you like a ton of bricks, sometimes the beauty of Nature can save you." To herself she thought, *Even if it has to whack you on the back of the head.*

"In honor of Fr. Hopkins' *God's Grandeur*, I think we should both take our shoes off," said Libby slipping her sandals off. She looked at David expectantly. He was going through the poem in his head and finally said, *"The soil is bare now, nor can foot feel being shod."*

"Well," said Libby, "the soil isn't bare, but the wet grass feels wonderful."

David leaned back against a tree and took off his shoes and socks. He wiggled his toes in the moss and grass. "Hmm," David breathed a sigh. "We should have done this in Poetry 101. I have never enjoyed poetry so literally and three dimensionally."

Libby replied, "But sometimes it is better not to think about the words too much and just let the loveliness wash over you."

David took her hands in his and looked into her eyes. "Libby, you are the most wonderfully alive person."

For a moment she was speechless. What could she say, "Almost dying will do that." Instead, she said, "Thank you," as her mother had taught her to do when receiving a compliment. She smiled and gently removed her hands from his. "I guess I should be going in. It was very kind of you to come over and check on me. I hope you won't think me ungrateful for not asking you in, last night was an extraordinary circumstance. I don't think it looks proper for me to be in the house alone with a strange man. I mean, a man I don't know well."

"If you're worried about appearances," David said, "I don't think anyone knows I'm here."

Libby was afraid she would seem priggish, but she wanted to be straight forward. "I don't think I should be alone with you, not just because it looks improper, but because it is improper."

"After all, character is what you do when no one is looking," David added helpfully.

"Exactly," she said relieved.

"I understand," he said picking up her sandals and handing them to her. " Good night, Libby. I'll see you tomorrow evening at the library."

Chapter 11

Thursday night David came to the library for his second computer lesson. Libby was a little shy around him after their last two encounters, but she got down to business. At the end of the lesson they had set up a free email account for David. The lights dimmed announcing closing time. Again he asked if he could walk her to her car.

"Mr. Baynard ..."

"David," he reminded her.

"Well, about that, David, this is a small town and I'm afraid tongues will wag if I let you walk me out to the parking lot all the time. Most people would say we still don't know each other very well."

"Would it help if you got to know me better?"

Libby hesitated, "I'm not sure."

"At least you didn't say, 'No'. Would you like to get some coffee?" he asked.

"Now?"

"Sure, you have your own car. You can drive yourself and leave whenever you please."

Libby realized she was hungry and David's suggestion sounded prudent. "All right," she said slowly. "I didn't really eat dinner."

"Good, follow me. I know a place that has superb carrot cake."

To heck with Atkins, Libby thought, *after yesterday, I'm going to eat whatever I want.*

David opened Libby's car door for her and then got into his truck which was parked next to her car again. She followed him out to the interstate, where he headed north. They went for a long way, and she was getting concerned. Finally, he exited at a truck stop and pulled into the parking lot. She parked next to him, and he helped her out. He offered her his arm and they walked into the diner, where they sat in one of the back booths.

A waitress came to take their orders, she gave David an admiring glance, "I'm Alexis and I'll be taking care of you tonight. What can I get for you?"

David nodded toward Libby. "I'd like a cup of hot tea with two creams," she said.

"I'll have a cup of coffee, black. Do you have any carrot cake left?" David asked.

"We sure do," said the waitress.

"How about it, Libby? Do you want to give it a try?" David asked.

"Sure."

"Good, a big slice of carrot cake and two forks," said David.

"Coming right up," said the waitress sticking her pencil behind her ear.

"It's strange. I've around lived here for almost twenty years and I've never come to this place," said Libby.

"Probably because it is designed to attract drivers passing through on the highway, while you tend to favor things closer to home," David suggested.

The waitress returned with their orders and she gave Libby her tea. "If you need anything else just give me a wave," she said setting the cake and David's coffee down in front of him.

After the girl walked away, Libby leaned across the table and said conspiratorially, "I think our young waitress fancies you."

"Well, I hope you fancy this carrot cake," David said as he carefully lifted a cream cheese frosting rosette onto his fork and raised it Libby's lips. She tasted it.

"Mmmm," she said rolling her eyes heavenward, "that is good."

David put the fork on the plate and pushed the cake closer to her.

"How come I'm the only one stuffing my cheeks?" Libby asked.

"Because I've already eaten and you haven't."

"And cake is one of my favorite food groups." She took a sip of tea and said, "Well, we might as well get right down to it. What do you want from me?"

"I admire your directness," David said.

Libby gave a slight nod and continued, "A week ago I'd never heard of you. Now I've seen you four times in one week. You can imagine how that might set off alarms."

"You worry that I am pursuing you because you might be a well-to-do widow?"

"Certain people around town might see it that way."

"Would it help if I could prove to you that I was very comfortable financially?"

Heat spread up from Libby's chest, she wasn't as self-assured about this as she sounded.   "You wouldn't need to prove it to me, you'd need to prove it to the gossips."

"Okay, more conspicuous consumption on my part. Check," David said marking off an item on an invisible to-do list.

Libby made a little snort, "Okay, that was easy. Now here is my problem. What's in this for you? You're intelligent, good looking, well off and younger than I am. I on the other hand have wrinkles, saddle bags, a double chin, a bum knee, graying hair and -"

"Those are all external things that could be cured if one wished," David interrupted.

"But, they are not 'cured' and I don't even know if I would want to."

"All that is irrelevant," said David. "You have a joy for living. You're kind. You're fascinating. You have the knowledge and wisdom that come from intelligence and experience. What's in it for me? You're good company and I feel at peace in your presence."

What objection could anyone have to that? Libby was flummoxed. "So," she said, "I could be like a big sister."

"I have no desire to call you 'sister' and I'm forty, not much younger than you are."

"So, you are telling me you like me for my personality?"

"If in personality you are including character and soul, then yes, I like you for your personality."

"That is almost a bad joke. When I try make matches for friends, if I say, 'Oh, she has a wonderful personality,' the guy will want to see a photograph thinking 'wonderful personality' is code for nice but unfortunate looking."

"There is nothing unfortunate about you," David countered. "Your eyes are this velvety blue that is almost violet. You have a womanly figure, which is so appropriate for a woman. You have a delightful sense of humor and a sincere smile. You have this presence. When you walk into a room, people's faces light up. When you greet someone, you look him in the eye and ask how he's doing. Then, you actually listen to the answer. That interaction with you may be the only time that person has really been seen and heard all day. You're like a comet that leaves a trail of light behind it that warms people."

Libby's cheeks were flaming, "I hardly know you, when did you make all these, these … observations."

"I've seen you around, in the library, the grocery store. Just around."

Libby was fanning herself with her napkin. She was hot and perspiring like mad. She wished she could open another button on her blouse, but now would not be a good time.

"I'm sorry, this just doesn't make sense," she said with false nonchalance forking up another piece of carrot cake.

"Why are you so determined to talk me out of my attraction to you?" David asked.

"Because it doesn't add up, it goes against my empirical evidence; BC I used to be a scientist."

"What do you mean BC?"

"BC stands for before children. In college I studied biology and physics."

"I thought you studied music?"

"My senior thesis was *The Physiology and Physics of Vocal Music.*"

"And what was your conclusion?" David asked.

"That the human body is like the body of an instrument. The volume and the density of the body make up the physical qualities of the sound chamber for the voice, just like the body of a guitar or violin. Like the violin and guitar, the voice is also a string instrument. The individual characteristics of the vocal cords make each voice unique, as unique as finger prints," Libby said holding up her hand palm up with fingers spread.

"That's another thing I like about you. You're interesting to talk to."

"You got me off on a tangent!" Libby said. "The point is, I like things to make sense. Biologically and culturally you should be seeking women as much as 20 years younger than you are. That's how it works at singles' clubs like Parents Without Partners. I would be attracting fat, balding, nearly-seventy-year-old geezers."

"Do you know this from experience?" asked David. "Have you had many relationships with septuagenarians?"

"No, and I'm not interested in having a relationship with anyone. It was my mother who went to those clubs for widowed and divorced people, when she was widowed twenty-four years ago. For ten years, I heard her stories."

"Why only ten years?"

"She remarried and was widowed again ten years later."

"That adds up," David said with a grin.

Libby rolled her eyes.

David continued, "Your mother sounds like quite the *femme fatale.*"

"She passed away recently, but she said senior dating wasn't that sophisticated. It was more like high school or even junior high. 'Jennie, don't turn around, but Walter is looking at you. Oh, oh, he's coming this way. I think he's going to ask you to dance.' Then it's 'Do you want to go steady? Will you wear my class ring?'"

"It sounds rather charming."

"Yes, it does, until the old guy puts his hand on your derriere or says, 'Do you want to come back to my place?' Wink, wink. Nudge, nudge. He has his line all ready, 'After all you can't get pregnant any more. I mean you're fifty years old, what are you saving it for?' To which my mother would reply, 'It's not that I don't want to have sex. I just don't want to have sex with you.'"

"Ow! I can see where you get your directness."

"My mother would say that just to bust the guy's chops. She was a good Catholic girl, who didn't believe in sex outside of marriage."

"Are you a good, Catholic girl?" David asked.

"Yes, of course." Libby regretted starting this line of conversation.

"So, in the meantime," David went on, "a man my age is consigned to twenty-somethings, as they're called today."

"Yes, especially if you are handsome and prosperous."

"Should I take that as a compliment?"

"You may take it as a fact."

"A complimentary fact," David said smiling. " According to your theory, I should be attending clubs and bars in search of a woman wearing those ridiculous sheep-skin boots with a cell phone permanently attached to her ear and a pair of sweatpants or shorts with words printed across her bottom. As she walks the words rise and fall -- 'Volley' 'Ball', 'Volley' 'Ball' or 'New' 'York', 'New' 'York'. I once saw a young lady whose backside was so prodigious that she could have carried off Mississippi." David was using his hands to give an example of the wave pattern the jiggling letters might make.

David's antics made Libby choke on her tea. She laughed so hard that it came out of her nose. She covered her face with a napkin, as tears rolled down her face, but she couldn't stop laughing. David came around the table and sat next to her so could he pat her on the back. He began chuckling. That grew into guffawing. In a minute they were both laughing like fools. Slowly, Libby regained her composure. She wiped her mouth and nose with the napkin. A few more giggles escaped her. She dabbed at her eyes.

"I'm all right now." Libby breathed. "I haven't laughed that hard in ages."

"Neither have I," said David.

"Now, where were we?"

"Butt shorts, I believe they're called," said David chortling.

"Don't start that again," Libby said, playfully cuffing him on the shoulder. "Those … items of apparel are more a college student style."

"But college girls are in their twenties. So, I invite a charming co-ed to dinner and we attempt to have a conversation. She says, 'Like, I was watching this reality show, you know? And my roommate was all up in my business like, 'How can you watch that shh…. , sorry I mean crap. Anyway then I'm like 'This totally gives you insight into real life, like when her belly button ring gets caught on her thong.'"

Libby pushed her fist against her mouth to keep from laughing again. Suppressing a smile she replied, "Fine, then look for an intelligent woman in her early 30's."

David shook his head, "They are all tied up in their careers and forget to have time for real life."

Libby shook her head, "You make fun, but you're being unfair to young, modern women. They have it tough. There is always a tug of war going on in their hearts, souls and minds between personal life and work. They have the idealism that every young person needs and confidence that they are going to be a success and change the world. Young people need that to give them the drive and energy to work hard. Meanwhile, a woman always has that and the primordial undertow of yearning for love, home and family.

"I wouldn't want to go back to my twenties or thirties. When you get to your mid-forties you have that reality check that corrects your expectations. You are probably not going to be the youngest CEO, law partner or college professor in history, and you begin to realize that it isn't necessary for a full, happy life, and that you are doing well just to get this far. I've learned that every person has a story that will surprise you, and everyone needs a dose of kindness at least once a day. That's the wisdom of an older woman."

David became serious. "That's the kind of woman I'm looking for, one who has lived and learned the most important things about life. Do you believe that you are a better person now than you were twenty years ago?"

"Yes," agreed Libby. "I have grown a lot since I got married and I've definitely become a better human being since I had children. My sons are the number one priority in my life. I would do whatever I felt necessary to raise them to be good men - move heaven and earth or even become a housewife, if that is what it took."

"Does that change consist in your feelings toward your children, exclusively?"

"No," Libby said thoughtfully, "at first, it included other children. I understood what made them happy or what hurt them – like not getting invited to a birthday party or having somebody eat something in front of them and not offer them any. Then it expanded to their parents. I knew how much it meant to me for someone to be kind to my child or how it broke my heart to see my child hurt. Eventually, I saw each person as somebody's baby or somebody's mother or father."

"Empathy leads to compassion," added David. "Women who are mothers have learned to love others more than themselves. You've learned that lesson three times over. That's why you radiate an air of kindness."

"That's all very flattering, but my being seen with you could still cause a scandal. Have you heard the expressions 'boy toy' or 'eye candy'?"

"I don't care what other people think," David said with a wave of his hand.

"I do care," said Libby, "I live here and my sons do, too, occasionally. I don't want to be a foolish, middle-aged woman running around with a younger man. It would be an embarrassment to my family."

"Is this because of the sexual aspect of such a relationship?"

"Yes, that's probably at the heart of it. It is hubristic for a woman to believe an attractive, younger man would be interested in her romantically … physically. There would have to be some other reason for the appeal, like money, fame, position or, worse, a mother figure. The younger man has to get something out of the relationship, other than sex with a saggy, baggy old woman."

"You are not a saggy, baggy old woman and being with you makes me happy. Isn't that a good enough reason to want to be around you?"

Again, Libby had nothing to say to such a simple, good reason.

"Would it help if I were homosexual?" David asked.

"What?"

"Could we be seen together if I was a homosexual? Then it wouldn't appear to be about sex."

"That's ridiculous. You aren't gay. Are you?"

"See, you aren't sure."

"David, you're making my head spin, and it's getting late. I have to go. Thank you for the scoop about the carrot cake. It was magnificent," Libby said as she slid out of the booth.

David stood up and picked up the check. "Wait, I'll drive out with you and make sure you get home safely."

"That's nice of you, but I know my way from here."

"Let me walk you out to your car," David said as they headed toward the cashier.

"This all sounds so familiar," said Libby wryly.

David smiled, his dimples deepened, "It's the way my mother raised me."

Again, he offered Libby his arm. They walked down the steps of the diner to their vehicles. Standing between his truck and her car, David opened her door and said, "There's still a lot you still don't know about me. We should go out to coffee again."

"Perhaps."

"I'll see you next Tuesday at dance class. That will give you five days of not seeing me at all, unless something comes up."

Chapter 12

Friday morning, Libby wondered if it would be awkward between her and Jesse after the incident at the beach. When the aide dropped him off, he looked at her in silence for a moment. "I was thinkin' maybe I wouldn't see you today."

"Oh?" replied Libby.

"I told my cousin about you, about how your husband died and everything and about why you come here, and she said maybe you were trying to kill yourself."

"Oh, no! It was nothing like that," Libby said quickly. "I just did some stupid things without thinking, like swimming alone at a place without a lifeguard."

"How could someone smart like you do that?" Jesse said almost belligerently. "You could have died." His voiced cracked a little. Libby wasn't sure if it was emotion or puberty sneaking in.

"I wasn't thinking. I was upset about something and I just didn't think. I'm sorry."

"What you so upset about?" he asked, narrowing his eyes.

"It's kind of embarrassing. My dog died and I was sad and hurt and I just wanted to get away."

"How did your dog die?"

"He got hit by a car."

"Oh."

"What makes it even worse is that it was my fault he got hit. He got out the front door before I could stop him."

"Yeah," said Jesse shaking his head. "My dog died last year."

"What happened?", Libby asked.

"He got sick," Jesse said. "The vet said there was something wrong with his heart, but my grandma said we didn't have enough money for the medicine Godzilla needed. So he died.

74

I was really mad about that. If we had more money, he'd still be alive."

"I'm sorry that happened to Godzilla and you."

Libby and Jesse sat quietly for a moment. "What are you working on in math this week?" she asked.

"Fractions and percentages. I don't get 'em."

"Do you like baseball?" Libby asked.

"Yeah," Jesse answered suspiciously.

"What does it mean to say someone is batting five hundred?"

"Nobody bats five hundred," he replied.

"Maybe not in the major leagues, but how about a little league player?"

Jesse blew air out through puckered lips, "Little League is for losers."

"Okay, what does it mean if a basketball player's free throw percentage is fifty percent?" Libby said taking a new tack.

"It means he needs more practice."

"And why is that?" Libby asked leading him.

"Because he's missing half his foul shots."

"Exactly," Libby said. "Who's your favorite basketball player?"

"LeBron James," Jesse said without hesitation.

"What are his stats?"

"His career free throw is about seventy-four and field goals fifty-seven."

"What do you mean when you say his free throw is seventy-four?"

"What do you mean, 'what do I mean'?"

"Doesn't it means if he gets to the free throw line a hundred times he'll get the shot in seventy-four times? These are all percentages. What if a player hasn't gotten to the free throw line a hundred times yet? Can we still figure out his statistics?"

Jesse looked puzzled.

"Sure we can. If you made ten foul shots and you got seven of them in ..."

Libby wrote on the white board 7/10 = 7 divided by 10.

"Give it a shot," she said with a wink and held out the marker to him.

He groaned at the pun, "Oh, that's bad," and took the marker from her.

When they finished working on percentages, Libby pulled out the *Indian in the Cupboard* for them to read. They read aloud until the end of their 50 minutes.

"Hey, can I keep this book?" Jesse asked shyly.

"I took it out of the library, so you have to promise to bring it back in two weeks. Deal?"

"Deal," he said giving Libby the best smile she'd seen from him yet.

Chapter 13

After Mass on Sunday, the choir director asked Libby to stay behind. She wondered if he wanted to work on a solo with her. "Mrs. O'Malley," he started out.

"Please, Derek, call me Libby." He was only three years older than her oldest son. She figured he was self-conscious about being an authority figure.

"Thank you ... Libby," he continued awkwardly, "you are the strongest first alto voice I've got." She smiled at him and was about to say thank you, but he rushed on. "So, when you're off, it really shows."

"Oh," said Libby.

"You've got the old material down perfectly, but in the new arrangement of this Sunday's psalm there are two G sharps that you sang as G's," he said pointing at the score. "We'll be using this again in a few weeks. I thought maybe we could go over it now while we're here by ourselves."

"Certainly, Derek," she said putting her purse down.

"Okay, here's the beginning of the phrase," he sat down and played the chords. "Now the first alto part, let's go over this section." He played again and Libby sang along. "You're still a tad flat. Let the organ guide you." He held a sustained G sharp. The awful realization came to her, she had trouble hearing and matching the tone.

When he said, "That's it!" She tried to feel it in her voice instead of hearing it. "You may be experiencing some hearing loss," Derek opined. "It's common as people get into their fifties."

Libby wanted to say, 'I'm only 47!', but remembered her mother was hard of hearing before she was fifty, so she just nodded.

Derek continued, "I'm thinking maybe you should stand next to Mrs. Stanton, she is as reliable as a pitch pipe. Try to blend with her until you're sure you've got it - then sing, gently."

Libby forced a smile and said, "I'll do that." Afterwards, she walked quickly to her car, slammed the door behind her and put her head in her hands. She was ashamed of messing up the song during Mass and not even knowing it, and worried because of what this might mean for the future. Might her hearing get so bad that she wouldn't be able to learn new music? If she had to quit the choir, on top of cutting her off from the joy of singing with the group, it would leave another empty night in her calendar.

So, when Tuesday rolled around again, Libby found herself eagerly looking forward to ballroom dance class. She arrived early, and David was waiting for her at the far end of the parking lot.

"Hello, Libby, darling," he called. He walked toward her briskly with perfect posture, and gave her an air kiss on each cheek. "How do you like my costume?" he whispered in her ear.

He stepped back to show his lilac polo shirt, close fitting chinos, penny loafers and lilac and pink argyle socks.

With raised brows she whispered back,"What are you doing?"

"I am showing you and everyone else that I'm gay, so you won't be afraid to be seen with me in public," he said.

"You're not a gay man, you are a caricature of a gay man," she hissed through clenched teeth that she hoped would pass as a smile if any one saw them. "Don't you dare go in there dressed and acting like this."

David's face fell. "But, I don't have anything to change into and I don't want to miss the class."

"This was a bad idea, David. You either have to change or miss the class."

Without another word, David turned and walked back to his truck.

Libby went inside. One of the women in the class showed Libby her new dancing shoes.
They were classic character dance shoes, taupe, leather pumps with ankle straps and a one and a half inch heel.

Libby smiled and said,"These are perfect. It looks like you're taking this dance class seriously."

The woman replied happily, "My husband and I are getting ready for our daughter's wedding."

"Congratulations!" said Libby.

Then Herb called the class to order, "All right let's begin with a brief review of last week's class. Libby, we're glad to have you back. We missed you last week."

"Thanks," Libby said.

Herb held his hand out to her.

"Would you help me refresh everyone's memory of the basic steps?"

She took his hand and they got into closed dance position.

"Music, Maestro," Herb called to the young man standing near the CD player. As Tony Bennett crooned *I Left My Heart in San Francisco*, Herb led Libby through a series of straight, turning and box steps, while describing each step to the class.

"Thank you, Libby," Herb said letting her go. "Okay, is everyone ready to try it?"

Libby left the floor to find one of the single ladies who might need a partner.

Soon after David walked in the door wearing a short sleeved blue
oxford shirt, comfortable looking black pants, black socks and the penny loafers.

After Herb and Libby finished the next demonstration David walked over to her saying, "K-Mart was open, but now I've missed the first two-and-a-half lessons. Would you mind tutoring me?"

Not sure if she would laugh or croak, Libby nodded her assent.

"I think I've got the basic rhythms down, so we can go right into dancing," David said. He held up his left hand and Libby placed her right hand in his palm. When he placed his hand on her back, she nearly jumped. She could feel the heat and pressure of each of his fingers through her dress. She felt warmth radiating from his chest and arms. It felt much more intimate than when she danced with Herb. She left six inches between their torsos as she remembered Sister Trinita's command at St. Joseph's High School dances, "Leave room for the Holy Spirit."

Thinking back to high school and college dances, Libby wondered how she let so many guys get so close to her in public? It was exciting at first with Frank, but the thrill of touching wore off over the years. They hugged, they kissed, they occasionally danced, but their touching had become a habit – comfortable instead of erotic. At this moment with David, she felt imminently combustible.

She worked to keep a serene look on her face, but her mouth went dry as her heart sped up. She wanted to lick her lips, but was afraid it would look suggestive, so she made the most common ballroom dance faux pas and looked down at her feet. She missed a step and kicked David in the ankle. What was it about him that transformed her from a sensible woman into a bungling mess?

"I am so sorry," Libby said wishing she could disappear.

"It was my fault I'm sure," David said gallantly, "let's start again."

Libby kept her head up with her eyes looking just over David's left shoulder so she didn't have to make eye contact. David led her around the floor, "You are an excellent partner for me," he said, "it's nice to have a woman who is closer to my height."

This made an impression on Libby, because she aware she was taller than most women and many men, too. Early on she was quite self-conscious of her height, like when she was twelve years old and was five feet nine inches tall weighing 150 pounds. She was nearly a foot taller than the boy she had a crush on in seventh grade. She probably had fifty pounds on him, too. She worried she was not as feminine as other girls because she was bigger than they were. She grew another inch by high school graduation. Back then her measurements were 36-27-36, which looked attractive on her, but the waif-look was already in vogue and she was never going to be a waif. After having three babies, she wore a size 10 1/2 W shoe and a size 16 W dress.

"Your being a woman of substance helps, too," David said.

Libby raised her eyebrows.

"Did you know," David asked, "that Marilyn Monroe was a size 14? I saw one of her costumes in a museum once. But as I was saying, dancing with someone with more substance helps with balance and centrifugal force." To demonstrate his point, he pulled her closer and executed a two-step pivot turn, which Herb hadn't taught yet.

He doesn't need dance lessons and he sure knows all the right things to say, Libby thought.

Herb introduced a new step – side car, where the partners stood hip to hip facing in opposite directions. Afterward, David claimed Libby as his partner again.

"I'm still not comfortable with this," she said getting up the fortitude to look him in the eye.

"I can't get what you're saying," David replied. He pulled Libby in close squeezing out any chance the Holy Spirit had. They danced cheek to cheek while they conversed, each one's lips near the other's ear.

"I'm still worried that rumors are going to fly about my spending time with you," whispered Libby.

"And why is that?'

"I don't think that's going to make my sons happy."

"It sounds as if your sons are very hard to please, or perhaps you only think they are. Wouldn't they be happier knowing you are out and about instead of sitting at home moping?

I can understand their objection to a 'boyfriend', but are they so puritanical that they don't want you to have any friends at all."

Libby considered that; perhaps she was projecting her concerns onto her sons. They probably didn't give much thought to whether their mother was sitting at home alone or not, they had their own lives now. They'd take notice if scandalous gossip about her made its way to them, wouldn't they? But who would bother gossiping about her? Who was she kidding! This was a small town and gossip was a small town's main source of entertainment.

Libby needed to weigh the costs and benefits. Did she want to spend time with David as much as he seemed to want to spend time with her? What were his real motives? The music stopped and she stepped away from him.

As class ended, the students applauded and thanked Herb. Libby helped him pack up his music, while David carried Herb's equipment out to his car. "Thanks," said Herb, "I want to get home soon so Bonnie doesn't come home to an empty house. Goodnight."

Again, David and Libby were alone in a parking lot, so he walked her to her car. "I have an idea," he said. "Let's do something fun and out of town so you won't have to worry about who sees us and what they say."

"What did you have in mind?"

"We both like music and dancing. Would you accompany me to the theater?"

"Really? I love plays."

"I happen to have two tickets to *Kiss Me Kate* in my pocket."

"This isn't part of your 'gay' persona, is it?"

"It isn't *La Cage Aux Folle*, and heterosexual men like musicals, too."

"It's just that I could never get my husband to go with me to one. He'd say, 'Why don't you go with your girlfriends?'."

David just smiled then asked, "Are you teaching anyone else computers besides me on Thursday? The tickets are for this Thursday night."

"That's short notice."

"I feared if I left you too much time to think about it you might back out."

"What if I said no?"

"I'd be disappointed and go by myself."

"Mrs. Palmeri has switched back to daytime classes," said Libby. "So if you're not coming, I'm free."

"Could we reschedule my class for Friday?"

"I have to take care of a friend's horses during the day, but I could make it Friday night. The usual time?"

"That would work perfectly."

"Where is the play?"

"It's at the Walnut Street Theater in Philadelphia. Did you want to meet me there or will you ride with me?"

"How about I meet you at the Park and Ride near the highway?'

"Always prudent," David said giving her hand a squeeze.

Chapter 14

     Libby told no one about this date; if it was a date. Weren't she and David just two people going to see a performance they would both enjoy? He had bought the tickets, before he even asked if she could go. Was he so sure she'd say yes, so sure she'd have nothing to do? Maybe he bought the tickets intending to go with someone else and she or he wasn't able to go. So, it's not really a date it's just keeping an extra ticket from going to waste.

     "Nice try, Libby," she told herself, "David bought those tickets and he is not about to ask you to pay for yours. This is a date. How did you end up going on one with a man you just met?" This wasn't the first time she'd had this conversation with herself in the last two days. Libby wished she could discuss it with Sue so she could help figure out if it was a date and how nervous Libby should be. Sue could also have helped Libby figure out what to wear if she hadn't been keeping it a secret.

     Since the issue of this being a date was unclear, Libby decided to dress according to the event. This was a professional performance of a musical comedy in Center City Philadelphia, she should really go all out. She hadn't been anywhere this fancy in ages, so she laid all her best clothes out on her bed. "Hmm, this blue suit is acceptable, but kind of business-y and not much fun. This black dress is too low cut, though I could wear something under it, but then it would be too warm. This might work."

     Libby picked up a royal purple coat dress. It had three quarter length sleeves with the cuffs turned back and held in place by large buttons covered in the dress fabric. Three more of the cloth-covered buttons came down the front. The open collar met two inches from the hollow of her neck, so the neckline wasn't too racy. She also loved the color and weight of the fabric. It was heavy enough to produce a drape that was forgiving of any figure flaws. The swing coat design left plenty of room to sit down. The exaggerated A-line skirt of the dress fell just to her knee, making a contrast with the slenderness of her calves. The only thing wrong with purple, blue or red clothes was that they did bring out the blue of her spider veins. She needed opaque tights to wear with this, so she rummaged through her drawer until she found a pair of black ones.

"Perfect! I can wear these with my black heels." Libby put on the pair of black patent leather, t-strap dress shoes with a low heel. She added her pearl necklace and pearl drop earrings. In front of the bathroom mirror, she fluffed and separated her curls and parted her hair on the side. She brushed clear gel onto her eyelashes, which made them look as if she had just come out of a pool. Using the gel on her eyebrows made them darker and shinier, and kept them in place. She put on some rose tinted lip gloss, after which she dropped the tube of gloss and a comb into a small black patent leather purse. She tried to put her everyday wallet into the dressy purse, but it was too big. She transferred only the essentials: her phone, driver's license, a credit card and some cash. She looked herself over in the hall mirror.

"You look mahvelous, Dahling," she said and blew herself a kiss.

The plan was to meet at the park-and-ride at seven o'clock. Libby maneuvered her mini-van into a spot furthest from the entrance, where the lot was empty. A late model Lexus backed in beside her. David got out of the car and opened Libby's door for her.

"Hello, Libby," he said, giving her a hand to help her from her seat. "You look lovely," he remarked as gazed at her head to foot. He gave her shoulders a squeeze and kissed her on the cheek. Libby was a little surprised, but being an affectionate person by nature, she accepted it as a friendly gesture at the start of a joint adventure. He took her hand and walked to the passenger side of his car.

"Your hands are nice and warm," David remarked.

"I used to be cold all the time when I was younger, except when I was pregnant. Now I am toasty most of the time," Libby answered. *Like most women my age*, she thought. David opened the door for her and helped her in. The car's leather interior was sumptuous and immaculate.

"This car looks brand new. It even has that new car smell."

"You could say this is it's maiden voyage. I purchased it yesterday. My truck wasn't appropriate for squiring a lady."

"Are you telling me that you bought this car just to go to the theater tonight?" Libby's voice was up nearly an octave, "That's crazy."

"I've had that pickup for quite a while now, and I couldn't see you climbing into the cab in a dress and high heels."

Libby was so glad that she worn a dress.

"I use the truck to do a lot of hauling for gardening."

"I have a hard time picturing you in overalls and a flannel shirt," said Libby, " and I meant to tell you, you look pretty spiffy tonight yourself."

David wore in a classic black power suit with a grey shirt and a red, grey and black paisley tie. Libby wondered if he was wearing suspenders again under his suit jacket. She liked the traditional look and he looked about as traditional as they came.

"Thank you, Madam," David smiled. "Would you like to listen to some music? The stereo system is excellent."

"What do you have in the way of CD's?"

"Look in the glove box and see if there is anything you like."

The first CD Libby pulled out was *A Sing Along with Mitch Miller: American Standards.* "This is perfect!" Libby said as she slipped it in.

The first song was *Shine On Harvest Moon* and Libby sang along. David joined in with a fine baritone and even sang some harmonies. Next up was *I've Been Working on the Railroad.* They had a grand time keeping up with the speed of the second chorus. *"Fee fi fiddley-I-O, strumming on the old banjo."* They continued until the CD ended.

"I can't believe you know all the words to those songs," Libby said breathlessly.

"My mother's family was Irish. They loved to sing. My aunts and uncles and cousins would come over on a Friday night, have a few drinks and sing into the 'wee hours of the mornin' as my grandmother would say. You're no slouch yourself."

"We didn't have relatives living near us, but my mother invited neighbors in. We had a player piano with rolls and rolls of old songs."

"I guess that was the predecessor of the boom box." David commented.

Libby laughed.

"I love it when you laugh," David said glancing over at her. "It's delightful; it actually is silvery."

What else could Libby do? She laughed again.

David used valet parking when they reached the theater. *How extravagant!* thought Libby. She and Frank had always pinched pennies. They needed to while the boys were growing up. They would have driven around for half an hour and ended up five or six blocks away with on-street parking.

As usual, David opened the car door for Libby and held his hand out to help her alight. He took her elbow and steered her to the inside of the sidewalk with himself on the outside, creating a protective barrier between her and the busy street. She remembered her grandfather doing this for her mother or any woman he walked with in public. Such chivalry made her feel elegant and treasured. Frank was not one for such courtliness.

She almost said something comparing her husband to David, but she remembered her mother's advice. "Never bad mouth your husband, living or deceased, it makes you look bad, twice. First, you look disloyal and make people wonder what you say about them when they're not around. Second, your husband's flaws are a bad reflection on you, after all, you married him. Let people think your husband adored you and treated you like a queen and that you expect nothing less from anyone else."

Libby purposefully turned her thoughts to the delights of the moment. David and she made small talk about the loveliness of the city lights and the charming old buildings. Arriving at the theater, they showed their tickets. Inside, David helped her off with her coat and checked it at the coat room. Libby excused herself to use the ladies' room.

Even this part of the theater was grand. Crystal chandeliers lit the way to the entrance to the ante room with its red brocade chaise lounge. The room was empty, so she sat down on the chair. She brought her legs up, she rested her head back and looked up at the dark red walls and gilded coffered ceiling; the room was a Victorian gem. She quickly finished her visit and returned to David before he wondered what happened to her. She didn't want to have to explain her enchantment with the decor of the restroom.

Libby rejoined David in the vestibule where he waited in line to buy refreshments.

"What would you like, Libby, a drink, some candy?" he asked.

"Sparkling water would be lovely."

David ordered a bottle of Perrier and a box of Raisinettes. He handed Libby a plastic cup and placed the candy box in his breast pocket. "For later," he said patting his pocket. He picked he bottle up and twisted the cap. There was a spray of bubbles and water. "Aaah," shouted David and quickly closed the cap.

"Oh!" Libby said bursting out laughing. David's face, hands, jacket, tie and shirt were wet. She grabbed some napkins and blotted his face and chest.

"I'm glad you asked for water," David said, letting her dry him off. He poured what remained of the drink into her cup and, taking her hand, led the way to the nearest entrance to orchestra seating. He handed the usher their tickets and she, in turn, handed him two programs.

"Please, follow me," the young woman said, smiling at David.

David drew Libby's arm through his as they walked down the center aisle to Row F.

"Here we are. Two on the aisle. I hope you enjoy the show," the young woman said. She gave Libby an appraising look before walking back up to the entrance.

David didn't seem to notice the look. "Would you like to sit on the end, Libby?"

"No, thank you, why don't you sit there so you can stretch your legs?"

David stepped aside to let Libby into her seat and then sat and did just that.

"This is so exciting," Libby said, hugging herself with a shiver of happiness.

"The actress playing Kate is supposed to be an up-and-coming star." David said, pointing to the cast listing.

"Yes, I've even heard of her. I forgot how many great musical numbers there were in this show," Libby said as she looked over the order of the scenes and songs. "Thank you so much for inviting me, David, and these seats are perfect."

"I hoped you would be pleased."

The lights flickered and dimmed. The overture began and David pulled his feet out of the aisle as the last flurry of patrons was seated. The curtains opened on the scene of the back of a theater in Baltimore. After a short dialogue, the cast swung into the first musical number, *Another O'p'nin, Another Show.*

As the orchestra and the cast neared the crescendo of the song, Libby's smile grew wider and wider. She felt the kind of thrill she felt at the finale of Fourth of July fireworks. As the last note ended, the audience applauded enthusiastically. Libby looked at David to see he was grinning right back at her.

On the way home, David asked Libby to look for another CD. In the console was an unopened album of *Kiss Me Kate* by the Broadway cast. "Oh! I love singing the songs from a show I've just seen," she said ripping off the cellophane wrapping. By time they got on the highway they were already singing the third song, *Wunderbar.*

When David launched into the gangsters' song, *Brush Up Your Shakespeare,* Libby laughed so hard she nearly had an accident. They rollicked all the way home. As they were about to pass a diner near the interstate exit, David asked if Libby would like to stop for a nightcap.

"Oh, David, I'd like to," she said with regret, "I've had such a wonderful time, but I have a full day tomorrow. I have to get up early to feed and water the Bannon's horses and then get over there later in the afternoon to exercise them and clean out the stalls."

"That sounds like a lot of work."

"Not really, besides Ray and Callie need the help and I love being with the horses."

A few minutes, later David pulled into the carpool parking lot, and again he parked next to Libby's passenger door. He turned off the ignition, got out of the car, came around to her door and helped her out. He walked her around to her car, where she fumbled around for her keys.

"We always seem to end up in a parking lot," David said as he took her purse out of her hands and put it on the hood of his car. He leaned his back against the car door and gently took her into his arms. Libby froze with her hands at her sides, she didn't say no, but she didn't give any encouragement either. He held her close, but after a moment, he pulled back to look at her. She gazed back at him remaining silent. He bent toward her and placed his lips on hers. His lips were warm and smooth as he held his mouth lightly against hers for what seemed like a very long time. One tear slid from the outer corner of her right eye. Just one small tear, but it held relief, remorse and recollection as it rolled past her glasses and down her cheek.

David pulled away again. With his thumb, he wiped the tear along her jaw line. "Why are you crying?" he whispered.

"It has been a long time since anyone has kissed me." Libby took a steadying breath. "I need to go home now."

Chapter 15

Although Libby's hands shook and her heart beat like hummingbird wings, she calmly drove out of the park and ride. She would have pulled off on the side of the road, but she knew David would stop to see if something was wrong with her car. Slowly she continued home.

The door to romance had slammed shut in Libby's face three years, four months and ten days ago when her husband died. Now this attractive, young man was pursuing her. Did she want this? Was she allowed to want it? "Dear God," Libby demanded, "what is going on? Is this Your idea of a joke? I didn't expect a second chance. Is that what this is or is it loneliness and desire leading me into temptation? Is this even coming from You?"

On more than one occasion, Frank asked Libby if she would remarry if he died. She knew the answer he wanted to hear was that she could never love anyone else. "I'll live in lonely mourning for the rest of my life," she would say melodramatically, "especially, if you die when I'm eighty."

"What if I die when you're sixty?" Frank would ask.

"Gee, Frank I could have another twenty or thirty years left. I'm the kind of woman who was meant to be married."

"Wouldn't you miss me? Would you cry at my funeral?"

"Of course, I'd cry at your funeral, but you're being ridiculous, Frank, you'll only be sixty-four when I'm sixty. You'd probably outlive me if you started exercising a little. What about you, would you remarry if I died?"

"No, absolutely not. I could never remarry. You know me I'm too shy and besides – 'Once burnt; twice shy'."

"Droll, Frank, very droll."

Frank didn't even make it to fifty-five. He had a desk job and never got into exercising. For fun he liked to read, watch TV and play online poker. Meanwhile, their marriage faded into a business partnership, the business of managing their home and raising their three sons. There was loyalty, family pride, friendship and the strong Catholic belief in the sanctity of marriage.

Libby knew part of the blame for the fire going out of the marriage lay squarely with her. She was disappointed that there wasn't more affection between her and Frank. They weren't even always polite. When she was particularly annoyed, she'd tell Frank, "Why don't you treat me like a stranger? You'd probably be kinder and more courteous."

Libby wasn't particularly interested in sex without kindness or respect. Sometimes she wasn't enthusiastic or she did not feel up to it and would pretend to be asleep. Now and then she would be blunt and they would get into an argument, "No! You haven't said one kind word to me in days, only 'I don't have any clean socks.' or 'What's for dinner?' or 'The house is a disaster.' or 'What have you been doing all day?'."

It was so banal, picking over the same petty things, but Libby felt unappreciated and so much less than treasured while Frank felt aggrieved and denied what he had a right to expect.

"You can't just take people for granted, Frank, and then expect them to be enthusiastic about sex," Libby scolded.

"I don't expect 'people' to be enthusiastic, Libby. I expect my wife to at least be willing. And, yes, I do think there are some things you should be able to take for granted in this life and sex with your wife is one of them."

Wasn't this a classic male and female battle? She wanted affection and he wanted sex. As they got older, they mellowed out. Frank quipped, "If God expected you to have sex after a certain age, He wouldn't have invented ED." He found TV commercials warning of 'an erection lasting more than four hours' both embarrassing and annoying. "People who put this stuff on before ten o'clock should be horse-whipped. It's indecent and kids are watching."

By the time Libby started menopause and wasn't worried about getting pregnant, she missed sex, yet Frank showed less affection and desire. She decided they needed to go to a marriage counselor. After all, they could be together for a long time; they should work this out.

Frank, however, was horrified. "You don't talk about sex to a stranger; we don't even talk about that kind of stuff to each other."

"That's just it, Frank, the kids are going to be out of the house soon and it's just going to be you and me. I know we can do better and be happier."

Despite his shortcomings, Frank loved Libby and if she wasn't happy in their marriage, he'd go to a counselor.

"Sex is the cement of marriage," the counselor said.

Frank shrugged his shoulders and looked at Libby, as if to say, "That's what I've been trying to tell."

The counselor continued. "It is one of Mother Nature's great ironies. Women suffer from a decreased libido, sometimes for physical reasons and sometimes because they don't feel loved. For men, sex is the way they show love and affection. A woman's libido can increase from going through the actions of making love. It's her body's reaction to the chemical effects of foreplay and intercourse. She responds emotionally to her husband's increase in affection for her, which has increased because he feels loving and loved. It is a natural cycle that can either spiral up or spiral down."

Talking about sex and the desire to bring the romance back into their marriage caused Frank and Libby to feel more affection for each other, and the timing was right. One weekend, while the two older boys were away at college, Brendan went on a school ski trip. Libby made Chicken Cordon Bleu and sauteed asparagus, some of Frank's favorites. Frank bought flowers and wine.

Frank and Libby ate the lovely meal and later drank wine in front of the fireplace. They talked and laughed. By nine o'clock, they were grinning like fools and hurrying upstairs. Libby slipped into the bathroom to put on a pink lace teddy held together by satin ribbons tied into bows. When she entered the bedroom, she found candle light and more wine. Frank sighed appreciatively and said, "Wow." They rediscovered the art of kissing and Frank opened the bows on the teddy like a present. He was a generous lover, doing his best and succeeding in pleasing Libby. They had just reached perfect satisfaction and happiness when Frank suddenly collapsed on Libby.

"Frank, get up you're squishing me," Libby said, playfully pushing him. Frank didn't respond. She pushed harder and rolled him over on his back. His eyes were closed, and she waited for him to crack a smile. When they were younger he would sometimes pretend to pass out after making love, then he would smile and say, "I thought I died and went to heaven." She put her head on his chest. She liked to listen to his heartbeat and his breathing in the afterglow, but his heart wasn't beating. He wasn't breathing.

"Oh, God!" Libby shouted.

She jumped out of bed and ran around the end of the bed, stopping for a second to grab a long flannel night gown out of her bottom dresser drawer. She was still pushing her second arm through a sleeve as she grabbed the phone off of the night stand on Frank's side of the bed and punched in 9-1-1. Holding the phone in one hand, she grabbed his shoulder with the other and shook him hard.

"Wake up!" Libby cried.

"Mizpah Volunteer Fire and Rescue, what is your emergency?" asked a woman's calm voice.

"My husband," Libby said, "he's not breathing. His heart stopped." The horror of the situation increased as she said the words.

"Mrs. O'Malley, it's Tess from the Post Office. Do you know CPR?"

"Yes, sort of," said Libby.

"I have you at 1700 Good Hope Road. Is that correct?"

"Yes."

"I'm sending an ambulance right away, meanwhile I'll talk you through the CPR."

Libby put the phone on speaker. She concentrated on breathing into Frank's mouth and doing the compressions on his chest. They lived out in the sticks and she knew it could be fifteen minutes before the volunteer squad reached them. She worried that she wasn't blowing or pushing hard enough. Frank's chest rose and fell with her breaths, but his body did nothing on its own. She was sweating from the effort. When she heard the siren in the distance, she became aware of Frank's nakedness. It would be undignified for him to be found naked in his bed especially by people he knew.

Libby couldn't reach his pajama drawer and do CPR at the same time, but she knew he wasn't coming back. Tears coursed down her face as she stopped doing CPR and got long pajama pants out of his dresser. She pushed and pulled the pants onto Frank's body, but she didn't think she could get a shirt on him in time. Victor was going berserk barking at the ambulance's siren and lights. Libby ran down the stairs. As she let the paramedics in the front door, she realized her nightgown was on inside out and backwards.

Libby cried for Frank for months, for years, really, when no one was around. It wasn't just the revival of their love life. She would have missed him without it. He was her best friend, her partner, the one who made her laugh and laughed at her jokes and the father of her children. She also felt tremendous guilt. She had denied him sex on a number of occasions when they were younger. When he got older and out of shape, for her sake, he took drugs so they could have sex again. Any ember of sexual desire had been doused with a bucket of water, stirred and stomped on. Smokey the Bear would have been pleased, the possibility of a wildfire starting in her heart was reduced to nothing.

Death was so big. There was no way around it. There was only time and living through it. Libby was numb and empty for a long while. She needed to function for the boys, especially for Brendan, who was still at home. As with many younger widows, her children were her greatest concern and her greatest help. Libby wanted the boys' lives to be as normal as she could make them. They would stay in the same schools and the same house. Their rooms would stay the same. She wouldn't open her mind to the thought of another man while Brendan was there. But now, Brendan was gone, gone to the West Coast.

Chapter 16

Libby needed a break from rethinking her evening with David and in the morning was glad get up early and go to the Bannons' place to feed and water the horses. Later in the day after tutoring Jesse and running errands, she returned to muck out the stalls. Using a pitchfork, she hefted the manure from each stall into a wheelbarrow, which she pushed a long way from the barn to the small mountain of straw and dung to be composted, where she dumped it. Zoe snorted and whinnied all the while; the young palomino was getting antsy with the brisk weather.

"You need to get out for a run don't you, baby?" Libby cooed and patted the animal's golden, dappled neck. Palominos were at their most beautiful at the end of the summer, in Libby's opinion. Their coloring went to light blonde with darker blonde spots, while their manes and tails were bleached almost white. In the winter, everything would become a few shades darker.

"I'll take you out as soon as I finish my chores," she promised the mare.

When the time came to get Zoe's English saddle Libby was dismayed at how skimpy it was. It had been a while since she had seen one. Keeping up a soothing patter with Zoe while saddling her, Libby remarked,"This is a bikini bottom of a saddle, isn't it?", gently placing it on the horse's back over the lamb's wool pad that served as a saddle blanket. Adjusting the stirrups and putting on the bit and bridle, she continued, "It's a whole lot lighter than old Baldy's saddle. Yes, it is." After leading Zoe to the riding ring, Libby used the fence again to stretch her hamstrings and to climb on to get into the saddle.

Zoe snorted and skittered sideways first left than right, she desperately needed to be exercised. She fast trotted several times around the ring, until Libby could slow her to a walk. When the horse calmed down, Libby rode her out of the enclosure and headed for the forest trail, where they trotted some more. When the trail opened up a little wider, Libby clicked her tongue and nudged Zoe to a slow canter. Putting her head down close to the horse's neck to dodge branches, Libby gave the animal free reign. Zoe didn't waste a step, and galloped flat out. The rush of trees and the wind were exhilarating.

"Yahoo, Zoe!" Libby whooped.

Out of nowhere, Zoe stopped dead and reared up. The momentum jerked Libby forward and she started to slide back off of the saddle and onto the horse's rump. Instinctively, she grabbed for a saddle horn, but the English saddle didn't have one, and pain in her knee kept her from tightening her legs over Zoe's ribs. The horse bucked and Libby flew off backward landing hard on her back and shoulders. Her head snapped back, hitting the ground with a thud.

With the wind knocked out of her, Libby lay on the ground trying to catch her breath. For an instant, Zoe looked down confused to see her rider on the ground, then the terrified horse turned and bolted toward the barn, her white tail flying behind her. Libby raised her head to see what had spooked the horse, but the world turned at an unnatural angle, and she thought she would vomit. She put her head down on the dirt and turned her eyes to see what was on the trail. Two box turtles appeared to be mating in a sunny spot on the trail. After all the ruckus, the male must have fallen and flipped over onto his back. The female was pulling him along behind her into the tall grass. Libby was pretty sure the female turtle winked at her before it disappeared. When Libby tried to raise herself up on her elbow, black spots clouded her vision. She now wished she had worn that stupid-looking English riding helmet instead of her straw hat. She closed her eyes and didn't try to move again.

"Libby!" "Liiibby!"

Libby heard someone calling her name. She opened her eyes, but couldn't see anything. After a moment, she realized it was night and remembered she was in the woods.

"Libby, where are you?"

Frank was calling her. Where had he been all this time? No, it wasn't Frank's voice.

"Libby, are you out here?"

"Yes," Libby mumbled through dry, dusty lips, but she could barely hear herself. She couldn't move. She called louder, "I'm over here," which made her head pound. She heard a branch crack and was shocked to see David kneel down beside her.

"Are you all right?' he asked, looking her over anxiously.

Libby tried to move her head, but she couldn't. "I can't move," she said.

"I have to get you out of here, but I can't get a vehicle down that narrow path in the woods. I'm going to have to carry you. Okay?"

"Okay," said Libby. Tears slid down her cheek and into her ear. She feared that she was paralyzed.

David slid one arm under Libby's shoulders and one under her knees. He had her a few inches off the ground when she cried "No! Put me down. It hurts." Her arms, legs, back, neck - everything hurt.

David put her down. "That's a good sign," he said, "if it hurts, it means you can feel."

He picked up her arm and laid it on her chest. He crossed the other arm over the first. "Maybe it will hurt less if your arms aren't dangling. Don't try to lift your head. I'll support your neck better with my arm. Okay, here we go again."

He lifted her effortlessly, but she grunted as pain flashed all over her. Though he tried to walk smoothly, she felt each foot fall.

"I went to the library for our class," David told her distracting her with chatter. "Sue told me you hadn't come in. When she found out we rescheduled class, she was worried. She said you never miss appointments. She told me to look for you at your house or the Bannons' farm. I went to your house, but you weren't there. When I pulled in here, I saw a horse with a saddle in my headlights. It was grazing on the lawn in front of the house. I saw some fairly fresh manure at the head of this trail so I took a chance and walked in calling your name."

"What happened to Zoe? The horse?" Libby asked.

"She trotted into the barn when she saw my headlights. I locked her in."

"Good. Thank you," Libby said. She grimaced and tried not to make unseemly noises.

Gently, David put her down on the back seat of his car. She groaned as she straightened out as much as she could.

He drove her to the local hospital, and stopped in the "No Parking" area in front of the ER doors. He ran in."I need a gurney," he told the nurse at the desk. An orderly brought one out through the sliding doors. Together he and David took Libby out of the back seat and put her on the gurney.

"Oh, God! Oh, God!" Libby moaned as they moved her.

The ER was quiet for a Friday night and David held Libby's hand as the orderly wheeled her into a hallway outside of a treatment room.

"Wait!" called a nurse. "Sir, you can't leave your car there and I need you to fill out some paper work."

David dashed out and parked his car then returned and answered as many of the nurse's questions as he could. Finally, they both walked into the treatment room where Libby lay with her eyes closed against the glare of the overhead lights. She was able to answer the remaining questions. "I don't have my insurance card," she told the nurse.

"We can call that information into you when she returns home," said David.

"I need a copy of the card." The nurse insisted.

"We'll fax you one later," David replied firmly.

David shaded Libby's eyes with his hand while she signed the forms with squiggly lines.   "Those will never hold up in court. Definitely signed under duress," said Libby faintly.   When David realized Libby was joking, he smiled and patted her hand.

A young doctor with a long foreign name came in and introduced himself shaking hands with David and Libby. "So what happened to you this evening, Mrs. O'Malley?" he asked with a melodic cadence.

"I was thrown from a horse earlier this afternoon. I couldn't get up so I've been lying out in the woods for a while."

"It is almost nine o'clock," the doctor said looking at his watch. "What time did you fall?"

"Around three o'clock, I think."

"Were you unconscious at any time?"

"I don't know. I slept for a while. It was light when I closed my eyes and it was dark when David found me."

"So, there is some time you cannot account for." The doctor made notes on Libby's chart. "How does your head feel?"

"I have a wicked headache. Earlier I felt dizzy and sick to my stomach when I tried to sit up."

"Mmm, hmm," the doctor said shining a small flashlight in her eyes.

"It hurts everywhere and I can't move," Libby added.

"We will get a CAT scan and some x-rays."

David stepped out of the cubicle, when a nurse came in to help Libby change into a hospital gown. Every move, the nurse helped Libby make, hurt. Afterward an orderly wheeled Libby down the hall to the X-ray department. She told him she needed to use the bathroom. The orderly left her parked out in the hallway, and quickly returned with a bedpan.

"Oh, no," said Libby.

"I'm sorry, Ma'am, but you can't walk to get into the bathroom." He put the bedpan down on the gurney.

"*You're* not going to do it, not here in the middle of the hallway."

"Let me see if I can get one of the ladies to help," the orderly said.

A female aide came and wheeled Libby into a dressing area. With great discomfort, Libby employed the cold bedpan. Afterwards, the orderly pushed the gurney the rest of the way to the x-ray room. When it was her turn, the orderly and the tech used the sheet beneath Libby to move her onto the x-ray table.

"Can you bend your knee up?" the tech asked cheerfully.

"Not too well," winced Libby as she tried to bend her leg.

"Just a little more." The tech slid Libby's foot closer to her behind.

"Ow!" yelled Libby.

"Hold it now," said the tech as she jogged into the glassed-in control room.

After performing a few more contortions, Libby wondered why anyone would ask someone, who might have broken bones, to hold these bizarre poses. A cold sweat broke out over her forehead from the pain and effort.

David was waiting for her when Libby was returned to the room from which she had started.

"I called Sue," he told her. "She was worried. She said to tell you she's praying for you." He paused and looked intently at Libby's face. "You look like you are in a great deal of pain. Can I get you something?"

"A glass of water and some aspirin would be wonderful."

"I'll be right back."

David returned with a nurse, who carried a paper container with two tablets in it and a cup with water.

"Your friend was insisting on aspirin, but this is a non-aspirin pain reliever, Mrs. O'Malley, just in case you have any internal bleeding," the nurse said shooting an annoyed look at David. To Libby she said,"Don't worry now, just drink this down." Libby did as she was told and the nurse turned on her heel and left.

"I guess she found me too assertive as a patient advocate," David said with a smile.

"My goodness, it's almost eleven o'clock," Libby said. "You don't need to stay with me."

"How will you get home?" David asked.

"I hadn't thought about that," Libby replied trying to keep her eyes open.

A while later the doctor knocked on the door and came in with his findings. "You don't have any broken bones and the CT scan looks good."

"There must be something wrong with me!" Libby said.

"Oh my goodness, yes, you have sprained your entire body. That is why you are in pain. I am also concerned that you may have a concussion."

"Do you have anyone who can stay with you for the night?" the doctor asked looking at David.

"No," said Libby, "I live alone and it is too late to call a friend."

"In that case, I will admit you for observation. You must be roused throughout the night to be checked for concussion." With that the doctor left.

Libby turned to David, "You have really been racking up the good deeds. Thank you so much for finding me and getting me to the hospital."

"You're welcome. I wish I could take care of you so you could go home this evening, but I know you wouldn't like the appearance of impropriety."

"You remember well," Libby said with a smile.

"I have to leave early for work tomorrow," David added. "I'm sorry that I won't be able to take you home when they release you. Will you call Sue?"

"Probably."

"I want to get you something from the car."

Libby dozed off while David was gone. When he returned she woke and saw him holding large plastic bottle. "This is a vitamin and mineral supplement I have custom made," he said.

Libby took the bottle and saw a faint outline of large capsules through the amber colored plastic. The red and white label listed vitamins and other elements, the percentages of daily dietary needs provided in each dose, a list of ingredients and the name and address of the manufacturer.

"I've found these very useful in speeding up recovery from sports injuries," David said. "Nutrition can make a difference in your healing. This is a new shipment, but I have enough at home for myself. You can have these. I guarantee you'll feel better sooner, if you take them. I'll put them on the lamp table. If you decide to try it tonight, take three capsules, three times a day for the first three days, then lessen the dose to two capsules for … Well, you don't need to know all this now. The instructions are on the label."

"You just happened to have those in your car?" asked Libby.

"Yes, dear, cautious Libby, I picked them up at the post office today, before I came to my appointment with you."

Libby was abashed. "I'm sorry, David. Thank you so much for everything. If you really think it will help, I'll take them."

"Good," said David sounding relieved. "I'll get you some water."

He returned with a cup of water with a plastic cap and a straw. He put it on the table and raised the head of the bed with the controller. Libby tried to open the vitamin bottle. "Unh," she groaned. "I'm too sore to open them."

David picked up the bottle, turned the cap, cracked the seal and handed it back to her.

"You said three, right?"

David nodded.

She shook out three opaque, liver-colored gel capsules into her palm. Libby took all three at once and drank the water.

"More water, please, the pills didn't go all the way down." Libby grimaced as she tried to swallow.

"Right away," he said, taking a plastic pitcher off the wheeled tray-table and pouring her another cup of water.

"That's better," Libby said after a long drink.

"I'll wait with you until they get you settled into a room."

"I can't ask you to do that. It is already late."

"You didn't ask me; I volunteered. Don't worry, I am a night owl anyway." David pulled a dry leaf out of her hair and smoothed her hair off of her forehead

Libby's eyes were heavy and it comforted her to have someone with her. "Thank you," she said.

"There is nowhere else I'd rather be," David whispered.

Hours later the nurse on duty said, "Hello, Mrs. O'Malley. I'm Esther. Do you know where you are?"

Libby opened her eyes and was disoriented for a moment. Then it came back to her. "I'm in the hospital. I fell off a horse." She looked around the dimly lit room. "Where's David?"

Esther took Libby vital signs and checked her eyes with a flashlight. "Oh, your friend wasn't allowed to accompany you to your room. He wasn't happy about it, but it was well after visiting hours and he wasn't a relative. I suggested he go home and get some shut eye and come back tomorrow. Your pupils are evenly dilated and your vitals are good. How is your pain level on a scale of one to ten?"

"It doesn't hurt if I don't move, but I don't know if I can sleep without rolling over on my side."

"You were sleeping well on your back, when I got here. I was sorry I had to wake you up. Would you like some Tylenol with codeine?"

Libby considered it. "No, thank you, Esther, I'll try to go to sleep again without it."

"If you need anything, push the call button, especially when you are ready to go to the toilet. You may be dizzy, so someone has to walk with you. We don't want you hitting your head again."

"Okay, I will. Good night, Esther."

"Good night, Mrs. O'Malley."

Libby was awakened every two hours throughout the night with the same routine. By dawn, she really had to go to the bathroom. She rang the nurse's call button as she had been instructed. She dreaded this moment; after being immobile all night she figured it would hurt like the dickens when she tried to get up. Esther hadn't gone off duty yet, and she responded to the call. "Good morning, Mrs. O'Malley. What can I do for you?"

"I'm ready to go to the bathroom."

"All righty, then I'll get you a walker." Esther said. When she returned with a walker, she began lowering the hospital bed closer to the floor and raising the head of the bed. She helped Libby to slide her legs over, put her feet on the floor and sit on the edge of the bed.

"That wasn't so bad," Libby said, relieved and surprised.

Esther maneuvered the walker so it stood between her and Libby.

"Good, now put your hands on my shoulders and try to stand up."

Libby did so.

"How are you doing now?" asked Esther.

"The room just got a little dark around the edges, but now I can see clearly."

"Any more dizziness?"

"No."

"Any pain?"

"No."

"Super. Now, put your hands on the walker and when you are ready, try a small step."

Libby took a deep breath and then pushed the walker a short way and took a step. "I feel a lot better than I thought I would. I'm a little sore, but not too bad at all." She took another step. "I really don't need this walker, I'm fine."

"Just humor me and use it to and from the bathroom," Esther replied.

Libby finished her trip and was back at her bedside.

"I have to tell you, I wasn't looking forward to coming in here this morning," Esther said.

"And why is that?"

"Usually the day after--what did the doctor call it?-- 'spraining your entire body,' the pain and stiffness are worse than just after the fall."

"I'm surprised that I feel as good as I do, too. In fact, I don't want to get back into bed. I'd rather walk around a little to loosen up more."

"That's a good sign," Esther said, "but take the walker."

Libby pushed the walker down a long windowed corridor with a view of the parking lots. It was 6:30 and the sun rise was in full bloom. She prayed softly, "Thank you, dear God, for getting me out of this mess with just a few bumps and bruises and for keeping that stupid Zoe safe. I would have felt terrible if something had happened to her. Thanks for Sue sending David to find me. I could have been out there all night."

Libby would wait to call Sue around eight o'clock. It was a Saturday morning, but her kids were sure to have her up by then. She remembered what David said about being at work early, not that she could have called him anyway, she didn't have his phone number. But he was turning out to be a regular guardian angel or, perhaps, a knight in shining armor.

Soon after Libby returned to her room a young woman arrived with a breakfast tray of juice, coffee, a fruit cup, hot cereal, eggs, pancakes, bacon, milk and toast. "Wow, this is a feast... Yvonne" Libby said reading her name tag.

"I didn't know what you wanted, Mrs. O'Malley, since we didn't have an order from you. So, I brought almost everything," said Yvonne, she looked like she was about Brendan's age.

"Thank you, Yvonne, you are a girl after my own heart."

"You're welcome."

"Have you been working here long?"

"No, I started this summer after graduation and now I'm studying Nursing part time at the community college."

"What excellent experience," Libby said. "Is it hard work?"

"Yes and no. Most people are nice and appreciate getting their meals, despite all the jokes about hospital food. The hours can be tough though. I work the day shift so I can take night classes. Sometimes it's hard to stay awake long enough after class to get my homework done and still wake up at five in the morning," Yvonne said with a rueful smile.

"That's impressive," Libby said. "When it comes to getting a job in the real world after graduation, you'll have it all over kids with no work experience."

"Well, I'd better go. Thanks, Mrs. O'Malley, I needed a little boost today."

"Good luck to you, sweetie."

Libby finished her breakfast and remembered the supplements David gave her and took three more. Finally, it was a reasonable hour to call Sue's house.

"Hello?" Lily, Libby's goddaughter answered.

"Hi, Lily, it's Aunt Libby. Is your mother there?"

"Mom! It's Aunt Libby on the phone."

Sue picked up immediately, "Oh, Libby, I was so worried about you. Are you all right? David called last night and told me you had to stay overnight for observation."

Libby clicked her tongue, "I didn't want him to disturb you at that hour."

"Wait, don't say another word," said Sue. "I'll be over around ten and then I want to hear everything."

Two hours later, Sue stepped into Libby's hospital room and embraced her gingerly. "How are you feeling?" Sue asked quietly.

"I'm fine," said Libby hugging her back. "I'm a lot less sore than I thought I'd be. I'm more embarrassed than hurt. Do the Bannons know?"

"You know this town. Everybody knows."

"Oh, boy," Libby said sheepishly, "people are going to think I'm an idiot getting thrown by a silly, little horse like Zoe."

"People aren't that interested in who threw you. They're fascinated that David Baynard took you to the ER."

"Oh, no," moaned Libby.

"I'm sorry, that was my fault. He showed up at the library saying he had an appointment with you. You hadn't called, and you didn't answer your phone; it was dark and I got worried. The first thing I thought of was sending him to look for you. He was right there and more than willing to go. He was very worried about you, too. I thought it was better than calling the police."

Libby sighed, "No, Sue, you did the right thing. I was out there for hours."

"Well, to make up for it, I brought you a change of clothes and your purse. Thank goodness for that spare set of keys you left with me," she said jingling a key ring.

Libby put on the clean clothes. Eventually, a doctor appeared to look at her chart and check her over. When he gave her permission to go home, she was delighted. Within thirty minutes, a nurse had given Libby her discharge directions and an orderly was pushing her in a wheel chair. They stopped in at the emergency room admissions desk and Libby let the clerk copy her insurance card. Sue was waiting in her car at the main entrance.

"So, where do you want to go?" Sue asked.

"Do you mind driving over to Ray and Callie's?"

"You're not going to get back in the saddle right now are you?" Sue asked in disbelief.

"No, no, but I need to pick up my van and to check on the horses. They need to be watered and fed before the Bannons get home. They're usually home by mid-afternoon and they'll both be tuckered out."

"What about you? Should you be doing this kind of stuff so soon."

"I feel remarkably well, but if you're worried you can help me clean the stalls," Libby said.

"Oh, shhhi…," Sue stopped herself.

"Exactly," Libby said with a grin.

Chapter 17

When Libby got home, there was a basket on her front steps. It was filled with an arrangement of live plants: white African violets, pink kalanchoes, purple cyclamen and primroses. Ivy, maidenhair fern and moss filled out the display. The card read "Eat well, sleep well, take your vitamins and get well soon. David."

"Oh, David, they're beautiful," Libby said aloud as she held the card to her chest. She still had no way to get in touch with David to thank him. "Well, I can at least take my afternoon dose of vitamins." She took the plants in and got some water for them and for herself.

Throughout Sunday and Monday, Libby did some gentle stretching and took walks in the woods, so she wouldn't decline after such a good beginning. By Tuesday evening, Libby was raring to go to dance class. She smiled broadly when saw David in the YMCA parking lot. She walked over holding her hands out to him. "David, thank you so much for the flowers. They're gorgeous!" She gave him a kiss on the cheek.

"I'll have to send you flowers more often," David said beaming at her. He raised an eyebrow, "Is it all right if we're seen walking in to class together?"

"Gee willikers, I guess so," Libby said shaking her head, "but no walking in on your arm, and you've got to dance with other people."

"Other women, I assume."

"Oh, brother," she said elbowing him in the arm.

Throughout class Libby and Herb demonstrated a review of old steps and introduced new ones. David invited various single women to dance. He held the proper ballroom dance position maintaining a few inches between himself and his partner. At the end of each song, he escorted the lady off the dance floor and asked another to dance. Libby danced with women without partners as well. At five minutes before the end of class, Herb announced a freestyle dance, where couples could try any dance steps they wanted.

Herb put on Jerry Vale singing *Three Coins in the Fountain* and David approached Libby before she walked over to another single woman. "I've been good all evening, may I have my reward now?" he said softly, holding his hand out to her.

David drew Libby to him and tucked her in close holding her hand to his chest. He bowed his head until his cheek touched her hair. Neither of them said a word. She closed her eyes as he led and she followed, perfectly synchronized. When the song ended, he stepped away from her and bowed slightly.

"That's it for tonight," said Herb. The class applauded and a few people called out, "Good class." "Thanks, Herb."

"Hey folks," Herb said, "this is the fourth class. We only have two more in this session. Don't forget to sign up for the next session. We'll be learning the waltz."

Again, David and Libby helped Herb take his sound equipment and music out to his car. Neither of them said much as Herb chatted on about how the class was going. He thanked them and drove off with a toot of his horn and a wave. Alone in the parking lot, David offered Libby his arm and walked her to her car. When they got to her car, he turned her to face him. "Dancing with you, being with you, makes me feel like there is nothing and no one else in the world. You are the perfect partner," he said. Then he opened her door and helped her into the driver's seat.

'Perfect partner', that was either the best line she'd ever heard or an amazing declaration, thought Libby with her mouth slightly agape.

Before closing the door leaned down and David continued, "You were saying that we didn't have much more you could show me on the computer. Could we play hooky this Thursday and do something else together?"

"You know," Libby said, "I'd like that. Let's meet at my house, say at seven-thirty, and I'll think of a class trip. I'll tell Sue that I'm not having class, so she won't worry."

David paused before asking, "Will you tell her that you're going somewhere with me?"

Libby didn't pause as she answered, "No."

Chapter 18

The next two days passed slowly. Gardening, reading, Mrs. Palmeri and choir practice couldn't keep Libby from counting the hours before she would see David again. Thursday evening her heart gave a little jump and she couldn't keep from smiling as David's car pulled into the driveway.

"Is there any place special you'd like to go?" David asked as they they stood on the porch.

"It's so delightful out I'd love to take a walk. There's an historic village just across the Delaware River called Old New Castle. It was founded in the early sixteen hundreds. There won't be much open, but it will be lovely in the moonlight and decorated for fall harvest. Would you like to go?"

"I'd like going anywhere with you," David said.

Libby smiled and blushed. "I'll drive."

On the way Libby filled David in on some local history. As they cross the Delaware Memorial Bridge she summed it up. "So, New Castle was settled and fought over by the Dutch, the Swedes and the English in the 1650's. The Brits were the winners and in 1682 William Penn's first step onto the soil of the New World was at New Castle."

"So, it was up and running well before Philadelphia?"

"Absolutely, old Billy Penn ended up leasing New Castle from Lord Baltimore as a port and a civilized place to set up the administration of the Province of Pennsylvania. Later, New Castle became the capital of the colony of Delaware and later the state of Delaware. It was a hot property until the 1840s when a train line was finished between Philadelphia and Baltimore. It bypassed the New Castle and left it a backwater, but that wasn't a bad thing."

"Why do you say that?" David asked.

"Because the growth rate slowed down, they didn't need to tear down so many old buildings to make room for new ones. They still had quite a few period buildings left by the time enough people got interested in protecting the historical architecture."

Libby drove along two lane roads until she came to the cobblestones that marked the beginning of the old village. The 'shoppes' and coffee houses were closed so she and David had the streets to themselves. She parked on a side street between two trees whose trunks grew past the sidewalk and into the street. The gas streetlights and electric candles in the windows of the two and three story brick row houses gave a golden glow to the night air. She and David saw scads of gourds, kale, pumpkins, mums and scarecrows in charming displays. Fallen leaves rustled as they walked arm in arm.

Libby led David down to the Delaware River to the landing with a sign announcing *"Near here October 27, 1682 William Penn first stepped on American soil."* They walked up the sloping river bank to Delaware Street.

In the middle of Old Town sat one of the oldest surviving courthouses in the country. The New Castle Courthouse was a stately brick building in the Georgian style. Two two-story wings flanked the three story center of the building. The main section was crowned with a cupola that was later fitted with a bell. It had been the courthouse and government house of the colony and later the state of Delaware. The court house had been home to the British government and courts in the colony before the Revolutionary War and the state capitol for one year after the war. Libby and David admired the open green with a charming church at the town center. "It's starting to get late," Libby said. "Are you ready to head back?'

"I'm ready when you are."

Libby led the way back. "There's the van over there."

"You have a good sense of direction," David complimented. Just before they got to her car, he disappeared behind a tree and returned to shower her with handfuls of yellow leaves. Libby laughed and bent down to grab leaves of her own to throw back at him. David caught her around the waist and wheeled her around until he held her against the tree trunk. He held her face in his hands and kissed her. Libby didn't freeze this time. She decided to accept this gift. She put her hands on his waist and kissed him back. He sighed and wrapped his arms around her and leaned in to kiss her more soundly. Libby reached up and hugged his neck. She was glad he was holding her and that she was propped up by the tree because her knees were turning to water.

Finally pulling away, Libby said, "We really should go." She wasn't sure she could drive just yet, "but maybe we should get some coffee first."

"Won't that keep you awake all night?" David asked. Looking more closely at her he added, "You looked flushed. Are you feeling all right?"

Libby smiled sheepishly. "I'm a little wobbly. How are you?"

"I feel wonderful," he said with a grin. "Would you like me to drive?"

Libby pulled her keys out of her pocket and handed them to David.

"Good bye, Old New Castle, I shall remember you fondly," David said as he drove through the narrow streets. He and Libby talked about decorative plants, gardens and trees. When they got on the highway, David reached over and held her hand. They continued their conversation all the way back to her house and his car. He went around to help Libby get out of the passenger's side of her car to switch over to the driver's side.

"I hate to let you go," he said.

"It's already eleven o'clock."

"If I really must, then just one more kiss goodnight." Several kisses later, he said, "Goodnight, Libby."

Libby was walking on air as she locked the doors of her house, turned out the lights and got ready for bed. She hugged herself, sighed and expected some sweet dreams.

Chapter 19

Friday morning Jesse met Libby with a big smile on his face. "Guess what!" he crowed.

"What!?" Libby asked enthusiastically.

"I'm gettin' a new dog. High five!" he cried, holding his hand up.

"What kind of dog is it?" She asked giving his hand a slap.

"Well, it isn't going to be a puppy, and it sure isn't going to be a girl," said Jesse.

"Okay. What else can you tell me?"

"Grandma said something about it being a ketchup dog."

"Are you sure she didn't say a hot dog or a wiener dog?"

"Did you just say wiener?" Jesse guffawed.

Libby laughed too, "Yes, they're these little dogs with short legs and long bodies. Some people call them 'hot dog' dogs or wiener dogs." She snapped her fingers, "What is the real name? Um? Dachsunds! That's it."

"I don't know nothin' about dock sons, and I never thought I'd hear a lady say 'wiener'." Jesse's face was red and he was laughing hard. "My aunt took us to a swimmin' pool this summer and there was a guy there …" he could barely choke the words out, "with a bikini bottom on, and …" more giggles, "my cousin called it a weenie bender."

He collapsed on a chair taking in big breaths. He wiped tears from his eyes. Now and then, a stray chortle escaped. Finally, he let out a big, happy sigh.

Libby pressed her lips together trying not to laugh at the weenie remark. "Okay, so why is it a ketchup dog?"

"It's a certain kind of ketchup," Jesse said.

"I can't imagine what it is," Libby said shaking her head.

114

"I remember. It's a Heinz dog," Jesse said.

"Oh, a Heinz 57 dog!"

"Yeah, that's what my grandma said it would probably be. So, what's it look like?"

"I think your grandmother means that you are going to adopt a dog from a shelter or something and it could be a few different breeds mixed together."

"You mean a mutt?" Jesse spat out the word.

"I would call it a mixed breed," said Libby. "They're the best kind. They tend to be healthier and more even tempered than pure bred dogs."

"Yeah?"

"Yes, and you can get the best traits of different breeds all in one dog. I had a friend that had a tea cup Chihuahua, a little, tiny dog and it mated with a dachshund, that short legged, long bodied dog I told you about. The puppies were adorable little, tiny dachshunds."

"Huh," Jesse said.

"Do you know what they called them?"

"What?"

Libby's eyes crinkled, "Cha-weenies."

Jesse snorted. "No way!"

"Honest to God," Libby said crossing her heart.

"You know, Mrs. O, you should get a new dog to make up for your old one."

Libby shook her head, "I couldn't do that. It just wouldn't seem right, at least, not yet."

"You're gonna be loyal to your dog like you are to your husband? He died a long time ago right?"

"My husband died over three years ago, but getting a new husband and getting a new dog are very different. Though, I guess you could say it's still about loyalty. How long did you wait before you started looking for a new dog?"

"A long time, since last Easter."

"So, is this going to be your dog?"

"Of course, it's gonna be my dog."

"I mean, are you going to be the one who takes care of him? Walks him, feeds him, brushes him and all?"

"My grandma usually does that stuff. I'm gonna play with him."

"A dog usually loves the person who takes care of him most of all. That's why Victor was my dog, not my sons' dog. He liked me best. He knew he could count on me to take him out and make sure he always had plenty of food and water and treats."

"Oh," said Jesse.

"Maybe you could make a deal with your grandmother that you'll take care of him, whenever you're at home."

"You mean like walking him, when I get home from school?"

"That, and getting up earlier in the morning and walking him before you go to school."

"Hmm? Maybe."

"Okay, now let's look at what we are supposed to do today," Libby said looking over the assigned class work. "It looks like you're pretty well caught up. We can spend some time reading. How do you like *The Indian in the Cupboard*?"

"It's good, but I think they stole the idea of toys coming to life from *Toy Story*."

"It's the other way around." Libby said. "That book was written at least ten years before the *Toy Story* movie came out. People have wished for inanimate objects things to come to life for thousands of years."

"What kind of objects?" Jesse asked screwing his face up.

"Inanimate. It means something that is not alive. There's a Greek myth about a man, who doesn't like any of the women on his island."

"You mean, he's gay?"

"No," explained Libby, "it's just that none of the women around him are the kind he's looking for. So he carves a statue of what he thinks the perfect woman should look like. Because the statue is so beautiful, he falls in love with it. The man, his name is Pygmalion, goes to the temple of the goddess Venus and begs her to bring his beloved statue to life. Venus grants his wish. The statue turns into a real woman. She and Pygmalion get married and live happily ever after."

"Ew, you just told me a love story," complained Jesse.

"Oh, please forgive me," Libby said with mock contrition. "Here's another example, Pinnocchio, the wooden puppet that becomes a real boy."

"Okay, I get it, but the Indian story is better than both of them," said Jesse.

"Then you are in luck, there are two more books in the series."

"That's cool," said Jesse coolly.

Chapter 20

Early the next Libby had an appointment for her usual cut and color with her hairdresser Hepsi.

"Hey, Libby!" the receptionist greeted her, "I see you got my reminder call."

"Yes, I did. Thank you, Karen. How's your little sweetie Amber doing?"

"She lost her first tooth. Wanna see a picture?" asked Karen. She pulled out her cell phone.

"She is adorable," said Libby, "but losing a tooth, that makes her about six. That can't be; I remember when she was born."

"She'll be seven in December, but we look as young as ever."

"That's right, now you're getting the hang of it," Libby said with a grin.

Hepsi walked over and gave Libby a hug. "Hello, girlfriend."

"I see you're a blonde for the moment," Libby laughed as she fingered her friend's short, spiky hairstyle.

"How do you like it?" Hepsi turned around giving Libby a view of the back.

"I love it."

"Wanna try it?"

"No, thanks, Hepsi, but it looks great on you, and people are used to you changing your hair color every week."

"True, and why would you want to change, Libby. You look fabulous!" said Hepsi.

"It's my hair stylist, she is a coloring genius and her cuts makes the most of my natural curl," Libby said fluffing her hair dramatically.

"I can't argue with that," Hepsi said with a little curtsy. "You look, I don't know, younger. Have you lost weight?"

"Maybe a little, my clothes fit better." Libby looked at her backside in the mirror. "Things seem to be shifting around or something. I've been doing some yard work and taking care of the Bannons' horses most weeks."

"I heard you got thrown by one of the horses and had to go to the hospital."

"That was embarrassing. It's been a while since I rode English. I even forgot to wear a helmet."

"You're lucky you didn't break your neck. How are you feeling now?"

"I feel great. I was really sore at first, but I seemed to bounce right back. Thank goodness."

"Your skin looks great, too. You have a glow about you."

"Really? I've been trying this new skin care stuff, you know, cleanser, moisturizer, masque and stuff."

"That sounds like more fuss than you're usually willing make."

"One of Brendan's friends at college was selling the stuff online. It cost a lot and I didn't want to waste money, so I've gotten regular about using it." Libby leaned toward the mirror to examine her face. She hadn't taken a close look since that first night of her new regimen. She made an exaggerated smile to check out her laugh lines and crows' feet. "I'll be darned, it looks like that stuff is working. I can really see a difference! Either that or I'm misremembering how wrinkled I looked before."

"I don't know if creams and lotions can explain that happy glow," teased Hepsi. "Is there anything else you'd like to tell us about?"

"Like what?"

"Like maybe a man?"

Libby turned red.

"Libby, you are the cutest thing. You're blushing! It has been a while since I've seen a grown woman blush," said Hepsi with a laugh.

"There is no man," protested Libby.

"I heard a tall, dark and handsome stranger brought you to the ER that night."

"You mean, Mr. Baynard? He had a computer class scheduled at the library that night. When I didn't show up on time, Sue asked him to go out and look for me, because she couldn't leave the library."

"Sounds like, Sue's looking out for you in more ways than one," Hepsi said smiling suggestively. "And then what happened?"

"Nothing happened," Libby said emphatically. "He took me to the emergency room like any decent human being would have done."

"Methinks the lady doth protest too much," quoted Karen, who had been listening.

"It's all right if you don't want to tell us about it, Libby, but you know your secrets are safe with us," said Hepsi.

"There is nothing more to tell. The ER doctor told me I sprained my entire body. They kept me overnight for observation in case I had a concussion, and the next morning Sue drove me home. Now, here I am safe and sound."

The salon was rumor central, Libby never said anything there she wouldn't want everyone in town to know.

"All righty then, have a seat, Libby, and let's take a look at you."

Libby sat in the chair and Hepsi lowered it to adjust for Libby's height. Hepsi put a black cape over Libby's clothes and began her inspection.

"The top has grown wild," Hepsi said as she drew up a hank of hair from the crown of Libby's head between her second and third fingers. Hepsi parted the hair down the middle and examined Libby's scalp in a way that always reminded Libby of orangutans grooming each other.

"Ooo, girl, have you got roots! Has it only been six weeks since we did a color?" Hepsi made inspections in several other places and dropped her 'girlfriend speak'. "Libby, this is really weird. You've got about a three-quarters of an inch of grey roots then you've got a quarter of an inch of dark hair below that."

"We always go a little lighter than my natural color, so the roots look darker."

"No, that's not it. Your hair is at least fifty percent grey and your grey is nearly white, so the dyed color is always darker than roots. I've seen skunk do's with the white stripe down the middle, but I've never seen two stripes of different colors." To more clearly explain the situation to Libby, Hepsi emphasized each sentence. "Your hair is growing in brunette. You're not going grey any more. Your natural color is coming back."

"What are we going to do about it? And by we, I mean you," Libby replied nonchalantly.

Hepsi ran her hand through her own hair. "I guess I'll do the grey roots a shade in between the medium brown on the ends and the dark brown at the scalp, but that's not the point Lib. We're talking abnormal. Something strange is going on."

"It's probably just some little fluctuation."

"Well, if you figure out what it is, let me know, because I either want to bottle it or bury it, so I still have dye jobs to do."

Chapter 21

That night Libby couldn't fall asleep, and a creak on the steps made her sit up in bed. She put every particle of her awareness into listening. She heard crickets chirping. A whip-poor-will made its familiar lament, which Libby found it haunting. An old man from the Pine Barrens once told her if she heard the bird's call three times at midnight it foretold a death. She didn't want to check the clock.

"What happens if he calls five times?" Libby wondered now in the dark.

She also thought about how strange it was that earlier today she felt more youthful in a good way, but now she felt the hard won confidence of her 47 years give way to the insecurities of her youth, when she had been afraid to stay alone in a house.

Once, when she was a teenager, her parents went away overnight for a wedding. She had to work so she didn't go with them. She returned to a dark, empty house. She barely got in the front door when a sound from upstairs made her bolt. She spent the night hiding in her locked car in the driveway.

When Frank left for a business trip for the first time in their marriage, Libby spent a few sleepless nights, terrified in her own home. After that, she invited a friend to stay over or she would go to someone's house for the duration of each of Frank's trips. Usually that friend was Marguerite, an eighty-year-old women, who had adopted Libby and Frank as her substitute grandchildren. Many a time, Marguerite had come into the empty house with Libby and brandished her cane saying, "Don't worry, Libby, I'll protect you."

After Marguerite passed away and the two older children were born, Libby had to learn to stay alone in the house for a few nights. The boys often had a way of making her better than she was. Since she had to be brave for them, she was brave. It helped that she could attribute little creaks and squeaks to the them moving in their beds. Matt and Will also had terrible allergies. She could hear them snoring and breathing through their mouths all the way down the hall. She stood in their bedroom and marveled at the noise they produced. As she watched them sleep, the contrast between their serene faces and the ungodly sounds they made, would give her the giggles, and she'd have to make a quick exit.

What amused her even more was when at eight years old Matt swore he never slept. He said he couldn't fall asleep all night and then it would be morning. She'd look in on him before she went to bed and he would be snoring away. She was tempted to put a note on his nose one night saying, "*I stopped by, but you were sleeping.*" She never did. She worried that it would freak him out that he slept so soundly that someone could sneak up on him and he never even knew it.

Tonight, Libby was all alone. She didn't even have Victor's presence to explain strange noises. Silently, she drew back the sheet and put her feet on the floor. Her bare feet made her feel vulnerable, so she pushed them into her slippers. She crept to the bedroom door, slid her hand past the doorjamb and flipped the light on. She waited for a reaction; there was none. She poked her head into the hall and looked down the steps to the front door. Nothing seemed amiss. She didn't want to go downstairs, but knew she would have doubts all night if she didn't. She grabbed the plaster saw she'd left in her room to finish cutting a hole in the wall for a new air conditioning return vent. It looked vicious with its long jagged teeth. She called down the steps with as deep a voice as she could muster, "I'm coming down, now, and I am armed. I'll give you three seconds to clear out. One …. Two …. Three." She thundered down the steps with the saw held high.

Libby went from room to room turning on lights. She checked the front and back doors. Both were secure. She checked the open window in the living room. The screen was fine, but she still closed the window and locked it. When she was satisfied that there was no one else in the house, she went up stairs.

For the first time since Brendan stopped being afraid of the dark, she went to bed with all the downstairs lights on. She left the hall light on and closed her door. She turned her closet light on and left that door ajar. Now, as she did years ago, she put the cordless phone under her pillow and pulled out her Rosary. She rolled on her side facing the door, even though she had a hard time sleeping with a light on, she wouldn't turn her back to the point where an attacker might enter.

Libby closed her eyes and began praying, "Almighty Father, please keep me safe. Please Blessed Mother pray for me and watch over me." She continued with prayers she had learned as a child. "Saint Michael the Archangel, defend us in battle, be our protection against the wickedness and snares of the devil. May God rebuke him we humbly pray; and do thou, O Prince of the Heavenly host, by the power of God, thrust into hell Satan and all evil spirits who wander through the world seeking the ruin of souls. Amen."

Truth be told, in the dark, Libby was as afraid of supernatural evil as she was of any human intruder. She started praying the Rosary. With the beads in her hand, she finally dozed off. She startled awake when she heard the door from the basement slam shut. She heard deliberate steps coming up the stairs to the second floor. Her eyes were open and she faced the bedroom door, but she could not move or utter a sound. The steps came closer and closer until they stopped outside her bedroom door. The door opened. Because of the hall light was on all she could see was the silhouette of a man. He walked across the room and stood over her. He sat on the side of her bed. Libby felt the mattress compress under his weight and she felt her body sliding toward the depression he made. Libby's heart was beating fast. She couldn't even breathe.

"I just came to see if you were all right," said a familiar voice, it was Frank. He reached out and touched her arm and she found she could move again. She switched on the lamp, but she was alone.

Was it a dream? Was it a ghost? Libby believed in spirits, like the Holy Spirit, angels, demons and the soul in each person. During the day she didn't believe demons could do her physical harm, but at night she wasn't so sure. What ever it was; Frank's visit left her feeling more sad than afraid. She was touched by his concern for her, but she felt terribly alone. The episode wiped her out physically and emotionally and she fell into a deep sleep.

Late in the morning Libby woke to a voice saying, "Help me." Her arm was stretched out over the edge of the bed with the cold, damp palm facing up. She was reaching for something or someone. The words that woke her had come from her own mouth and she felt like a weight had been placed on her chest. Inside her heart fluttered like a moth in a bottle, crashing against the hard, glass wall, making its attempt to escape more frenzied. She hadn't had a panic attack in years. As frightening as they were, she preferred them to the crush of the nothingness that usually came afterward.

Libby was now fully awake and agitated. She had no plans for the day and didn't know what to do with herself, but she couldn't stay in the house much longer. She splashed water on her face, brushed her teeth, ran her fingers through her hair and pulled on the same clothes she had worn yesterday. If the house had been on fire, her need to flee wouldn't have felt more urgent. She got into her van and drove toward town. Where could she go? There was only one place.

The church was quiet and dark inside. Nobody was there, but One. The red sanctuary light was burning. The church was a modern, suburban, box type with the tabernacle off to the side, instead of in the center above the main altar. She didn't care for the modern church's architecture, but it suited her needs. She walked up to the golden door set into the wall like a safe and sat on the step beneath it. She leaned into the brick wall below, and sat at her Jesus' feet.

"Lord, please help me. I didn't know what to do or where to go, so I came here. I don't know what is happening to me, but I feel the darkness closing in on me, like I'm on the edge of the abyss again. Please hold onto me; don't let me fall." She sat with head against the wall and breathed.

Twenty-five years ago she and Frank went to the Grand Canyon. They arrived after dark. It was off season, and there were no electric lights. She wanted to see the canyon anyway. There was enough natural light to see the leaves of the trees near her face, but a few feet away was the purest blackness she'd ever experienced.

She couldn't see the canyon, but she sensed the emptiness. She was drawn to it and terrified at the same time.

Depression felt that way to her. She'd had bouts of depression at various times in her life, even before she knew what it was. It threatened to swallow her up after Frank died, but the boys needed her. So, she did what she had to do, she saw a therapist once a week in the morning hours of a school day, leaving enough time to recover from the crying jags that accompanied the sessions. She also took Wellbutrin and Prozac faithfully and got through it, but now the Noonday Demon had caught her unawares. She wanted nothing. She wanted to do nothing. She feared the serenity she had cultivated with years of prayer, reading and counseling was evaporating.

Libby heard the front door of the church open and sunlight poured in. She rolled up on her knees so she would be kneeling before the Blessed Sacrament, if anyone saw her. A woman genuflected and knelt in a pew near the back. Libby felt it was time to leave. She walked down the side aisle as silently as she could. The woman didn't look up from her prayer book. Outside, Libby sat in the van wondering what to do next. Everything about life seemed sour. She didn't want to be seen by anyone she knew. The very thought of the people she would normally see annoyed her. Mrs. Palmeri, Jesse, … suddenly they all seemed dense and needy.

Libby decided to drive to the new mall about ten miles away. She walked through a big department store's jewelry and perfume section. The cleanliness and order of the place soothed her. She roamed through the main plaza of the mall with its skylight and fountain. She had tea and a scone at a cafe. The tea was hot, but the scone was dry and bland. She drank the tea until it became tepid, ate half of the scone and threw the leftovers away. She wandered through stores, browsing the sale racks. Nothing really appealed to her. She found a sweater and a blouse in her size that were marked down seventy-five percent and bought them. She picked up a pair of khakis and a striped polo shirt for Brendan. By mid-afternoon, she was exhausted and went home. At the house she left the shopping bags with the receipts in the trunk. She knew she would return all of it eventually.

Libby disconnected the phone, went up stairs and pulled down the shades and closed the curtains. She turned on the window fan more for white noise than for cooling. She got into bed and pulled the blanket up over her head leaving just a little crack near her nose to breathe through. It felt so good to lie down and be covered in darkness and white noise. The best part was not needing to think or decide. Sleep was good for her, wasn't it? It was a safe and healthy thing for her to do - she could do it in good conscience.

Libby slept for hours. When she woke up, she had a dull headache and felt groggy. She rubbed her face feeling more tired when she woke up than before she had taken this epic nap. She went downstairs and made a pot of tea and some toast. After several cups of tea, she felt better. In the waning light, she went into the garden and pulled some weeds. Looking around she noticed the lawn was in need of mowing again, so she got the mower out of the shed and mowed on autopilot. She worked to tire herself out so she could get to sleep at a decent hour and, hopefully, sleep through the night. She was successful.

At dawn, Libby woke up with the urge to use the toilet. The back of her nightgown felt wet. "Don't tell me, I'm incontinent now," she thought grimly. She was shocked to see blood in the toilet and then pulled the back of her nightgown around to where she could see it. There was blood there, too.

Libby started laughing. "You have got to be kidding me! I'm having my period?"
It had to have been a year since her last one. She thought she had gone through the change, but a period could explain everything – the anxiety, the depression, the exhaustion. It was all just one monumental bout of PMS?! She laughed again with relief. She remembered back to her childbearing days when she had these black days and nights. She would go to bed early assuring herself and the men in her life everything would be better tomorrow, and it usually was. But what could explain the onset of her period now?

Libby dug around in the linen closet to find a few sanitary supplies left. *Oh, boy, that'll raise eyebrows if I go through the checkout line with these at the grocery store*, she thought. She decided she would go to a drugstore in another town.

Chapter 22

When she got downstairs she saw the voice mail message light flashing. She pressed the play button. "Libby, it's David. I'm calling to invite you to my home, tomorrow at dusk. Sunset occurs at six nineteen. Don't be late. I have something I want to show you." He left his phone number and address.

Libby thought it over. Was there any reason she shouldn't go to his house? She'd have her car and could leave when she wanted. The thought of seeing David made her happy. She called him back, but there was no answer. She left a message saying she would be there.

The Google Maps' directions to David's house showed a good portion of the drive would be on two lane roads out in the country. Libby left early, giving her more daylight time to travel and a ten minute cushion in case she got lost. She arrived at the turnoff for David's driveway just before sunset. It was a long, tree-lined dirt road wide enough for a large truck, although the top might brush the tree branches. When she saw the house, a light bulb went on in her head. The driveway was wide enough for a team of horses to pull wagons or other farm equipment. The three-story Victorian house was flanked by mature oak trees. The clapboard siding was a buttery shade of yellow with first floor windows about eight feet tall. A deep porch wrapped around the house at the right corner of the house; the porch ballooned out into a gazebo. Pointing up from its elaborate octagonal roof was a brass finial that had weathered to green. The second story was decorated with six sided cedar shingles in the same shade of yellow, while the third floor was indented by various roof lines covered with slate tiles. Gabled windows cropped out on the three sides of the house that Libby could see. Crowning it all was a turret on the front left side with curved windows capped with the traditional conical roof. The gables and turret were covered with row upon row of differently shaped shingles giving the illusion of ripples. The porch was supported by ten-foot tall round columns. Purely decorative spandrels connected the tops of the columns with fanciful designs that looked like wooden lace. Turned spindles supported the railing going up the steps and lining the perimeter of the porch. All these elements were painted white as were the window and door frames. The overall effect was elegant and calming.

Libby climbed the stairs. The front door was wide, tall and solid looking, she raised the pineapple shaped brass knocker and gave it a few taps. No one answered. The sky was getting a bruised look as the sunset approached its full glory. Libby walked to the back of the house, which looked out over a cascade of hills. It was a wide open view and she could see out to the horizon. It had been a long time since she had seen a sunset from a hilltop clear of trees, she stood in silence and watched.

"It is beautiful, isn't it?" said David, appearing at her side.

Libby jumped with her hand on her heart. "You startled me!"

"I'm sorry," said David, "I didn't want to call out to you from the house and disturb you. It was fascinating to watch the colors changing on your face. You seemed to be in another world."

Libby smiled at the compliment. "This world is wonderful enough for me. I was very much in the moment. Sorry, I came around to the back uninvited. I thought perhaps you weren't home yet, and I couldn't resist the colors of the sunset."

"Oh, but you are invited. However, we've got to hurry to see what I wanted to show you." David put his hand to her elbow and turned her toward the south side of the house. As they turned the corner, she saw a glass conservatory. It was about fifty feet long and thirty feet wide. The corners of the roof were rounded, converging into an onion-top dome.

"This is amazing," Libby said.

"This is only the frame," said David. "The real art is inside."

David walked quickly with Libby in tow. He opened the door for her to an interior where the air was warmer and more humid than the early autumnal evening that was unfolding outdoors. David led her quickly past huge elephant ear plants and banks of green and white caladium. "Oh good, we're on time," he said as he stopped in front of a plot of plants about two feet tall with dark green foliage and small purple buds.

"What is it?" Libby asked, nonplussed after the showy greenery in the entryway.

"Just wait," he whispered. They waited and watched. Suddenly, a long blue petal flipped out from one of the buds, then another petal on another bud. Libby realized the flowers were moving, they were opening right before her eyes. In less than a minute, the first blossom's four petals were fully opened. She laughed and clapped her hands with delight. On and on, blooms unfurled like slow-motion fireworks that did not fade and fall to the ground. The fully opened blossoms were four or five inches wide with petals the color of the sky on a clear summer day.

"Look up there," David said pointing excitedly to a vine rising ten feet high, spiraling around a supporting column. Libby stared as among the large heart shaped leaves a 4 inch long bud began to unwind counter clockwise. The resulting flower was the size of a dinner plate and creamy white.

"A moonflower!" Libby said. "I've always wanted to see one, and the blue of these … ." She gestured to the shorter flowers

"Four O'Clocks," finished David.

"This blue just about breaks my heart," Libby sighed. She looked around her and walked toward a small fountain and pool. In it were red water lilies pushing their spiked blossoms open.

Libby breathed in the scents. "The smell makes me want to eat some of these flowers," she said laughing and then more seriously, "This is what I imagine the Garden of Eden was like."

"It's called a moon garden or a midnight garden," explained David. "Most of the plants are night-blooming. They use smell more than color to attract insects, especially moths, to pollinate them, some nights I leave the door open for them."

Night fell slowly and discreetly placed low-wattage lights came on among the plants.   "Did you do this yourself?" Libby asked.

"The conservatory was here when I moved in, but the garden was in a terrible state. I work on it at night, I had over 3 cubic yards of dirt delivered. One of the things I plan to use the computer for is finding more nocturnal plants."

"I just love going out to my garden. It tickles me to no end to see the seeds and bulbs sprout and the shrubs and trees leaf and bud. I go out every morning and check to see what's new with my babies. I never thought of a night garden. That's such a great idea since you are gone most of the day."

"I think everything is awake now. Come into the house, there is something else I want to show you."

David brought Libby in through the front door. The entry foyer had a twelve-foot ceiling where a brass candelabra chandelier hung in the center. To the left was an imposing curved staircase, its handrail and steps were stained the same light oak shade as the front door and floor. The sturdy balusters and newel post were the shape of Grecian urns and painted white. The procession of balusters and railing went up nearly twenty steps, turning to line the upstairs hallway. On the stairs was an Oriental carpet runner in a royal blue, black and white arabesque design. A wider runner with the same pattern decorated the hallway, which had two doors leading off to front rooms and then fell into shadow toward the back of the house, presumably in the direction of the kitchen.

David slid open a pocket door on the right and Libby stood at the entry to a square and airy parlor. The first thing to catch her eye was the dark red of the walls. In a smaller room the deep shade might have seemed claustrophobic, but in the generous proportions of this room it felt welcoming, though still grand. The dentil crown molding at the ceiling was nearly a foot tall and the window and door molding at least six inches. In modern homes, this substantial molding made rooms look unbalanced as they just didn't have the dimensions to carry it off. Here, though, the balance and harmony were precisely the elements that gave the room its classical charm. The satiny cream color of the woodwork softly reflected the light coming from the lamps. The lines of the room were further softened by the curves of the furnishings. A peach velvet sofa sat between two wing back chairs covered in brown and gold brocade.

Scrolling wood framed the arms and bottoms of the furniture and the legs ended in claw and ball feet. The pillow backs and cushioned seats were overstuffed and rounded. An Oriental rug covered the center of the floor while the wooden floors shone as if recently waxed. Floor-to-ceiling bay windows looked out over the lawn toward the conservatory. They were covered with lace curtains that moved with the freshening evening breeze.

"David, your house is simply beautiful."

"Thank you," David said distractedly as he anxiously paced around the room. "Please sit down. Can I get you something to drink?" He opened up a glass breakfront with crystal cut decanters and glasses.

Sitting down on the plush sofa, she asked "Do you have any tonic water?"

"Certainly."

As David filled a glass from a soda siphon, Libby heard scratching at the door leading to the back of the house.

"I didn't know you had a pet."

"I didn't, until just recently," he said pushing a hand through his hair. "That's what I wanted to talk to you about."

The animal became more insistent with high pitched barks.

"It sounds like a little dog."

David opened the door and a little, red Pomeranian dashed into the room and bounded on to Libby's lap.

"My goodness, he looks just like Victor!" she laughed as the dog licked her face then she scratched behind his ears until he calmed down and curled up in her lap. Out of habit, she rubbed the animal's paws and found only two and half toes on his front right foot.

"Good God in heaven," Libby whispered picking up the dog and staring into his face. "Victor, it is you." Her scalp and neck prickled and everything went black. When she opened her eyes she was lying on the sofa with her feet propped up on the arm. David knelt next to her, patting her face with a cold, wet cloth and Victor, standing with his front paws on the edge of the sofa, licked her hand. Dumbfounded she gaped at them.

David opened his mouth and lifted his hands in supplication, but no words came out.

"How? ... What?" she murmured. "Did you clone him? No, that's impossible, he would be a puppy and his toes were crushed after he was born."

"No, he isn't a clone," David said slowly. "I ... reanimated him."

"Reanimated? You mean with electricity, like a, a Frankenstein dog?" Libby stuttered.

"No, more like a Dracula dog."

"What?" Libby thought she must have heard wrong. She tried to sit up, but her head spun and she lay back down.

David went on, "Remember what you said about him having a mortal soul and how sad you were because this life was all there was for him? Well, I tried an experiment."

"An experiment!" she cried. Victor jumped up on her and she put her arms around him and glared at David. "Wait, did you do come back and dig him up when I was asleep?"

"No, ... I never buried him. I put him in my car before I filled in the hole."

"What would you have done if it hadn't worked," Libby voice went up an octave, "double bagged him and thrown him in the garbage? I put a tree over an empty grave."

"I didn't think about what I would do if I failed." David looked down at the floor.

"It sounds like you didn't think about much at all, like asking me if I wanted you to experiment on my dog with some weird science."

"I thought carefully about what I was doing. You and I discussed the pure goodness of his nature. I hoped he would behave instinctively and his instincts would incorruptable. And he *is* a good little vampire dog. He sleeps all day and is perfectly happy to drink beef blood that I get from the butcher."

"What exactly did you do to him?" she demanded.

"I don't think you want to know the details."

"You're wrong, I want to know precisely what happened to him."

"Then I'll tell you. As you feared, he wasn't completely dead. There was a spark of life left, but he wouldn't have regained consciousness, if he had been buried."

"Oh, God," Libby said putting her hand over her mouth, but still held Victor with her other arm.

"What then?" she asked shakily.

"I drained him of his blood and transfused him with my blood."

Libby took a slow breath to keep herself from retching. "How is possible for a dead dog to come to life with human blood transfusions? Why would he want to drink beef blood?"

"This is what I've been afraid to tell you. My blood isn't human blood."

Libby eyes widened. "Are you telling me that you're an alien or something?"

"I guess I would be the 'or something', Libby, I am a vampire." David said with a simple shrug of resignation.

"Why do you keep saying that? Dracula? Vampire? That's not possible," Libby said as much to herself as to David. Then looking him in the eye, she said, "There are no such things as vampires."

"You said it yourself, Libby, that is Victor. How else would I be able to do that?"

Reaching for the dog, David said, "And now Victor needs to feed. He's been well behaved, but I don't know what would happen if he got really hungry."

Her arms were empty now, but her eyes stayed on Victor.

"You still look pale," David said, "I'll make you some tea, if after that you want to leave and not see me again, I'll understand. All I'll ask of you is to keep the truth of my nature a secret." He turned and took Victor into the kitchen.

Libby's mind was reeling, *A vampire! A vampire? David must be out of his mind. I have to get out of here. He lied about burying Victor, and somehow that is Victor. But, however he did it, I can't just leave Victor here drinking beef blood for the rest of his life.* She thought about leaving and getting Victor back some other time, but she didn't trust her legs to carry her to the door, and there was no guarantee that she'd ever see Victor again.

Libby jumped when the door from the kitchen swung open. David returned with a tray laden with a china tea pot, cup and saucer, sugar bowl, creamer and silver teaspoon. "Do you think you can sit up?" he asked as he placed the tray on the table in front of the sofa. He sat in the arm chair off to the side. His mouth was tense and his eyes were bright.

Libby sat up slowly and swung her legs down to the floor, furiously trying to plan a getaway. *I'll wait until Victor comes back and then I' ll ask if I can take him for a walk outside,* she thought.

Hoping to gain strength, she poured herself some tea.

David's face relaxed, "You don't believe me, do you? You think I'm crazy."

"I don't know what to think," Libby said, stirring her tea and willing her voice to be steady, "Victor's being alive complicates things."

"Do you have any questions for me?"

"Of course, I do."

"Let me start with the basics. I am a vampire - the whole Anne Rice thing with some exceptions. I need human blood to sustain me, though in a pinch I can use animal blood. With blood, I can live indefinitely. I have more acute senses and strength than a human being and my physical body does not age. I rest while the sun is up and rise at sunset. The special exceptions to date are that I cannot fly or turn into vapor or a bat. I believe in and obey the laws of physics, especially the conservation of mass and energy."

A short, hysterical laugh escaped Libby. She covered her mouth and nodded for him to continue.

"I also can't control the weather or people's minds. For the record I do not shine, sparkle, glisten or anything else in sunlight. I neither own a night club nor have vampire buddies, housemates or nest-mates."

"You aren't cold to the touch," Libby said, thinking of how his fingers had seemed to burn through her clothes when they danced, "or sickly pale."

"Anne didn't get that right either. More accurate European folklore depicts us as warm blooded and having a ruddy complexion. But all the books and folktales agree on the most important thing, I have no soul."

"It sounds as though you've done your homework."

"I had to get information about what I've become any way I could. Although I can vividly remember seeing the person who made me what I am today, I saw him only once. He attacked me and the next thing I knew I woke up in the dark in an abandoned mine shaft outside of Leadville, Colorado."

"When was all this supposed to have happened?" Libby asked.

"In 1941. I was born in 1900, by the time World War II rolled around I was too old for the first draft, the maximum age was 35. Still, I was a mining engineer, and the war caused a big demand for a mineral called molybdenum; it's used in making alloy steel. It makes the steel stronger, yet molybdenum's lower melting point makes it easier to weld, and it also prevents corrosion."

David warmed to his role as history teacher. "So, it was used in making armored vehicles, large charge casings and other military equipment. The highest concentration of molybdenum found in the US is in the Climax Mine near Leadville, Colorado. Leadville grew up in the gold rush and though there wasn't much gold there, there was millions of dollars worth of silver, copper, lead, zinc, manganese, bismuth and molybdenum."

"I don't want to seem rude, but could you cut to the part where you turned into or got turned ..."

"Yes, of course, I'm sorry, I got off on a tangent," David said sheepishly. "I loved my work." He cleared his throat and continued, "I was in Colorado on a job. I was driving a truck around in the mountains between Camp Hale and Climax looking for another location to open up a mining operation. Camp Hale, renowned for its extreme winter weather, was an Army training camp specializing in mountain warfare. Well, an early snowstorm blew in from nowhere and stranded me. Visibility was almost zero and I was afraid I'd make a wrong turn and go over a cliff. When I stopped the truck and got out to reconnoitre, I saw firelight coming from an old mining shack. At the time, I was amazed at my good luck.

"I knocked on the door. A normal looking guy in his early twenties opened it and invited me to come in out of the storm. The guy said his name was Dale. He was very hospitable, telling me to stand in front of the fire to dry my coat and boots, sharing a can of beans and giving me melted snow water to drink. He said he was in training at Fort Hale, but had gotten separated from his platoon during exercises in the blizzard. Dale looked legit with a crew cut and white camouflage parka and snow pants. A rucksack and cross country skis and poles were standing in a corner. We talked for a while, then I told him I needed to get some shut-eye. I settled down on the floor next to the fire, while Dale looked warm and comfortable sitting in a chair nearby. Next thing I knew, Dale was on me, holding me down with no trouble at all. He opened his mouth and I saw large, sharp fangs. Shoving my head over to the side, he sunk those teeth into my neck. It was the most terrifying thing I ever experienced." David stopped talking and stared into the middle distance, reliving that moment.

David shook his head and looked back at Libby. "At some point, I guess I passed out. When I came to, I was in an old mine and had a raging hunger and thirst. I could see well enough to find my way outside. It was night with the sky was as clear and black as I'd ever seen it. I heard a twig snap and in the distance, I saw a deer stripping bark off of a tree. Without a thought, I was running after it like a wild animal. I caught it, took it down and broke its neck in seconds. I had never ... an instinct just took over. I bit through the deer's hair and hide and into a vein in its neck and started lapping up its blood like a dog," he said sounding both amazed and disgusted. "I drank the animal blood, but somehow I knew what I really craved was human blood."

"Have you ever drunk, uh, … human blood?" Libby asked weakly.

"Yes, many times, the first being that very night. I was drawn to the army camp by the scent. Some poor guy was doing guard duty. I sneaked up on him and tapped him on the shoulder. When he turned around, I punched him in the face. I wasn't starving like I was the first time. I felt like I was outside of myself watching what I was doing. I bit into his jugular vein, blood spurted everywhere, but clamped my mouth over the wound and sucked the blood down. I pressed on the bite with my tongue to apply pressure. My saliva causes blood to coagulate and wounds to close up, but I didn't know that at the time. When I took my mouth off the wound, I saw the damage I did to his neck ... I closed him in the guard house and ran off.

"I felt an urgent need to return to the old mine and ran to it with no trouble. When I got deep into it, I fell asleep. When I woke up it was night again, sneaking into the Army camp hospital to find another victim, I discovered bottles of blood for transfusions in a kerosene powered refrigerator and took them out in a rucksack. I needed to get out of the area before people figured out what was happening. I found the truck, packed the bottles in snow and headed toward home. At night I'd find blood ... supplies and then look for secluded places to hide the truck and dig holes in the ground for sleeping during the day. I went back to Denver to be near my family and lived in the mountains outside of city for a while, but I couldn't let my family or friends see me like this. Eventually, everyone I knew from my former life died or moved away. Now, I live on the fringes of society and move on every so often."

"Let me see if I got this right," Libby said, "You were born over a hundred years ago. You were attacked in 1941 by someone who appeared to be a normal, young man. You never saw him again and since then you have been living on the blood of animals and bottled and um ... fresh human blood. Right?"

"Basically."

"You said earlier that you have no soul. How do you know that?"

"Everybody knows that."

"I don't know it, and I'd like you to explain the evidence that convinced you."

"All the accounts of vampires say we have no souls."

"So one day, you were a normal human being and the next this guy came and took your soul. Is there some kind of vampire bible that tells you this or are these just stories you tell around the campfire or morgue or wherever vampires philosophize?"

David ignored her sarcasm, "You think you know more about vampires than I do?"

"I don't know anything about vampires. I don't even know that they exist, but I do know a little about souls. Did you become a vampire of you own free will?"

"No, of course not!"

"Then, I'm sure God wouldn't give you up so easily. You were born human and you believe you had a soul. Right?"

"Yes."

"People can't lose their souls. Even if you did something seriously wrong, that you knew was wrong and you chose to do it, you would still have a soul. It would be in a state of mortal sin, but you'd still have it. As of right now, I can tell you have a mind, self knowledge, free will and you know right from wrong. That sounds a like sentient being, who has a soul, to me."

"I know what human beings say is right and wrong, but I am not a human being. I can't and don't live by the same code of ethics. To meet my needs, I've had to develop my own moral code."

"Doing things that are wrong to meet your 'needs' is like any human being following his baser instincts. Seriously, where did you get your information about vampires?"

"I've never met another vampire. All that I know comes from reading every major book about vampires that I could find and from my own experience."

"How did vampires come into being?"

"It all goes back to the devil."

"I hadn't thought of that," said Libby, "but not even Satan can't create something from nothing."

"No, he took a human being and corrupted him, desecrated him, having him sell his soul for immortal life!"

"You mean sort of a Dorian Grey arrangement?"

"Perhaps."

"That could work for the first vampire, but you'd have to have every subsequent vampire agree to the same arrangement to give the devil that kind of power. Somehow vampires are part of Creation just like any other being."

"So on the eighth day God created vampires," David said flippantly.

"Haven't you ever heard of evolution?" asked Libby.

"I didn't think Catholics believed humans descended from monkeys."

"Oh, come on. Gregor Mendel, the 'Father of Genetics', was a Catholic monk."

"Didn't the Pope reject Darwin?"

"The Church states there is nothing in Catholic theology that prevents the faithful from believing in evolution. God could have created the universe in any number of ways. Science is our way of figuring out how God did it and what His laws are. The only catch is…"

"There's always a catch," said David shaking his head.

"Yes, there is and it's that there had to be something special about the creation of the first man and woman so that God could give them souls."

"Fine, and now we are back to the soul, which my vampire bible tells me I haven't got."

"Your body isn't really immortal, is it? You can die, can't you?"

"It isn't easy, but, yes, a vampire can be killed."

"So, if the world came to end, your body would be destroyed along with everything else."

"Yes, I would think so, but it wouldn't have to be that cataclysmic."

"By what? Sun, wooden stakes,…"

"My instincts tell me the sun would make me very uncomfortable. I don't know if it would kill me. I usually can't stay conscious when the sun is up, so I am defenseless. From my reading, it seems vampires can die from fire, decapitation, a stake through the heart and starvation. Speaking of which, I am getting hungry."

David stood up and walked toward Libby. She gave a little gasp.

"Won't you join me?" David asked as he walked around her toward the kitchen door. "Don't worry, I've already got provisions."

David held the swinging door to the kitchen open for her and then snatched a damp cloth from the sink and wiped traces of blood from Victor's muzzle. David picked up the bloody dog bowl and quickly rinsed it out. Meanwhile, Victor ran toward Libby with his tail waving like a flag. She couldn't resist, so she scooped him up and cuddled him.

David opened the refrigerator. There was some food visible on the shelves, but when he pulled out the big drawer on the bottom it was filled with the same type of plastic bags Libby saw at the blood bank when she made a donation. "Is that real blood?" she asked.

"Yes, doctors can get it for private patients they treat outside of the hospital. I have my source in a town quite a ways from here."

"Does he know about your secret?"

"No, we've never met. It is understood that I pay promptly and well and he asks no questions. Everything is done by express mail and insulated containers to a business mailbox rented under a pseudonym."

"How do you earn your living?" Libby asked waving a hand around her indicating his house and belongings.

"I had a career as a thief for a while. I'm fast and quiet and can see well in the dark. After I got my grubstake together I invested in things - mining and precious metals and then stocks and foreign currency."

"So, when you told me you were working, that was a lie."

"Yes," David said abashed.

"I see," said Libby, "did becoming a vampire make you more … attractive than you were as a human being?"

"No, not really, I was good looking before," David said dryly.

Libby grimaced at his attempt to make her smile.

"Well, it's getting late and you have a lot to think about," said David.

"Yes, you're right, I'll take Victor home now."

"No," David quickly and took the dog from her, "I'm better equipped to take care of him here. Besides, how would you explain him to people?"

"Good question," Libby murmured.

"Please forgive me for not walking you out to your car," David said as he opened the door for her. "Seeing you has excited Victor, and I don't want to leave him alone in the house."

Driving away, Libby heard Victor howling for all he was worth. Looking in the rearview mirror she saw the turret and roofline of David's house silhouetted by the moon. What had seemed a quaint Victorian to her a few hours ago, now resembled a haunted house from a horror movie.

Chapter 23

For the first time since Victor died a month ago, Libby noticed she wasn't sad when she entered her house. She was too astonished to be sad and somewhat hopeful about Victor's getting a second chance. But ... vampires? Somehow, David brought Victor back from the dead. She tried to sleep, but she was too keyed up after seeing Victor and hearing David's stunning explanation.

Giving up on sleep, Libby got up and paced around the bedroom. Finally, she went downstairs and turned on all the lights. She tried doing some housework, but her heart wasn't in it. Nothing new about that. She sat at the computer to catch up on some emails, but she couldn't concentrate so she gave up and did a search on vampires. This struck her as so ridiculous that she closed the lid of her PC. She sat in her pink, Queen Anne styled, velvet recliner and began to pray, but finally fell asleep.

She knew she was dreaming because she was back in the bedroom she slept in as a teenager, when she heard a loud crash. Out the window she saw a moving truck stuck on the steep incline of the road in front of her childhood home. The back doors of the truck hung open and furniture and boxes slid out onto the road. Libby ran outside in her pajamas, and found a high school friend named Lynn was standing amid the pile of belongings behind the truck. Libby went to console her, remembering that Lynn's little sister had just died in a freak accident.

The girl was on a hayride with her church group and sat on the front edge of the wagon where it was hitched to the tractor. When the wagon bumped over a large rock, she lost her balance and fell backwards between the tractor and wagon. Her skull was crushed by the wagon wheel.

Lynn looked forlorn surrounded by ripped boxes, scattered clothes and books lying on the ground. The trail of broken furniture extended down the hill. Lynn saw Libby coming toward her and knelt down to pick something up. When Lynn stood up, she held out a delicate bottle made of thin, clear glass. Inside it was transparent golden liquid. Lynn said, "I want you to have this, Libby, because it's the only thing that isn't broken."

Libby awoke with tears in her eyes and was left wondering about her dream. She wished she could call Sue, with whom she discussed her strangest dreams, but it was four in the morning. Libby sat up determined to figure out the message her subconscious might be sending her through the dream. It was clear that she was being given an important gift. What was the gift and who was giving it to her? Was Victor the gift? Was David giving it to her? Was David the gift? Thinking about it was making her head hurt. She fell back to sleep.

Libby called Sue later in the morning.

"Libby, come on over and tell me over a cup of coffee I have here with your name on it."

Libby arrived and told Sue the dream.

"Oh, that is so beautiful," said Sue. "It makes me want to cry. There's your friend, her life is literally falling apart around her and she gives you the only thing she has that isn't broken."

"I think I should call her," Libby said, "it's been a while since I talked to her."

"That's a good idea, but I don't think that's what the dream is about," Sue counseled.

"No, I don't either."

"In a psychology course I took a few years ago," Sue recalled, "I think it was Jung who said all the major elements of your dreams represent you. It could mean you are giving yourself ... to yourself."

"I have problems with that theory. I got that I was receiving something important, but not quite that I was giving myself to myself."

"Libby, it sounds like something really big is coming down the pike, but I can't figure it out yet. Is there anything else you can tell me?"

Libby pressed her lips together and shook her head.

"Getting up to go to the bathroom at night seems to be helping you remember more of your dreams," Sue said. "I know I remembered a lot more dreams in vivid detail when I was pregnant and getting up every couple of hours."

"Ironically, that's getting better. I don't have to get up as much in the middle of the night, but I am having trouble sleeping."

"What do you think that's all about?" Sue asked.

"I can't say," Libby said, trying to avoid outright lying.

Chapter 24

Later that afternoon, Sue called Libby. "Mr. Baynard left a message on the library voice mail. He's canceling his lesson for tonight."

Of course, he did, she thought, but she just said, "Oh."

"Libby, you still there?"

"Yes, I'm here."

"You sound disappointed."

"No, that's fine. Thanks, Sue, for letting me know."

Libby went to the library anyway on Thursday evening, just for something to do. She futzed around until eight, hoping David would change his mind. After all that vampire jazz, she'd feel more comfortable if they met in public. She wished they could go back to where they were before his big revelation. However, he said he wasn't coming and he didn't show. She went home, had a light supper and went to bed early, but lay awake thinking about how easily she'd gotten used to having David around. Being with him was exciting and fun, it gave her something to look forward to. She realized this more acutely being alone again, but being alone now was her choice. David hadn't banished her! She knew where he lived and could go to his house and try to work things out.

"But the guy thinks he's a vampire," she told herself, "Dracula, human blood, fangs ... It's a kid's Halloween fantasy run amok." She put her face in her hands. She was just going round and round. Maybe he was testing her or joking with her though he certainly seemed serious. What about Victor? Victor was real. She was getting worked up again, and decided to use one of the relaxation techniques her therapist had taught her. Lying back on her pillows, arms at her sides, she got comfortable.

Libby flexed her toes tensing all the muscles in her feet while keeping the rest of her body relaxed. She moved methodically up her body until she was clenching all her muscles and then letting them go slack. The next phase involved controlling her respiration. She took a long, slow breath in through her nose, held it and then slowly blew it out through her mouth. She concentrated on and counted each breath. She would count ten breaths. If she thought of anything else during the count, she would start again. On the third round, she fell asleep before she got to ten.

Chapter 25

In the morning, Libby was surprised to see she had a message on her machine. It wasn't there when she came in last night, and she hadn't heard the phone ring. She kept the ringer turned off on the phone in her bedroom, but she usually heard the downstairs phone. She played the message.

"Hello, Libby, it's David, if you're willing to give me another chance, I'd like to see you. I can pick you up at seven o'clock tonight. Bring your walking shoes."

Before she lost her nerve, she returned the call. It rang four times and went to voicemail. "All right, David, I'll be ready by seven."

Libby was relieved to get an answering machine, but when she thought about it she realized it was morning and a person who said he was a vampire, would at the very least not answer his phone during the day.

She thought back on her many interactions with David, realizing how very little she knew about him. He'd always arrived at night, using work as a reason for not being available during the day. He dressed as if he was coming from some sort of business or professional office. Did he dress like that just to come to the library to see her? On one hand she was glad she had already committed to seeing him again, on the other she was appalled that she was doing so.

Libby busied herself with housework and took a long nap in the afternoon, but the day dragged by. By quarter to seven, she was ready, dressed in twill pants and layers on top - camisole, a purple short-sleeved shirt, a marled grey cotton pullover sweater-and her walking shoes. When she saw the headlights of David's truck coming up her driveway, she went out on the front porch to wait. She still felt strange about being alone with him in her house.

"But it's just fine and dandy to go off with him in his car. No one will even know where you are. It's hard to be discreet and safety conscious at the same time. Dear God, don't let this be a big mistake. Please keep me alive and well." Libby shook her head in wonder that she was going through with this.

"I'm glad you're willing to meet with me. I need to talk to you more about the other night," David said. Libby nodded and said, "Thank you," as he opened his passenger door for her and gave her his hand to help her up into the cab. Now that he was here she didn't know what to say, they drove along in silence for a while.

"Where are we going?" Libby finally asked.

"A fishing cabin on the river," David said glancing over at her. "The moon is full and the weather's mild, I thought you might enjoy a walk. We should be back by ten o'clock. Is that all right?"

"Yes."

More awkward silence.

"What is Victor doing tonight?" Libby found herself asking.

"I gave him his dinner before I left. He has the run of the kitchen and the mud room. I closed the doors to the rest of the house, I'll take him for a walk when I get back."

"I used to leave the radio or the TV on when I went out, just so he wouldn't feel lonely," Libby suggested.

"That's a good idea, I'll try that next time. Seeing you the other night made him happy, but, now, I think he misses you."

David pulled off of the roadway onto a gravel road that would have been easy to miss. They drove through the woods where the road deteriorated from gravel to dirt. The truck thumped over ruts and roots. After about a quarter of a mile, an opening in the forest showed in the path of the headlights. It was a wide semicircle of something green, moss or grass, to the left was a cabin.

David stopped the truck and helped Libby out. He took her hand as they approached the cabin, where steps led up to a covered porch with two rocking chairs. "Sit here," David said brushing some pine needles off of a seat. "There is no electricity out here, but I have some lanterns inside."

As Libby sat her eyes grew accustomed to the dark and her ears to the sounds of the forest. David came out with a camp lantern, which cast enough light to walk by. "Come down to the river," David said taking her hand again. "There are roots and rocks that can trip you up, so I'm going to keep hold of you." Once they got from under the trees, the river and its wide grassy bank were illuminated by a big, orange moon and its reflected twin was on the water.

"This is lovely," Libby whispered not wanting to contaminate the quiet.

David smiled and said, "Let's walk a little then we can go to the dock." They walked on a path of beaten down grass. Occasionally, a startled frog plopped into the water. Behind some cattails migrating ducks quacked sleepily. When an owl screeched from a nearby tree, Libby jumped and grabbed David's arm.

David laughed. "Maybe you'd like to head to the dock."

"I think I'm ready."

When David and Libby got to the dock, he said, "Would you like to do a little night fishing?" He nodded toward a broad row boat with two seats and a tackle box.

"I haven't fished for quite a while," Libby said.

"Do you like fishing?"

"I do."

"I knew my instincts about you were good," David said with a grin. "We'll need to get some bait first."

A pitch fork rested against a tree. Libby noticed it earlier and thought it looked out of place. David picked it up and pushed the tines deep into the ground. He planted his feet on either side of the fork and with both hands shook it back and forth.

"I remember that old trick," Libby said. "The worms feel the vibrations and think it is raining, so they come up to the surface."

"Exactly," said David. "Shine the lantern around my feet."

A few seconds later an earthworm came wriggling out of the cool, damp soil.

"There's one!" Libby called. "Where are we going to put them?"

"Here," David answered unbuttoning his breast pocket.

"They're going to be a bit gritty," Libby said.

"I don't think the catfish will mind."

"No, I meant for your shirt."

"Oh, this is an old one I use for fishing. It won't be the first time I've had night crawlers in it."

"They're certainly earning their names tonight. Look at them."

By now, four were squirming around on the ground. "Do you want me to pick them up?" David asked. "You'd have to be the rain maker," he said using his chin to indicate the pitch fork.

"No, no, you're doing a good job. I'll get them," said Libby.

"Okay, but hurry up before they figure out it isn't raining."

Libby bent down and grabbed each worm with her right hand and put it into her left to hold. When she stood up, David stopped shaking the handle for a second and pulled open his shirt pocket and she dropped in the worms.

"Good going, Libby. I knew you wouldn't be squeamish." Looking down he said, "Quick! There are more."

Libby scooped up three more. David stopped moving and she put them in his pocket, too. "That should be enough for now," he said buttoning the pocket flap over the squirming lump. She was about to wipe the dirt on her hands on her pants.

"Wait," David said. He pulled a handkerchief out of his back pocket.

"Thanks," said Libby, "you sure are prepared. I bet you really were a Boy Scout."

"One of the founding members of my troop," David said.

"No wonder, you had that salute down," Libby replied, poking him in the shoulder.

With a chuckle David pulled up the pitchfork and laid it back against the tree. "Let's go," he said taking Libby by the elbow. They walked down the dock. He got into the boat lithely, put the lantern in the bow and helped her in. Along side of the tackle box there was a hefty hoop net.

David pointed to the tackle box, "There are two telescoping rods in there. Would you mind getting them out while I row to a good spot?"

"I'll give it a try," Libby said.

"There is no try; only do," David said as he sat down in the stern seat. Libby cocked her head and looked at him.

"I was quoting Yoda from the second *Star Wars* movie," he explained.

"Oh, yeah, I remember," she said, "Yoda is training Luke to be a Jedi on some swampy planet ..."

"Dagoba!" They said at the same time.

"Aye, aye, Captain," said Libby.

David laughed and set the oars in the oarlocks. He cast off from the dock and rowed out into the river's slow current. "This is the easy part," he said, "the pool I like to fish in is downstream from here."

"How far away is it?" Libby asked.

"Only about ten minutes."

Libby got the rods ready. "Can you tie on the hooks and sinkers?" David asked.

"Sure, which ones do you want me to use?"

"Use the egg sinkers and the biggest hooks in there."

"Got it."

"Did you hear that?" David whispered.

"What?" Libby whispered back.

David pulled the oars in and a minute later said, "There. The fish are jumping."

Libby heard a splash in the distance. "Cool!" she whispered. "It's magical out on the water in the moonlight."

"We don't really have to whisper; the fish probably won't hear us," David said.

A large bird flew out of the woods on the bank and over their heads down the river. "But the birds might. That was a night heron, I think," David said as he started rowing again.

"Wow, you sure can see well in the dark," Libby commented.

"It comes with the territory," he said. Before Libby could say anything he announced, "We're here."

David anchored the boat and pulled two worms out of his pocket. He handed one to Libby. "For you, my lady." They baited up their hooks. "Have you ever fished for catfish before?" he asked.

"Nope," said Libby.

"We want to get the lines down to the bottom. It's about five feet deep, so take about eight feet of line out and just toss it out there." David said. "You take the starboard side and I'll take port."

Libby's line dropped close to the boat.

"Try again," suggested David, "it's a little different from regular casting."

Libby pulled the line up and swung it underhand. It dropped a few feet from the boat.

"That ought to do it," David said. "Now, we wait."

"That part of fishing I'm familiar with," Libby said settling into her seat.

After a while David said, "What would you say if someone offered you immortality?"

"I'd say, 'Already got it, but thanks anyway.'"

"You're talking about life after death," David countered. "That's not the same thing, because you have to die first. The body you have now will become sick or injured or die of old age and turn to dust."

"Believe me, I know about physical deterioration," said Libby, "but the part of me that makes me who I am is my soul, and that doesn't die."

"I can glimpse your soul in your aura. It is beautiful, but are you so sure of life after death that you are willing to bet this life on it?"

"Wait, how can you see my soul?" Libby asked.

"Twice now you've mentioned that I have excellent night vision."

"Well, just now when you saw the heron ... ," she thought for a moment, "and the first night we met when you lifted me off my feet just before I stepped into that pothole in the library parking lot."

"That's right," David said with a grin. "After I was changed, I experienced a big improvement in my vision. I could see better in the dark, and I could also see a wider range of color, hues and intensities. I could see beyond the light spectrum I saw as a human. I don't understand it completely, but there is a kind of psychic energy that the mind produces when a person thinks or feels emotion and it gives off heat that causes low level light. I see it as an aura or a halo. I noticed a correspondence between the brightness and color of light surrounding people and their behavior. People, who are kind, calm and spiritually wise have a soft, white glow and yours is pure and unwavering. When I told you that you're like a comet leaving light in its wake, it was because that is what I saw."

Libby was speechless and just stared at him.

"But, let's go back to the question of life after death," David said. "Tell me what you know about it."

"I can tell you what I believe, but nobody knows exactly what it will be. 'Eye has not seen, ear has not heard, nor has human mind conceived what God has ready for those who love Him.'"

"That's very poetic," said David.

"That's a quote from the Bible, and nowhere does the Bible give details or a clear description of heaven."

"So far, you're not helping," said David.

"Stay with me for moment. When I was a kid, I learned that animals didn't have immortal souls, so my horses and dogs weren't going to be in heaven. I didn't think I even wanted to go to heaven, so I asked my priest why it had to be that way.

"He asked me, 'Libby, what do you like so much about horses?' I said, 'Horses are beautiful and strong and I love the way I feel when I ride them. When I ride at a gallop I feel like I'm flying, I feel free.'

"And he said, 'God is the source of beauty, strength and freedom. You will be surrounded and filled with these and all good things. Your heart's desire for them will be satisfied. You will be in a state of blissful contentment.' That's what life after death has over immortal human life. Can you say that you are content?"

Libby asked looking into David's face in the darkness.   "Wait! I got a bite," she shouted. Her rod was pulling toward the bow.

"Give him a little more line," David said. "Okay, okay, now hook 'im."

"Man, this thing is fighting." Libby said breathing hard as she jerked her rod and started reeling in the line.

"Good, good. Get him a little closer." David grabbed the net and shifted in his seat to get closer to Libby's side of the boat. The fish lashed with its tail, splashing them both.

"Woah!" Libby cried.

David scooped the catfish up.

"It's probably 4 or 5 pounds!" said David.

Libby was beaming. "That was great," she said.

"We can clean him and cook him over a fire," David said as he handed Libby the net and grabbed the bucket. He reached overboard and filled it with water. "Let's unhook him and put him in here."

"Here's more bait for your hook," David said taking a worm out of his pocket. Soon Libby's line was back out in the water and they both settled down.

"So where were we?" David asked.

"I was explaining how life after death was better than mere longevity, because it included blissful contentment if you went to heaven. Then I asked you if you were content."

"Right. And the answer is no, I'm not usually content. I am sometimes, like when I'm with you," David replied. "Clearly, you are someone who loves life."

"I do love life," Libby said. "I try to find beauty and joy … in every regular, old day. I try to do good and stay away from evil. But I have to tell you, sometimes the freedom to do what I think is right wears me out. Look at my life right now. I stick to my morning routine like a man overboard holds onto a life raft. If I think about all the things I could do each morning, I would be out of my mind before breakfast. I did that for a while after Frank died. After the boys left for school, I'd run through possibilities for hours until I was paralyzed by … restlessness. It was a terribly state to be in. Then I found my way and my purpose, but now, I'm at another stage of life, another crossroad. Once again, I need to find ways to make my day-to-day existence mean something. Figuring out what to do with myself now is bewildering and exhausting. In this life, there is always worrying, wondering and … wanting.

"When I was young, I wanted to be finished with school. Sitting in a class, I was so pent up with desire to get out into the world, I could have hurled myself out a window. When I was finished with school, I wanted to work, to find my career, find fulfillment. After working for a bit I started thinking about throwing myself out a window again. I wanted to be married and start real life. After I was married, I wanted to have children. After I had children, I have to say I was content for a while, probably because I was too tired to be restless," Libby said with a laugh. "Even as a mother, though, I often wanted to rush through the phases of the children's lives. I wanted them to be able to walk, to talk to me, to learn. Now I wish I could have it all back again."

"How can you be so sure that creation, redemption and heaven and hell, that it's all true?"

"Remember we talked about how being a mother helped me to be a better person?"

"Yes, I remember."

"Well, becoming a mother helped me to understand God better, too," said Libby. "Before I had Matthew, I don't think I really knew what true love was. Then there was this child that Frank and I helped to create 'in our own likeness and image.' He already had Frank's nose, for heaven's sake! Everything that child did - move, smile, sleep - just his *being* delighted us, just like in Genesis. It all made more sense to me, God created us and just loves us for just existing. He is much greater than I am so He would be a better parent than I ever could. He could love me more than I could love my own child. If I did for my children what I thought was best for them, He could do that and more for me. If I could forgive my children for just about anything, He could forgive me anything. If I would do whatever I could to save my kid's life, He could and would do anything to save me." Libby stopped.

They contemplated their fishing lines silently for a while.

"I am in the difficult, restless state you described," said David. "I don't know if redemption is possible for me. I still can't believe you're right about my having a soul, but I have hope that you can help me find out if I have one or how to get it back. But, how can I prove to myself that what you believe is true?"

"You can't," said Libby. "It's faith and it's a gift. The first thing you could do is start praying for the gift of faith, and the best that I could do is pray for you, too."

"I think there is something else you could do for me," David said.

"What is that?"

"Lead by example and let me follow you. I could be the project for the next phase of your life."

"And what would the goal of that project be?" she asked.

"To be a companion, to help me find my purpose in life."

Libby couldn't come up with a reply.

During their discussion, the moon had darkened. Now, the wind picked up and clouds were moving in fast. Pointing to the sky Libby said, "We better get back to shore. A storm is coming in."

The two pulled in their lines. As David started rowing, fat drops of rain fell, and thunder rumbled in the distance. David rowed more briskly, but the storm was faster. Lightening flashed and the rain came down in sheets. Libby struggled to get the fishing rods and tackle back into the box.

"Can you see where you're going?" she called over the noise of the squall.

"Almost," David yelled back.

The thunder crashed almost simultaneously with the lightening flashes. Libby calculated that the lightening was close and was anxious about being on the water. She murmured prayers, but couldn't see a thing through the pouring rain.

"There's the dock," David shouted.

"Thank you, God," Libby said blowing out a sigh. David gave the lantern to her and hurriedly tied up the boat. He got out with the bucket and gave Libby a hand getting onto the dock.

"Let's get inside," David shouted. He and Libby ran down the dock, across the moss and onto the covered porch of the cabin. They were soaked to the skin. Water ran off of their noses and hair and dripped from their clothes. Libby tried to find something to wipe the rain off of her glasses. David poured some water out of the bucket to make it lighter and handed it to her.

"You take the fish and the lantern in, I'll get some firewood," David said and pointed to the woodpile on the porch.

The dampness from the river and the rain pervaded the cabin and Libby felt it when she opened the door. David came in soon after her with an armful of logs and the wind banged the door behind him. Libby shivered and rubbed her arms with her hands.

"There are some towels and spare clothes in the bedroom," he said. "Why don't you dry off and change?" He handed her a box of matches. "Do you need help lighting a kerosene lantern?" He indicated three of them sitting on the table.

"No, I can manage." Libby lit one and carried it to the bedroom. On shelves in the bedroom she found slightly musty towels as well as sweaters and pants. After undressing she toweled herself off and then wrapped a second towel around her head. She hoped David's clothes wouldn't be too small for her.

She had had an embarrassing experience as a teenager. On the spur of the moment she was invited to stay overnight at a petite friend's house. The family offered her their older son's clothes and Libby spent the evening covering the fact she was unable to button the pants with a long flannel shirt. Luckily, David's pants had a drawstring waist and were very forgiving. His sweater was thick and plenty wide in the chest so it didn't cling to her bra-less torso. She turned up the sleeves and returned to the living room with her wet clothes.

David smiled at her, "Don't you look fetching." He had drawn two wooden chairs up to the fire. "Spread your clothes out on the hearthstones," he said pointing to the one foot high floor of the fireplace that extended out into the room. "I'll be back in a minute," he said as he headed to the bedroom.

Libby spread her clothes out and warmed her hands. The fish made a noise in the bucket. "Sorry, old boy, looks like you're what's for supper."

David returned in khakis and a sweater drying his hair with a towel with one hand and his wet clothes in the other hand. "That storm sure came up fast," he said, laying his clothes out in front of the fire.

"I didn't even know they were calling for rain," remarked Libby.

"Neither did I. There may be some stuff left in the kitchen by the previous owners. I think I can manage to cook that catfish, but I don't know what if anything is in the cupboards."

"I ate before I left," said Libby, "but all this excitement is making me hungry again. Grilled catfish sounds really good."

"Excellent! I'll clean the fish. You look through the cupboards and see what we have. "

"How long have you had this place?" Libby asked as she rummaged through cabinets and drawers.

"Less than a year," David replied.

"So, whatever food I find will be at least a year old."

"At least," he said.

She found metal plates and cups and silverware. "There's some pepper and salt ... and flour. No bugs in it so far as I can see."

"Perfect," David said as he lifted a good sized fillet off of the cutting board. "Do you see anything to cook on?"

With a little more searching, Libby came up with a cast iron Dutch oven. It had metal handle that could suspend it from the big hook in the fireplace "Ta dah!" she said holding it up triumphantly. "You won't believe this, but there's some Crisco down here, too."

"Is it any good?" David asked raising his eyebrows.

"This stuff can last for years, if it is stored right, and ... the lid is tight," Libby said prying it off. She looked in and sniffed. "It looks and smells fine to me. I'll wash out the pot and dishes."

"The pump handle over the sink works,"said David. "It only brings up cold water, but it's clean."

Soon the smell of fresh fried catfish filled the cabin. David swung the cooking hook and pot out of the fireplace. He used an old dish towel to take off the lid. "Bring a plate on over, Libby."

David spooned steaming chunks of catfish onto Libby's metal plate. "Here's one for you," she said, handing him a second plate.

"Oh, no thanks, this is for you. I'll join you at the table for a drink," said David.

"You're not going to have any fish?" Libby asked.

"I don't really eat much of anything," David said.

"Oh?" Libby thought back to the carrot cake. "Oh, I see. You can't eat anything else?"

"No, but I do drink water and the water here is delicious." They sat at the table, Libby with her dinner and David with his cup of water.

"Mmm, this is good," Libby said after taking a bite.

"When you've been cold and hungry, everything tastes good."

"That's true," Libby said, "but I wasn't that hungry until you started cooking." She took a sip of water. "And this well water is good."

David smiled, "I'm glad you like it."

Libby savored the fish. Eventually, she sat back. "I'm full. I can't eat another bite."

"I had hoped the rain would let up by the time we were ready to go," David said, "but it's still coming down hard."

"Well, I still need to clean up." Libby took her plate and cup to the sink.

"That's not necessary," David said.

"No, I insist. You did the cooking; I'll do the dishes. Has that Dutch oven cooled off yet?"

"There isn't any soap to wash with," he said as he brought the pot over to the sink.

"Well, we don't want to wash a cast iron pot with soap any way. I'll just wipe it out and rinse it. Too bad we don't have something to wrap the rest of the fish in. I guess we can put it out in the woods for an animal to eat."

"I'll take it out," David offered.

"Boy, is it rainy out there," David said when he returned brushing the rain off of his shoulders and running his hand through his hair, "and windy, but I guess ... we should go."

"I'm ready to go; time to face the storm." Libby picked up their clothes from the hearth. "Almost dry." She said as she tucked them under the sweater she'd borrowed.

David pulled the remaining wood and embers away from each other. Using the fire place shovel he covered the embers and small flame that was left with ashes. It smoldered. Then he drew the metal screen across the front of the fireplace and said, "It'll burn itself out; let's go."

Out on the porch, David said, "We'll have to make a break for it. Don't run though; it's slippery out there." He put out the second lantern and held the other one up to see them out. They both pulled the necks of their sweaters up over their heads and left the shelter of the porch roof. They were soaked again when they got into the car.

David turned the truck around. Visibility was poor and the dirt road had turned to mud, so he drove slowly into the forest. He hit the brake hard to avoid running into a big limb that had fallen across the path, causing him and Libby to jerk in their seats.

"Hmm," David grunted. He shifted into reverse, and the back tires just spun in the mud.

"Should I call Triple A?" Libby asked as she looked through her purse for her cell phone.

"I don't think there's any reception out here," David answered and turned on the overhead light.

"You're right," said Libby, "not one bar." She tried to call anyway but nothing happened. "Now what do we do?"

"We either spend the night in the truck or go back to the cabin."

"Oh, dear," Libby said uncomfortably. "You can't control the weather, can you?" She sounded a little suspicious.

"No, I think that's the X-Men," David said with a smile. He turned off the ignition and reached into the backseat. "We'd better relight the lantern," he said."It's going to be very muddy on the road. It might suck your shoes right off. We'll be better off walking on the pine needles and leaves on the side of the road."

Chapter 26

David and Libby put their original clothes under their sweaters again. David took Libby's hand and he helped her down from the cab, and began guiding her back to the cabin. He was right about the mud, her shoes squelched across the road to the forest floor, which was less muddy. The trees cut the rain a bit, but it was still torrential and the wind tore at everything, their hair, their clothes and the tree tops. By time they reached the porch she was breathless. Wiping their feet on the porch they pushed through the door into the cabin.

Inside, David said, "At least it'll be easy to restart the fire. You should probably change again so you don't get sick."

Libby changed back into her own clothes and dried her hair with another towel. She bestrewed the wet clothes around the hearth again. "As the great Yogi Berra said, 'This is just like *deja vu* all over again'," she said with a laugh.

The realization of what spending the night meant started to dawn on Libby.

"What will Victor do if you don't come home before morning?" Libby worried.

"He'll be all right, I have his bed set up in the pantry. There are no windows in there and there's a doggy door in the pantry door so he can get himself in there. He's never had to be told it was time to find a dark place to stay for the day. It really is instinctual."

"What about you, where will you go when the dawn arrives."

"Don't worry, I can sleep in the truck."

"And you said you left him his ... dinner, right?"

"Yes, believe me he'll be fine," he said reassuring her and then asked, "Do you think you can drive my truck, it's a stick shift?"

"Sure, I learned to drive stick when I was a kid."

"That's my girl," he said with a smile.

They sat and stared into the flames.

Suddenly, Libby looked at David, "Have you eaten?"

David shrugged and said, "I was planning to do that when I got home. I guess I didn't think of everything."

"Can you go all night without food?" she asked.

"It would be unpleasant."

"What can you do?"

"I could go out and hunt around in the forest."

Libby looked at the window. Heavy rain was still falling along with lightning and thunder. "Are there any deer or other large animals around here?"

"Not this early in the fall. They tend to stay further north until it gets colder."

"And you swear that you didn't know about or have anything to do with this storm?"

"Cross my heart and hope to die," he said making an X over his heart.

"That's a rather lame oath coming from you," Libby said.

Libby was used to dealing with bad boys. She decided to call his bluff. "How much blood do you need?" she asked David giving him a long look.

"No, I couldn't ask you to do that," he said shaking his head.

"Would it do something bad to me to let you have some of my blood?" she asked wondering about being turned into a vampire, then thinking it was absurd to even consider that.

"No, I could be very careful, but …"

"Feeding the hungry is an act of Charity. It doesn't say anywhere in the catechism that you can't give somebody your blood," she told him and herself. He was gaping at her now realizing she was serious.

"How much do you need?" she asked again.

"A pint would hold me over," he answered.

"That's how much I give when I donate to the blood bank and it's been several months since I was there last."

"I usually get my blood from a blood bank," he conceded almost hopefully.

"We'd just be cutting out the middle man, I guess," Libby said with a feeble smile. She couldn't believe it was getting this far. "When do you want to start?" she asked.

"Whenever you're ready, I guess," David said shrugging and lifting his hands helplessly.

"I guess there's no time like the present," she said pulling her collar out a little and bending her head to expose her neck.

"There's more to it than that," David hurried to say.

"All right, lead on McDuff," she said lightly.

"For starters you need to take off your sweater," he said stepping closer to her. He reached for the top button.

"I can handle that myself," she said unbuttoning the sweater and pulling it off. "Okay, what next?"

He took Libby into his arms and kissed her forehead, her eyes, her cheeks, her mouth, her neck.

"What are you doing?" she asked keeping her voice calm.

"I am trying to get you to relax. This might hurt a little if you are not in the right frame of mind."

"Relaxed is not the word I would use to describe how this is making me feel."

David laughed. "All right my lovely Libby."

He started quietly singing an old song.

If you were the only girl in the world

and I were the only boy

Nothing else would matter in the world today

We could go on loving in the same old way

A garden of Eden just made for two

With nothing to mar our joy

I would say such wonderful things to you

There would be such wonderful things to do

If you were the only girl in the world
and I were the only boy.

As David sang, he slowly waltzed her around the room, and then steered her into the bedroom. After spinning her under his arm he picked her up and placed her on the mattress with her head and shoulders on the pillows. He picked up Libby's left hand turned it palm up and placed it under her head. She felt as if she was lying on a hill looking up at the clouds, but her eyes were on his face. The singing stopped. Gazing at her intently, his pupils widened until they were surrounded by only thin gray and yellow circles. He unbuttoned her blouse, never breaking eye contact with her. His stare seemed to bore into her mind. She was frozen with fascination and could say nothing.

"Here my mark will remain hidden. Only you and I will know," he whispered lying down beside her. Ducking his head to the hollow where her arm joined her torso, his tongue rasped across the stubble of her shaved underarm. Passing his tongue over one more time he explained he was lubricating and anesthetizing the spot with healing saliva. His movements were slow and deliberate, then his body tensed and sharp as knives his fangs pierced her skin. A charge went through her and muscles contracted all over her body, causing her back to arch of it own accord. There was a warm trickle and then the movement of his tongue, like an animal lapping water. As he took a deep draught, she felt blood being pulled from the punctures. Her body relaxed, her eyes closed and her mind opened. She was not alone in her mind or in complete control of it. Something effervescent was on her tongue, a taste and smell of heavy sweetness. Sweet, sparkling, red wine and lilacs came to mind, so much better than cold, plastic-tasting bagged blood, she sensed David nearly swooning.

Visions passed through her consciousness. A bright blue sky, so beautiful, David was seeing it with her or through her. The pure morning light was shining on grass and golden leaves. He missed that. They felt the thrill of clean, cool sheets on warm skin, then soft, chubby arms around the neck, wet kisses on cheeks. The tenderness of maternal love flooded David's and Libby's joint consciousness. There was a vision of Brendan turning with a box of CD's and books, smiling as he looked back from the door of his dormitory. Pride, heartbreak, tears. Voices sang. Surrounded by sound, Libby's voice dipped into the lower register, trilling in lively triplets. A chord vibrated in and around her. Many made one with the music, encompassing the whole being, it filled all need for meaning.

Libby saw people and things she didn't recognize. A woman dressed in an "*I Love Lucy*" kind of dress held the hands of two children. Libby didn't know them, but felt contentment. They were gone. A handsome young man's face loomed above - panic, cold fear, darkness. Looking into a mirror she saw David's face, she felt his confusion give way to self-loathing. More people and places flashed by and desolation stabbed the heart.

Here were places and people she knew, but from a different perspective - Main Street, Sue, the woods, the choir, the river, Fr. Larry, the library, Mrs. Palmeri. In each scene, Libby saw someone she knows, as one knows in a dream, is supposed to be her, but does not look the way she normally sees herself. There is a glow around her. She felt something coming from her. It felt like … hope.

Libby was aware of David's will pulling away, like a bubble about to break. Pop! She was alone in her mind. Disoriented, she opened her eyes and saw only blackness. "What happened?" she whispered.

.   "For a moment we shared the same cognizance," he replied quietly.

"Yes, I sensed what you saw and felt..." she said slowly, "but now I feel so sleepy."

"Yes, dear heart, you'll need to rest, but let me get you something to drink first."

David got up and got her a cup of water. He sat on the edge of the bed as he handed it to her, she gave it back empty. He placed the glass on the floor under the bed.

"Now, scoot over and give me some room," David said. Lying down beside her again he wrapped his arms around her, pulling her close to him. She put her head on his shoulder and her arm across his chest. Picking up her hand, he kissed her palm. She wanted to stay here awake for a long time, but she couldn't.

When Libby awoke, she was alone. "David?" she called. There was no reply. She walked from room to room as the morning sun came through the windows facing the river. As she opened the front door a piece of paper that had been closed between the door and the jamb fell at her feet. It was a note from David.

"Dearest Libby,

I don't know how to thank you in writing, I will try in person tonight.

The truck is up on the gravel part of the road, so it won't get stuck in the mud again. I am in the truck bed shielded by the cap. Do not open the back of the truck until 6:20 PM tonight. Drive to my house then and let me out.

Love, David"

Libby noticed the word '*love*'. It made her stomach flutter. She walked out onto the porch. No truck, no David. She got her things together and started up the side of the road on the leaves and pine needles. She passed the big, fresh ruts, the truck tires had made last night. The tree limb was on the side of the road. About a quarter mile more and she saw the muddy truck on the graveled part of the road. She checked it, the driver's door was unlocked and the keys were on the front seat.

"*How did David move that tree limb and get the truck out of the mud?*" Libby wondered. "*Maybe he went to a pay phone and called Triple A. ... Is he really in the capped truck bed?*" She climbed into the truck, turned on the engine and saw what time it was. The clock read seven forty.

"Sugar, honey, iced tea!" Libby cried. She had go home, get cleaned up and be at school to tutor Jesse by ten o'clock. Thankfully, the engine turned over and the car lurched forward spitting gravel behind it. As last night's happenings came rushing back, she started talking a mile a minute aloud, "Oh, dear Lord, I stayed out all night with David. I let David suck blood out of me. Oh man, how am I ever going to explain this to Fr. Larry?

'Well, you see Father, I met this man. I think he is a man, he told me he was a vampire. I wasn't sure I believed him, but he brought my dog back to life and then I let him bite me and drink some of my blood. If he's not a vampire, there is definitely something different about him.'"

Thinking more about last night a hushed, "Wow" escaped her lips. Could parts of it have been a dream? Driving faster than usual, hoping not to be seen in David's truck, she took a curve a little fast, and heard something bulky shift in the back. This was maddening. She couldn't look in the back, David told her not to - in the note. The note was real, but she could not decide if that was comforting or not. Driving into her driveway, she parked the truck under some trees. *"Oh, David, I don't know if you like it warm or cool. Since you're in the trunk, I'm going to go with cool."*

Rushing around the house, she went through her morning routine in fast forward, grabbed a banana for breakfast and ran out the door. She drove her van to the school and got to the mentoring room just as Jesse arrived.

"You're cutting it close, huh, Mrs. O?" Jesse said.

"And hello to you, too, Jesse,' Libby said.

"What are we doing today?"

"Hmm? Oh, I don't know yet." Libby said distractedly looking through the red folder.

"You trippin' today, Mrs. O," Jesse noted.

"Well, you'd be tripping, too, if you had the night I had. I got stuck out in that big storm last night."

"Did you get stuck all by yourself?" he asked teasingly.

"Why would you ask such a question, Jesse?"

"You're not answering it and you're turning all red."

.   Libby put her hand to her face and it felt warm. "Oh dear," she said, "maybe I caught a cold."

"Yeah, right," Jesse smirked. "You acting like my mother when she has a new boyfriend."

"Ah, here we are. Oh goodie, we're going to diagram some sentences."

"Oh no," Jesse said with a groan.

"Let's start with this one," Libby said. On the blackboard she wrote, *Children should not speak flippantly to adults.* "Can you underline the verb of this sentence, Jesse?" she asked handing him the marker.

"What's that flip word mean?" he asked sourly.

"That is a new vocabulary word for you." Libby said as she traded him the marker for a dictionary from the bookshelf.

When the bell marking the end of class rang, Libby gasped.

"Man, you sure are jumpy, Mrs. O," Jesse said.

"I've got a lot to do today," she replied, "I'll walk out with you."

"Aren't you forgetting something?" the boy asked.

Libby had already replaced his folder and turned out the lights. "What?"

"Your glasses? You keep taking them off and leaving them places. They are over there on the desk."

"Oh! Thank you, Jesse, I didn't even notice I wasn't wearing them."

"You should get one of those necklaces that you tie on to your glasses to wear them around your neck when you're not using them."

Libby winced, "I always thought those were for old ladies, more specifically old librarians."

"Out of the mouths of babes," Jesse said.

Libby looked at him and ruffled his hair, "Where did you learn that?"

"My grandmother always says that when I say stuff about her being old," he said making a point of brushing his hair back into place with his hand. Libby folded her glasses and put them in her purse.

"Aren't you going to wear 'em after all that?" Jesse asked with exasperation.

"No, something must really be off with this prescription. I can see just as well without them."

Jesse cocked his head to look up at her, "You look better without 'em."

"Thank you, Jesse. I hope you have a good weekend. Say hello to your grandmother and your aunt for me." Libby waved as she hurried into the main office to sign herself out. She slowed down as she realized she still had seven hours to wait before sunset.

Chapter 27

At 6:18 PM Libby was standing next to David's truck in his driveway. With his keys in her hand, she waited until exactly 6:20 to unlock the tail gate. Inside she saw a queen-size air mattress covering the entire floor of the truck and on top was a lumpy, unzipped sleeping bag. After a moment at the darker, far end there was movement. David crawled toward the opening and smiled up at her almost shyly. "Thank you," he said.

"Now that's what I call a truck bed! Did you, uh, sleep well?" Libby asked as he climbed out.

"Yes, very well," David said as he took her hand and kissed it. He pulled her into his arms and hugged her.

"Let's go in and feed Victor," David said as he took Libby's hand again and led her through his front door. Victor greeted them with happy barking. Libby brought him outside to play in the twilight while David went into the kitchen. Ten minutes later he called out the door, "Come, Victor! It's time to eat."

Victor looked up at Libby and ran to the door. She followed him into the house, but as he began slurping noisily she averted her gaze.

"David, how did you get the car past the tree limb in the road and out of the mud last night?" she asked.

"I went out after it stopped raining. When I got to the car, I saw the tree limb wasn't as big as it seemed earlier, so I pulled it off the road. To help the wheels get traction in the mud, I piled pine needles around the rear tires, and then rocked the car back and forth between reverse and first gear and eventually it moved. I figure it would be better to park up on the gravel."

Libby cleared her throat. "So, you really are a vampire, huh?"

"I said what I meant and I meant what I said," David said with a smile. "I've already dined, while you were out with Victor. Can I get you something to drink?"

"Tea, please."

"Tension Tamer?"

"You have some?" Libby asked.

"I got it a couple of days ago."

"I've been thinking about what we were talking about in the boat last night, about immortal life. Many widows would see your longevity as a point in your favor."

"Oh?"

"Right after upsetting my sons, being widowed again is one of the main reasons I'd be afraid to marry again. Losing Frank is the hardest thing I've ever had to live through, I'm still living through it. Having the boys made it worse, because of their loss, but it also gave me the strength or at least the motivation to scrabble along. If it was just me mourning alone, well ... I don't even want to think about it."

They sat silently for a few minutes thinking about things neither of them wanted to talk about.

"Have you ever been married, David?"

"Yes," he said.

"I guess you've been widowed, too."

"Not in the traditional sense," David said sadly.

"Why is that?" she asked.

"I lost my whole family twice. The first time was when I became a vampire. I watched my wife and children mourn for me and then saw my wife marry another man, who would also be the stepfather to my children. He was a decent man, a good husband and father, but I resented him for taking what was mine even though or, I should say, especially because I could never have it again.

"The second time was when my wife died. I couldn't attend the funeral, it was held during the day and besides I couldn't go near the church. There wouldn't have been any comfort for me in the minister's promise that we would all be together again in Paradise. I would live forever in this world with no chance of ever being with her again. It happened again with my son and then my daughter as they aged and died. I didn't stay close to watch over my grandchildren, I didn't want to get attached to any more mortal descendants."

"I'm so sorry, David," Libby murmured putting her arms around him. "You've lived with losses I can't even imagine."

David rested his head on Libby's shoulder as they sat on the sofa. She caressed his face and held him close with her chin resting on his head. She felt him tremble and sigh. His warm tears trickled down her neck. Her own tears trailed down her face and into his hair. She wanted to comfort his decades of lonely sorrow.

Into the night, they sat this way. Finally, David lifted his head. Libby dried the tears on his face. "Why are you letting yourself get attached to me?" she asked.

"When I saw the glow around you, I knew you would be a joy to be around and hoped that joy would bring back an enthusiasm for my life, such as it is. I haven't laughed so much or been as happy, as I am with you, for sixty years. I don't know why, but with you, I have hope."

"That's a lot to live up to," Libby said.

"You don't have to do anything but be yourself," David said taking her hand in his, "and let me be with you. I love you, Libby."

"How can you say you love me, when you hardly know me?" she asked.

"You could say it was love at first sight. Of course, I had the advantage of knowing exactly the kind of woman I was looking for."

"You were looking for a matronly, middle-aged widow?"

"Why do you continue to describe yourself that way? It's maddening," David said.

"I take it you weren't looking for someone w1ho is maddening," she teased.

"No, it's just an unfortunate side effect in a hardheaded woman," he said with a smile, "and I mean that in the most complimentary way - sensible, clear-thinking."

Libby laughed. "My husband would certainly have agreed with you on the hardheaded part, but with an emphasis on stubbornness. He used to say I had a 'whim of iron'."

"Whim of iron, I like that," said David. "Your husband was clever and probably smart. That's why I'm sure he saw that you would be good for him. Living with you day to day he may not have noticed you growing into the redoubtable woman you are. Certainly, some of that growth comes from living through marriage, raising children and being widowed. Now you are the woman I need, to become the man I hope to be."

David took Libby into his arms and kissed her.

Libby smiled at him, "Unfortunately, I think I should go now. If I spend another night with you …," she trailed off.

"I understand," David said kissing her fingertips, "but remember that nights have the innocence of days for me."

Libby was exhausted when she got home, having put in a full day and on into the wee hours of the night. She went upstairs to bed and as she closed her eyes she thought, "I'm in way over my head. I'm calling Fr. Larry as soon as I get up."

Chapter 28

Father Larry was an Oblate Father. He lived in a retirement home for priests run by his order. It had originally been built as a seminary, but now it was a retirement and retreat center. The campus included a medical wing, dormitories, offices, meeting rooms and a chapel. It was situated out on several acres of farm land and landscaped gardens. The Oblates rented the land to local farmers, while the priests kept their own gardens and cemetery. Care had gone into the landscaping and there was a great hedge that formed the logo of the order. Mature trees lined the walkways; under them were benches where residents and visitors could pause for reading and thinking. Walking trails were lined by flowering shrubs, and there were two meditation gardens. Boxwoods lined the priests' cemetery, the headstones were simple and inset flush with the ground. The dates went back hundreds of years to the first priests who had come to the colonies from England. The chapel was only about 85 years old as the earlier one had been destroyed by fire.

The older priests' residential area was completed just fifteen years ago. It had all the modern accommodations for the elderly or infirm. It was a one story structure with wide hallways and doorways for wheelchairs and gurneys. The hallways fanned out like rays around a circular common room with a nursing station on one side. The common room had floor to ceiling windows and a skylight. The hallways had rooms on one side and windows on the other. The daylight and constant view of nature kept it from feeling like an old age home. It always smelled like fresh air, too.

Libby walked down the hall to Fr. Larry's room. She knocked on his door and was invited to come in. His bedroom doubled as his office, where he had a desk and chair, overflowing bookshelves, a recliner for himself and comfortable armchairs for guests. Discreetly tucked away under the windows was a simple bed that looked like it could have been in a college dormitory, except that it was neatly kept.

"Hi, Fr. Larry, thank you for seeing me on such short notice."

The short, chubby priest pushed himself up out of his recliner and gave Libby a hug.

"Certainly, my dear, you've been coming to me for Confession every three weeks for over twenty years. When you call early, I know it must be something important. Sit down, now, and tell me what is on your mind. Do you want to go to Confession?"

"Yes, Father, but mostly I need some spiritual guidance."

Sitting down again, Father pulled out the long, narrow, purple stole worn for Reconciliation. He kissed the red crossed embroidered on the back of it and put it over his shoulders. "Let us begin then. In the name of the Father and of the Son and of the Holy Spirit," he said entering into the sacrament.

Libby began, "Father, I met this man, this person. He's intelligent. He's kind. We like the same things … "

"It's about time," Fr. Larry said bouncing a little in his seat. "I don't need to tell you the rules. No sex outside of marriage and so on…" He beamed. "I'm so happy for you."

Libby raised her hand. "Wait," she warned, "this is going to sound crazy, but he says he's a vampire and I believe him." She told him the story about Victor and David's confession.

The priest sat quietly through her explanation. Afterward, he shook his head and said, "Why am I not surprised?"

Libby's eyebrows shot up. "That is not what I expected you to say. I thought you'd be … shocked, horrified, incredulous?"

"God's plans are so intricate. You and I met years ago through Susan. I was retired and had time, you needed a spiritual advisor. It seems so ordinary. Then you meet a man and he confides in you that he is a vampire, which is extraordinary. But what is even more remarkable is that I am one of the few people in the world, who knows a vampire monk."

Libby sputtered, "That's, that's … I want to say impossible, but now I know that it is possible, so I guess it's … amazing."

"Yes, dear, it is." Father Larry continued, "I wasn't supposed to know about him, it was an accident, and I promised not to tell anyone until it was God's will."

He hesitated. "I'll tell you the story, but without the details of where it took place, and you must promise to keep the secret, too."

Libby nodded, "I am bound to secrecy by my friend, and that's why I told you about him under the seal of the confessional."

"All right," he said, "and you'll be bound by a promise made in the confessional, too."

He took a deep breath and began, "I thought I wanted to be a monk, so I went to ... . Let's just say I went abroad to an abbey to discern my vocation. One night I stayed in the chapel after night prayers to do some more praying and thinking. I must have fallen asleep, because the next thing I knew I heard voices. This was unusual because the monks don't talk in the chapel. They pray out loud and hear Mass, but they don't converse, and these two were laughing. I looked up from a back pew and saw the abbot talking to a monk I'd never seen before. Then the abbot said something about the brother helping him and this young monk reaches down and lifts the corner of the altar. This was one of those old, big marble altars, it must've weighed a ton. The abbot lies down on the floor and reaches under there and pulls something out. When the abbot crawls out, the other fella gently puts the thing down. It was an unbelievable sight, so I gasped. They both turned toward the noise and saw me. The abbott beckoned me to them and I had to explain myself.

"The abbot made me promise never to tell anyone what I saw. 'But what did I see?' I asked him. The faintest light of dawn was showing through the stained glass window to the East and the strange brother inclined his head saying, 'I have to go, Father, whatever you decide to tell him will be fine with me, I sense that he is trustworthy.'

"So, the abbot told me his story.

'Around the year 1200 AD, Brother Alerick, who had recently taken his vows and been consecrated, disappeared, sometime later he reappeared in a distraught state, he had been attacked by a vampire. Instead of killing him the vampire transformed him into one of the undead. Alerick was separated from the community and kept in a crypt behind a locked silver door. He refused to feed on human beings and suffered greatly.

'It was customary for the brothers to bring the Precious Body and Blood of Our Lord to sick monks in the infirmary. The abbot, Father Lorenzo, ordered the same be done for Brother Alerick deep in the bowels of the monastery. Alerick could not eat the Communion bread, but he drank the consecrated wine transubstantiated into the Blood of Christ. This sacred drink, which we have always believed was the real blood of Jesus under the form of wine, sustained and satisfied Alerick. This was the way God gave our brother his daily bread.   In time he was able pray together with his brother monks, he was especially well suited for all-night vigils before great feast days. On ordinary days, when the whole community of monks awoke before dawn for chanting the morning office and attending Mass, Alerick stayed with them until sunrise. Lorenzo even changed the daily order of prayers to Mass first, and then singing the Liturgy of the Hours so Alerick could take Communion with the other monks before his night ended. Afterward, the vampire monk would retire to his cell in the crypt for the rest of the day.

'Alerick had a keen mind. His work involved studying theology, philosophy and natural philosophy, which was the study of nature and the physical universe before the advent of modern science. His longevity contributed to the monastery's studies, as he contemplated the new and remembered the old.

'The abbot was wise. Like Holy Father Benedict before him, he knew Brother Alerick needed physical labor as well as prayer, study and writing. His chores included feeding and cleaning up after animals and helping the monks who awoke in the middle of the night to make fresh bread for their brothers' breakfast.

'For decades, the holy men lived in harmony, Alerick did not age physically and hence was present at the burial of many of his friends. The abbot of the monastery was an old man, when he sent a delegation to the head of the order to explain the plight of the 'undead' monk. At first, the abbot General was skeptical, he feared the far flung community of monks had lost its way and become Satanist heretics. He demanded that Alerick be brought to him.

'So, a party of seven monks including the abbot made the long trip with a wagon pulled by four mules, transporting Alerick in a coffin draped with cowhides to protect him from sunlight. When they arrived in Rome, Father General questioned Alerick at length. He found the seemingly young monk sound in his faith, and steadfast in his insistence that he was a vampire.

To prove himself Alerick devised his own test, he asked to be buried in the earth in a coffin in the monastery's crypt for twenty-four hours. On Friday evening just before midnight the selected monks dug a deep grave, carefully lowered Brother Alerick in a coffin into it and shoveled dirt in on top of him. Afterwards, two burly monks stood guard outside the only entrance to the crypt. They were not told what they were guarding. The door was also secured with the Father General's great wax seal, which would be broken by any attempt to open the door. Inside the crypt were four more monks, two from Alerick's abbey and two of the most trustworthy from the main abbey. The monks had enough food and drink for a day and hay for bedding, and took turns keeping watch over the grave. Before midnight on Saturday, the Father General and Abbott Lorenzo rushed to the crypt. Despairing that the young man had suffocated, the head of the order chastised himself for letting Alerick perform this test. The red wax seal on the door had to be broken for the two older men to enter. The Father General watched anxiously as the monks, who had stood guard inside the crypt, re-dug the grave. They pulled the coffin to the surface with ropes

'Brother Alerick, come out,' called Father Lorenzo, who carried with him in a covered chalice containing the Blood of Christ and a fragment of the consecrated Host from the morning's Mass. He knew Alerick would be very hungry.

'Alerick pushed up the wooden lid and sat up. He stepped out of the casket and fell on his knees before Lorenzo.

"*Corpus et sanguis Domini nostri Jesu Christi custodiat animam tuam in vitam aeternam, Amen,* (May the body and blood of our Lord Jesus Christ preserve your soul onto eternal life, Amen)," Lorenzo intoned.XXX

Alerick drained the chalice like a man dying of thirst and fell to the floor with open but unseeing eyes.

"Oh, dear God, no!" cried the Father General as he rushed toward Alerick's rigid body, but Lorenzo raised a hand stopping him, "Do not touch him, he is in an ecstasy."

After a long while, Alerick awoke as from a coma. He embarrassedly wiped tears from his face, he had wept copiously during his ecstasy. He sat up and offered to perform other feats and answered more questions. "No, my son, I believe you," said Father General humbly.

'The Abbot General swore all those present to secrecy, decreed that Alerick would go on living quietly in his home abbey and asked him to share, anonymously, notes from his studies in science, philosophy and theology with the monks at the abbey in Rome. Finally, he asked if Alerick had any questions.

'Alerick had only one question. 'How will I ever get to my Heavenly Father?'

'The Abbot General put his hands on Alerick's shoulders, 'I am sorry, my son, I do not know how to answer you. You are being asked to do something none of us has ever been asked to do before. Neither you nor any of us has the authority to end your present life. Clearly, your Father in Heaven has not abandoned you, He sustains you from day to day and He will find a way to bring you home, in His own time. Until then we must wait and watch His plan unfold.''

Finished with story Fr. Larry smiled, "And now, Libby, I am telling you this secret because you and I have become part of that plan as well. You are one of very few people who know there is a eight-hundred-year-old vampire monk. We must offer your friend this opportunity to seek spiritual counseling, if both he and Brother Alerick are willing."

Chapter 29

Libby appeared on David's doorstep at sunset and told him about her visit to Fr. Larry.

"So, you felt it necessary to immediately expose the secret I told you in intimate confidence," David said coolly turning his back on her and walking away.

"Wait," Libby said following him. "I didn't tell Father Larry who you are, your secret is still safe."

"How many men are you keeping company with, Libby? It wouldn't be hard for someone who knows you to deduce who the vampire is."

"David," she said as she placed her hand on his shoulder to turn him toward her, "I told Father under the seal of the confessional. He is obliged to keep silence and take your secret with him to his grave. Your circumstances are beyond my understanding, so I went to Father Larry, because I didn't know what to do for you. Then he turns out to be the one priest in thousands who knows about another living vampire. David, don't you see? It's Providential."

Holding his face in both her hands, she looked into his eyes. "I did it, because I care deeply about you. I think meeting Brother Alerick may be one of the most important things you do in your life."

David's frostiness melted, "You care deeply for me. What an extraordinarily wonderful thing to say." He took her hands in his and kissed each one then he placed her hands around his waist and pulled her tightly to his chest. "My love for you is growing day by day until my heart is overflowing. This is all so strange, but if you really care for me, I will trust you. I'm placing my life in your hands, and if you think I should talk to this vampire monk, I will."

Libby called Fr. Larry and asked him to contact the monastery. The next day, she visited him again. She had never seen the little, old priest so animated. When he heard her confession, prayed or said Mass he was serene, now he was nearly hopping with excitement. "I spoke to the new abbot, and he said that Brother Alerick is willing to see your friend. ... What shall I call him?"

"David," Libby replied.

"Very good, tell David I'll arrange everything," Father Larry said. "I have a benefactor who will lend us the use of her private jet with no questions asked. This way we can control the timing of our travel so we can take off and land at night. We will be crossing time zones, so it will be daylight for a few hours during the flight, but the jet has a large windowless room where your friend can safely stay."

"You've really been thinking about this," she remarked.

Fr. Larry smiled, "Oh, yes, since the moment you left. All this is no coincidence, Libby. I truly believe that the Holy Spirit is at work here. It's so wonderful to know we are carrying out God's work," he said finishing with a sigh. "So now, we'll fly out from a private airfield that is literally in a field not far from here. We'll land in Italy on another airstrip owned by the Vatican. It may take a week to work everything out."

"I have another detail you'll need to work out. We need to take my dog, Victor, with us."

"Ah, yes, how could I have forgotten dear little Victor," Father Larry replied. "If this travel plan will work for a vampire, I think it should work for a vampiric dog. Yes, yes, and this way there will be no problems with customs or quarantine for Victor."

Libby used the days to prepare for the trip. She paid bills that would come due soon, packed her suitcase and readied the house for her absence. She was lucky Fr. Larry had his connections. Her passport was out of date and David didn't have one. Libby attended choir practice and her classes with Mrs. Palmeri and Jesse. At each, she explained that she would be away for at least a week. "A last minute visit to see friends," she explained.

The evenings, Libby and David spent together. They attended the last dance class with Herb. The rest of the time they were at David's house passing the time learning some Italian, watching movies and canoodling.

The day before the flight was Sunday and Libby sang at Mass with the choir. Dexter asked her to stay after again. *"Uh oh,"* Libby thought and hoped she had been singing on key.

"Mrs. O'Malley, I mean, Libby, you have been spot on since we talked. Thank you so much for taking my suggestions with such good grace. I was out of line with my remark about you not hearing well, obviously, I was mistaken. Who knows, maybe it's my hearing that's off."

"Well, whatever it was, I'm just glad that everything is back to normal," Libby said.

"I know you're going to be away next week. I was wondering if you would be willing to start practicing some solos for Advent, when you come back?" Dexter asked a little sheepishly.

"I'd be delighted," said Libby.

"We could do an oratorio from *The Messiah.* I was thinking of *'Arise, shine for thy light is come.'*

"I love that one!" Libby said, "Thank you for thinking of me."

"You're welcome. Thank you, for saying yes. Where did you say you were going?" Dexter asked.

"To see some friends," Libby said.

Dexter hesitated as if expecting her to say more. He continued awkwardly, "Okay, then, um, I guess we'll see you when you get back. I hope you have an amazing trip."

"I'm sure I will," Libby replied.

Libby hurried to her car, because she feared she would cry again, but this time for joy. Sitting in the driver's seat, she hugged herself and prayed, "Thank you, dear Father in Heaven, I'm so glad my hearing is okay, and I hope you like my singing, Lord, 'cause I plan to be doing it for a while longer."

Chapter 30

     Libby, David and Fr. Larry ended up leaving on Halloween night. Libby rarely got trick-or-treaters at her house so far out in the country, but she did enjoy going to the library dressed up as a character from a book and seeing the children's costumes. This year she went as Little Bo Peep. She cringed, however, when she saw a few little Draculas with dripping blood and fangs parading around.

     When David arrived at Libby's house at 1:30 AM that night to pick her up, she was ready to go. He picked up her carry-on bag, "This is it? You've got everything you need for a week in this one little suitcase?"

     "Usually, I have to carry my own luggage, so I've learned to pack light," she said.

     As she got in to the car, Victor barked. David had him ready to travel in a doggie carrier.

     "Hello, Victor, I'm happy to see you too," Libby cooed, touching his nose through the mesh. "We'll get you out of there as soon as it's safe."

     Together they drove to pick up Fr. Larry at the retreat center, where he was waiting for them in his black suit and Roman collar. Libby greeted him with a hug. "Father Larry, I'd like you to meet David. David, this is Father Larry."

     "I am happy to meet you, David," said the priest, "I hope this trip benefits you."

     David inclined his head, "I hope so, too," he said and put the older man's suitcase in the trunk.

     "How ever things turn out," Fr. Larry continued, "your identity and your secret shall be safeguarded. Only those who absolutely must know about you will know. For example, I don't need to know your surname and so I do not know it. No one involved in transporting us needs to know your name or the purpose of our trip and so they do not."

"Thank you, that's very considerate of you," said David.

Fr. Larry got into the front passenger seat and Victor barked his greetings.

"Victor!" the priest said turning around in his seat, "It's good to see you."

David opened the back door for Libby, and she slid in next to Victor. Fr. Larry directed David to the airfield. Once there David handed his car keys to Libby, "Would you hold these in your purse for me?"

"I'm not always the best at keeping keys," Libby said.

"Perhaps, but you always end up finding them," David said with a smile.

No introductions were made between Libby, David, Father Larry and the flight crew. One of the crew members helped stow and secure the luggage on board the corporate jet. Included was a large cooler that David had told Libby contained blood supplies for him and Victor. The plane took off at four o'clock in the morning. When the pilot announced that they had reached their cruising altitude, Libby let Victor out of his crate. He jumped into her lap, bounded off again and sniffed around the cabin. Fr. Larry swiveled around in his chair and said, "If you'll excuse me, I'm going to try to get some sleep. You may want to do the same Libby, once we arrive, we'll have a full evening ahead of us. David, when you and Victor are ready to retire, the door toward the aft of the plane leads to a sleeping area with no windows. I don't know how your body will react to jet lag, but with the eight-hour flight and the plus six-hour time change, our estimated time of arrival is 6:00 PM local time, which will be almost an hour after sundown. Well, good night, all."

With that, Fr. Larry took a set of headphones and his rosary beads out of his flight bag, positioned his seat to nearly horizontal and settled in for sleeping.

"You must be exhausted," David said to Libby as he stood up and reached across the aisle to push a stray lock of hair behind her ear. She smiled at him and agreed, "I am fading, the hour and the excitement of the trip are catching up to me."

David bent down and kissed Libby tenderly. "Close your eyes and sleep, my dear. I'll take care of Victor, and soon we will meet the amazing Brother Alerick." He reached up and opened an overhead compartment and pulled out a blanket and pillow for her. He handed her the pillow and draped the blanket over her. Soon she was sound asleep.

Libby awoke to Fr. Larry saying. "Good morning and good evening, Libby. We'll be landing in about an hour."

"Good morning, Father," she said stretching.

"I hope you slept well," he said.

"I must have, this is the first I've been up. Have you heard anything from those two?" Libby asked pointing her chin toward the bedroom door.

"No," said Fr. Larry, "but it's still about half-an-hour before sunset here. I don't know how this time difference is going to affect them, but at least they will be safe from the sun and from anyone who might wish them harm."

"Who would want to harm them?" asked Libby.

"This is a whole new world for me, I don't know what the potential dangers are, but I feel responsible for their well-being. I'm trying to be vigilant."

"Did anybody at the monastery give you information on how best to transport David and Victor?"

"Don't worry, Libby, they set up the flight times and set up the permission to land and the specifications for the sunproof chamber, everything to insure their safety is being done."

For their breakfast Father Larry found ham and cheese sandwiches in the refrigerator of the jet's galley and the wherewithal to make tea. They were cleaning up when the doorknob on the bedroom door turned and David came out.

"Good evening," he said imitating Bella Lugosi. Fr. Larry started, but Libby put her hand over her mouth to cover a laugh. Victor barked and ran through the doorway.

"You're in rare form today," Libby remarked, "you must be well rested."

"I think I can speak for Victor as well as myself, we feel fine," David said as he picked up the cooler of blood and scooped Victor up with the other hand. "I'm going to feed Victor in here, Father Larry, you might find it a little unsettling. We'll only be a few minutes," David said closing the door.

"Well," said Fr. Larry, " he certainly seems happier than when I first met him."

"He's probably excited about meeting Brother Alerick," Libby said.

"You know, we can hear you in here," David called through the door.

"Forgive me, David," Fr. Larry said, "we'll wait until you come out."

Libby shrugged and smiled sheepishly.

There was an awkward silence until David and Victor reemerged a few minutes later.

"How are you, David?" asked Fr. Larry meekly.

"I am happy. I usually feel splendid when I'm around Libby, so, it's a pleasure to start my day with her," David answered smiling at Libby. "This trip," he said gesturing to the plane, "all of this, is for Libby. She thinks it is most important for me to meet Brother Alerick, so I will meet him and be open to what he has to say to me. I trust Libby's judgment and her good intentions toward me. I trust her and she trusts you," he shifted his gaze to Fr. Larry, "so I have no qualms about this venture. Am I hopeful for an improvement in my situation? I don't know. I do know that I care about Libby and want to do what makes her happy. So, what is the schedule for tonight?"

Fr. Larry took a slow breath and said evenly, "First, I want you to know, David that I care very much about Libby, too. For over twenty years she has been like a spiritual daughter to me. However, what we are doing here is for you, for your salvation. Making this first move for Libby's sake is adequate, but at some point, if you want to change your life, you will have to will a change in yourself, for yourself.

"Now to answer your question, we are outside of a small town about two hours from the monastery. We will stay here tonight and tomorrow during the day. Tomorrow evening we will be driven to the monastery to meet with the abbot and Brother Alerick."

There was a loud thump and Libby jumped.

"It is only the landing gear being lowered," Father Larry said patting her hand.

A moment later they heard, "This is your pilot, we will be landing shortly please take your seats and buckle your seat belts."

David stepped forward to catch Victor and put the dog into the carrier, which he stowed under his seat. After a bumpy landing, Father Larry spoke up cheerfully, "A car is waiting for us here, so shall we go?"

The pilot never showed his face or bid them farewell. Someone opened the plane door from the outside and pushed a set of stairs into place, but nobody was there when the four of them disembarked. A black limousine purred a little way off the tarmac. They couldn't see a driver as all the windows were tinted black. As they approached the trunk popped open, so David put the luggage in the car. Libby carried Victor in his travel bag. There were two rows of seats facing each other in the back of the vehicle.

They rode in silence for a while, watching the dark countryside out the windows. Turning to Libby, Fr. Larry said, "I know you've never been to Italy before, Libby. You might enjoy strolling around the town and getting something to eat. I'm not much of a walker anymore and I have a boring diet, so why don't you and David go out, I'll watch Victor. Since we're keeping a low profile on this trip, don't use your credit cards. I received some Euros before we left, so use these." He handed Libby about two hundred Euros in a variety of coin and paper denominations.

"Thank you, Father," Libby said, wide eyed, "This is very generous of you, but we won't need this much." She started to hand some of it back.

"No, no, my dear," Father Larry said, "keep it and only use cash. Credit cards leave a trail."

"Father Larry," she said with admiration, "I never knew you were so good at this cloak and dagger type stuff."

Father Larry just smiled.

They rode a while longer, then Fr. Larry said, "I'll ask the driver to let you out here." Sliding the glass window between the passengers and the driver, he said to the driver, "*Si prega di fermarsi qui e lasciate che questi due fuori.*"

The driver replied, "*Si, Padre. Quando devo tornare per loro?*"

Fr. Larry translated, "He wants to know what time he should pick you up?"

"What do you think, Libby? Would two and a half hours be enough?" asked David.

"Let's make it an even three hours," she said. "We could even walk back if we knew where we were going. What is the name of this town anyway and where are we staying tonight?"

"Without trying to sound even more like an undercover agent, the less you know the better. Oh and it's a little late to ask now, but did you remember to leave your cell phones home?"

Both Libby and David nodded.

"Very good," said Father Larry, "All this secrecy is to protect David and Brother Alerick."

"Yes, of course," said Libby thoughtfully.

"So, we'll meet the driver here at twenty-two hundred. Shall we synchronize our watches?" David said with mock severity, then they all laughed

"Off with you, now," said Fr. Larry.

David opened the car door and slid out of the back seat. He offered Libby a hand to help her out. The car pulled away. "*Arrivederci,*" Libby called as she waved goodbye.

David took her in his arms and kissed her, "Fr. Larry is a fine fellow, but I've been dying to be alone with you." He put his arm around her shoulders. "Here we are in a romantic Italian village, where no one knows us. We are just two lovers out of hundreds of others, who've walked these streets."

Before Libby got a chance to comment on his use of the word, 'lovers', David quickly added, "and I bet the seafood here is great."

"Why do you say that?"

"I can smell a tang in the air, I'm sure we're close to the sea."

"Is that one of your special spider sense? Smelling things?"

"My sense of smell is rather keen. It's all part of the instinctual predatory nature. Are you hungry?"

"Famished!" said Libby

"Let me hunt you up some fresh calamari."

"How did you know I liked calamari? Is that another one of your gifts?"

He took her hand again and pulled it through his arm, again securing her on the inside of the sidewalk furthest from the street. "No, it was a just a good guess. Who doesn't like good calamari?"

They walked along the cobblestoned main street for a bit before Libby pointed at a large wooden sign with a fish painted on it. "It looks like a fish market," she said, "but it's closed."

"But look behind it! There's a little restaurant and I bet they have very fresh fish," countered David.

They walked past the market and then through the alley to the rear of the building. On the street behind the market was the entry to *Ristorante di Pesce*. In contrast to the quiet street, the restaurant was bustling with most of its tables occupied. "It's crowded; that's another good sign," David said. He opened the door for Libby. They walked into a candlelit room that was warm and smelled of garlic.

"Wow, that's a lot of garlic," David said.

"Oh, no. Is that offensive to you?"

"Not too much, but if you eat it and I don't, kissing you later may be less pleasant. But we are in Italy, I can't imagine garlic not being on the menu."

"I have gum," Libby said brightly.

"That'll do it, maybe a little tiramisu and espresso, too."

"But we hardly know any Italian," said Libby.

"We know at least four words – *calamari, tiramisu, espresso, vino*. That's probably all we need."

As the host came to them saying, "*Buona sera*", David held up two fingers and they were on their way. David ordered red wine and Libby got everything she wanted with a few more words, '*per favore*' and '*grazie*'.

Crispy on the outside, tender on the inside, the calamari were served over homemade pasta. The tiramisu was creamy and sweet; the coffee was strong; it was an exquisite meal. The restaurant was a little loud for private conversation, so they mostly enjoyed the ambience of watching Italians be Italian.

Once they were outside again, David looked at his watch and said, "We have about an hour and a half left. Let's find a place where we can talk." They walked on, hand in hand, eventually coming to the town piazza. It had a small fountain and a waist-high stone wall at one end. They walked to the stone wall, which overlooked the hills. In the distance there was a black void, but a bright light swung across the horizon.

"That's a lighthouse beacon," Libby said, "you were right about being near the sea."

"That reminds me of something my grandmother taught me. Do you know what the three sweetest words in the world are?"

"Most people would say they're 'I love you'," Libby said.

"Having been a married woman you might agree with my grandmother that the sweetest words are 'You were right' followed by 'I was wrong'."

"She sounds like a wise woman," Libby said with a chuckle. "She must have been married a long time."

"Sixty years."

Further along the wall, a half circle patio opened up with benches facing the sea.

"Would you like to sit here for a while or is it too chilly?"

"It's a little chilly, but the view is worth it."

"Come here and I'll keep you warm," David said as he sat down and pulled her to him. She perched on his knees.

"Ohh!" Libby exclaimed as he slipped his arms under her arms and under her knees to lift her completely onto his lap. Then he put both arms around her and held her close.

"Now I can see two beautiful views, you and the sea, at the same time."

Libby put her arms around his neck and nestled her cheek next to his. She hadn't sat on anyone's lap since her school days, Frank told her she was too heavy after a couple years of marriage. David made her feel girlish again, she sighed contentedly.

"Libby," David said after a while, "I want to tell you some things, now, tonight, before we go to the abbey." He took a big breath and blew it out. "I love you. I want to be with you as much as I can for as long as I can."

David picked her up off of his lap and sat her on the bench. Libby stared at him wide eyed and dumbfounded as he knelt down on one knee and took a box out of his pocket.

"Elizabeth O'Malley, will you marry me?" he asked. He opened the box. Inside was a gold ring in the shape of a rose with a small, fiery diamond in the center. "This was my mother's ring."

"Oh, David, it's so beautiful," Libby said putting her hand to her heart. "You are beautiful, but I can't say yes to marriage. Even putting my sons and your being a vampire aside for a moment, we don't know each other well enough. Your opinion of me is based on some fairy tale you are inventing from only a few weeks of being together."

David looked intently into her eyes, "It is not an opinion, it is a fact that I can see with my own eyes. Your psychic energy radiates more strength and goodness than anyone I've met since my transformation."

Libby shook her head, "But, there's so much you don't know about me. You see me in an unrealistic light, literally it seems. I know I am not that good. This may the best I've become so far, but it's taken fifty-two years to get this way. I've done things in the past that make me sick to remember."

"I find that hard to believe."

"That's just it, I can't let you believe this fantasy version of me."

"From the beginning you've felt a need to disabuse me of my good opinion of you."

"I just want you to know the truth."

"All right, then, tell me the truth," David said getting up and sitting next to her.

Libby raised her hands trying to find the right words, "I was arrogant, ambitious to the point of vindictiveness ..."

David shook his head, "I see nothing left of that."

She continued, "Twenty-one years of marriage wore off some of my rough edges. My husband and I were like steel on steel. Both of us were stubborn and proud. Most of our marriage was a power struggle. Through the whole thing we had so many arguments, some terrible and some childish.

"Having babies helped, they are the great humblers. It is hard to stay high and mighty when you're wiping a dirty bottom or walking around with baby spit-up down your shirt. I gave up my career and became an 'at-home' mom. I never intended to do that. I told my boss, 'I'll be back in six weeks. Don't give all my projects away.' He was a father of three at the time and he advised me not to rush things. 'Put in for a six-month leave. You can always come back earlier, but extending a leave is a paperwork nightmare.'

"After six months, I just couldn't do it. I was completely besotted with my baby, throw in good old-fashioned Catholic guilt and I couldn't leave him with someone else for ten to twelve hours a day, so I quit. After I stopped being a 'rising star' in my company, I couldn't even bring myself to go to my high school ten-year reunion. I had gone from 'Most Likely to Succeed' to being a housewife, I'd also gone from a size 10 to a size 16. I never got into the housewife thing, but I did get into being a mother. By time the fifteenth reunion rolled around, I was armed with pictures of my boys and a pair of 'Spanx'. By that point, I had become a little too proud of being an at-home-mom."

"A pair of what? Spanks?" David asked.

"Never mind, it's a 'foundation garment'."

"Oh, you mean like a girdle or a corset," David assisted.

"Yes, like that." Libby said, sorry she'd mentioned it, she waved the idea away.

"That doesn't sound so bad," David said.

"I saved the worse for last, hoping I wouldn't have to go into it."

"You don't have to go into any of this. Nothing you say can change my opinion of you," said David putting his arm around her.

"No, that's exactly why I have to tell you the worst," continued Libby pulling away from his embrace and looking him in the eyes.

"I used to have a terrible temper. When I lost it, I went berserk, breaking things, punching walls, ... I cursed like a Marine, too, which I learned that from my father, who was a Marine. I never swore in front of my parents, because I'd get punished. My mother was very ladylike, although she did break a lot of china during arguments with my father. And my father? He had a strict double standard between what was appropriate for him, a man, and me, a girl.

"I behaved perfectly in school, because I wanted my teachers, my classmates and their parents to like me. Also, because if I didn't behave, it probably would've gotten back to my parents. My father was strict in other ways, too, he believed in corporal punishment and when he lost his temper he just beat the living daylights out of whoever was closest. He shot a staple into my hand with an industrial staple gun, because I didn't do something right while we were putting a new roof on the barn. He threw my mother against the wall so hard, her head made a hole in the plaster."

Libby took a breath, stared at her hands which were clasped tightly in her lap and then went on.

"At some point, our family doctor told my mother if she brought any more 'accidental injuries' to him, he'd have to tell the authorities. Mom told Dad he had to get help, he had to stop hurting us or she'd leave him. He grabbed her and said, 'Do you want to send me to prison and break up the family?' I heard that part. My mother told me years later that he whispered in her ear, 'If you ever leave me, I will find you. I will kill your mother and your father and the kid in front of you and then you last.' So, my mom blinked first. She stopped going to the doctor for 'injuries'. She went around to different emergency rooms, but only if it was absolutely necessary. When I got older, my father became more subtle. He would hurt us in ways that wouldn't leave visible evidence for long.

"It's strange, but for some reason, what he did to my pets upset me more than what he did to me. Once, he punched my horse, Honeycomb in the mouth. He'd been hitting her, because she stepped on his foot or something. She reared up, more to get away from him than to hurt him, but he held onto the reins. He pulled her back down, wrapped the reins around his hand so she couldn't move away and started punching her in the face. He must have hurt his hand, because he eventually let go of the reins. He tried to kick her in the rump as she ran away and he fell on his own rump, I liked that," Libby said with a quiet laugh. "But my horse was never the same after that, she was nervous and flighty. He sold her about a year later.

"Before that, I had a puppy named Harry. We were having a hard time housebreaking him. If my father was home when Harry went on the floor, my father would grab him by the scruff of his neck and push his nose into the mess. One day we came home and Harry had had three accidents in the house. My father grabbed him by the choke collar and took him outside. He attached the tie out rope to the puppy's collar and swung him over the low hanging limb of tree, he hanged him. The message wasn't lost on me, being a kid, I figured if he could do it to Harry and get away with it, he could do it to me." Libby told the story as if she was a reporter reciting the facts. There was no emotion in her voice.

"Senior year in high school, I couldn't imagine my father letting me get away from him by going off to college, even though it would look bizarre if I didn't go, since I was the salutatorian of my class. My mother helped me and we did whatever was necessary to for me to get out, including forging my dad's signature on admissions and financial aid applications. With a full ride to a small Catholic college, I escaped. A few months before I had to move back home for the summer, I fell into a deep depression, so I went to a campus therapist. She was a master of understatement," Libby said and shook her head. "She said I had some repressed anger, but she did help me find a job at school and year-round housing. I never lived at home again.

"After college, I married Frank, with him I felt comfortable enough to show my anger. I'd scream terrible things at him and he fought back in his own way - a little shouting and maybe the silent treatment for a day or two. It was upsetting, but not frightening, Frank's eyes never went black like my father's did when he went into a rage.

"After Will was born and I was home with the two boys all day long, I tried hard to be calm and patient, but then something would happen and I'd explode, usually when the boys fought with each other. That really pushed my buttons. I would get right into their little faces and shout horrible things. If I got really angry, I would punch the wall or break something. If I ever hit them, it would be a couple of swats on the seat of their pants with my hand or a wooden spoon. Sometimes I picked them up and 'firmly' put them in a chair or in their beds, but I was determined not to be the parent my father was."

Libby sighed deeply and continued. "When my third baby was on the way, I was so tired. I had gotten into the habit of napping when the youngest child napped and by then it was practically an addiction. Anyway, this one day Will wouldn't go down for his nap because Matt was home from preschool and they wanted to play. I couldn't keep my eyes open any longer, so I put a four-year-old in charge of a two-year-old. Setting them up with a video usually did the trick for thirty to forty-five minutes. About fifteen minutes later, I was dead to the world until a blood curdling scream woke me up. I ran down the stairs and saw that Matt had locked Will out on the back porch. Matt was pointing and laughing at him through the sliding glass door. I bore down on Matt like a freight train. He must have heard me, because when he turned toward me his face went white and his eyes were huge. I grabbed him and threw him down on the floor. I tore open the door and brought Will inside. He was fine; he was just … angry.

"I turned to dress Matt down and stopped in my tracks. His nose was swollen and bleeding. He was crying and holding his arm. I reached toward him and he flinched.

"I had finally injured a child in a fit of temper. I was horrified by what I had done, but I was also afraid that I would get in trouble. I thought I had broken Matt's nose and I wondered if he needed to go to the Emergency Room. I kept trying to shush him. I got him put ice cube in a face cloth for his nose and sat him on the couch. 'Where does it hurt?' I asked kneeling down in front of him. 'My arm, my arm,' he wailed.

"I said, 'Matt, look at me. I have to take you to the doctor. When the doctors and nurses ask you how you got hurt, you have to say you fell. If you tell them I hurt you, they might put me in jail.'

"Planning the lie was so familiar. It was like déjà vu, except now I was the monster. Matt stopped crying and looked up at me, his big, blue eyes magnified by his tears. 'Okay, Mom,' was all he said.

"I thought I would throw up, but I had to pull myself together. I had to lie convincingly, too. So we lied - to my husband, to the ER doctor, to the x-ray tech and to the orthopedist, who put the cast on Matt's arm. His nose wasn't broken, but his arm had a green stick fracture.

"That night and the next day, each time we were alone, I told Matt how sorry I was. I told him I was wrong and promised I would never hurt him again, I remembered my father saying that to me. I don't know if Matt believed me, but I wasn't sure believed myself. I felt like the lowest scum, I'd never heard of a physically abusive mother.

"I felt so … evil. I needed to get to confession. I called Fr. Larry and asked if I could see him right away. He was my spiritual advisor and I'd been going to him every three weeks for Confession and counseling for a few years, so he already heard so much, but I dreaded having to tell him this.

"'I got angry and I hurt Matt,' I said bursting into tears from shame as much as remorse.

'What happened?' Father Larry asked.

'I broke his arm.'

'Father gasped and, for a second, a shocked look passed over his face. He had never reacted emotionally to anything I had confessed before. He took a breath and very calmly said, 'This is a very serious sin. I know you've had trouble with anger before, but I didn't realize the extent of the problem. Is the child safe, now?'

"'Yes,' I told him. 'I took Matt to the emergency room yesterday. I lied about how he got hurt and I told him to lie, too. Now, he and his brother are home with my husband.'

"Fr. Larry nodded his head, 'Before I absolve you of these sins, you must promise to get psychiatric counseling.'

"I told him, I was afraid to tell anyone what I did, because I could be arrested or the children might be taken away from me. Father pressed his lips together into a white line and then said, 'I am qualified to counsel you for now as a beginning and as your confessor I can't divulge what you tell me.'

"I explained sometimes a wave of fury would come over me, I didn't know how to control it. He told me that control was something he could help me learn. He gave me a book off of his shelf and told me to read certain chapters and to come back to him the next afternoon. He checked to make sure I wasn't going to be alone with the children. I told him my husband would be home for the next few days for Easter vacation.

"He said, 'Good. For your penance I want you to sit before the Blessed Sacrament and read and pray for an hour. Now say an Act of Contrition.'

"The book was about anger management. It helped me understand the most important thing: you can control your anger. You do it all the time when it's for your own good. It gave the example of a driver being harassed by a gang of Hell's Angels. The guy might be angry, but he's not going to shout at them, make obscene gestures or take any other aggressive action, because he knows it would put him in danger.

"I realized then that I had done exactly that kind of thing. Sometimes when I was in the middle of a shouting tirade, the phone would ring, and I could turn off my anger in a second and answer the call with the sweetest hello."

"Did you ever tell your husband?" asked David.

"Yes, but not until years later."

"What did he do?"

"He was horrified, but he said he wasn't completely surprised. He said, 'I've seen that dark look on your face sometimes when we argued. I remember especially one time when you said you hated me, that look made me believe it'." Libby stopped talking and looked up at David.

"What else did Fr. Larry do?" David asked.

"He helped me to forgive my father. My dad was already dead, but Fr. Larry said it would help heal me if I forgave him. Fr. Larry had me make a list of the worst things I could remember, then he did the most amazing thing. He took the place of my father. We sat side by side not facing each other. He'd say, 'Libby, I'm sorry for all the times I hit your mother. Please forgive me.' And I'd say, 'I forgive you, Dad.' He went through the whole list."

Libby paused and said, "Now, you can see why I trust Fr. Larry."

"Yes, I can. Was he able to heal you completely that way?"

"No, there was a lot more to it. Fr. Larry found me a Christian therapist. I saw her once a week for about ten months and we went through my childhood experiences. Her theory was my father was probably mentally ill. He was an orphan raised by extended family. His father died before he was born, and his mother was committed to an asylum. Anyway, the therapist said he may have been neglected or abused growing up or maybe there was some inherited mental illness. I didn't like hearing that, but more importantly she helped me to analyze and defuse my anger. She helped me to see that I shouldn't take what the kids did personally. She told me, 'When they're raising hell over whose turn it is with a toy, it has nothing to do with you at all. They're not screaming because they want to 'get you'. The only thing they care about is getting the toy'."

Libby shifted in her seat, sitting up straighter. She talked about her subject as a student of human behavior. "She also helped me to figure out that there were three different kinds of events. Some I could do something about, but weren't important. Some that were important, but I couldn't do anything to change them. And a few things I could do something about and that were important enough to get involved in trying to change them. So I could shrug my shoulders at about two-thirds of the things that might have set me off before and say 'That's life' or as my mother would say, 'That's the way the cookie crumbles'."

"So that's it? 'That's the way the cookie crumbles' and you're cured?" he asked.

"No, it is an act of my will. I can't afford the luxury of anger. It is something I can't have. I can be irritated, annoyed, exasperated, or some other thing, but when it comes to being angry, I have to turn my emotional self off. I laugh. I walk away. I do deep breathing exercises. I picture in my mind what I have seen done in anger and what I have done in anger." Libby looked up at David and said, "That's the worst of it and that's what I had to tell you."

David folded his arms around Libby and placed his chin on her head. "I still love you, Libby. I'm sorry these terrible things happened to you. It must be painful to go through the telling."

Tears had been rolling down Libby's cheeks. David kissed the tears away, "Thank you for trusting me with the worst things of your life. I promise I will never bring it up or use it against you."

Libby began sniffling and David handed her his handkerchief. "Libby, this only makes me surer than ever that you are the person who can help me. How can an angel who has never sinned help me fix my life? You've lived through evil and come out whole and even stronger than before.

"I still want to marry you. You've made it clear that you don't want to share an immortal life. Although - who knows - in time you might change your mind, but meanwhile, we could have the rest of your life together. Or we can go our separate ways now and have fond memories. I would move away, of course, since we live in your family's home town."

"I don't want to lose you," Libby answered. "I think I've finally figured out what I am supposed to do with my life right now and it has to do with you. Helping you find salvation, both of us making each other happy. But can't we just continue as we are for now?"

David shook his head slowly, "We both know love can't stay static, it has to grow or wane. I don't think you would be willing to be lovers without the benefit of marriage."

Libby looked down at the ground, "I haven't really worked out the sex part."

"So, you want me to be your boyfriend, just like those octogenarians you told me about. We could go steady or something?" David's voice wasn't sarcastic. He was just trying a thought out loud.

"Is that something you would consider?" she asked.

"I love you. I love being around you. I would do whatever you wanted me to do. Sex isn't necessary right now and maybe you would consider marriage later." He held her at arm's length and looked into her face. "As long there are hours of you lying in my arms, long talks and just being together."

"I would like that very much," Libby said.

"I don't know what you'll say to your sons and friends."

"I'll have to work on that, too. We'll keep mum on the vampire part."

"Yes," David agreed, "that would be best."

"You're probably right that the boys aren't as concerned about the 'boyfriend' thing as I think they would be, if I'm discreet. Maybe they'd rather hear me talk ecstatically about you, then listen to me complain about them not calling me or visiting me?"

She was silent for a moment. "I don't know, I guess I'll need to broach the subject with them somehow."

"In the meantime, I have some good news," David said as he picked her up in his arms and swung her around, Libby let out a delighted shriek. "Even though the end of autumn makes you sad, winter brings longer and longer nights. By December twenty first, we'll have fifteen hours of nighttime to spend together."

"Brendan will be home by then, but I guess we'll drive off that bridge when we come to it. I know! You could come to Midnight Mass with us."

"We'll have to see what Fr. Larry and Brother Alerick say about that." David paused and added, "Please keep the ring. It won't be an engagement ring. Even if you don't wear it, it will be a symbol of hope for our future."

"For the first time in years, I'll look forward to after sunset," Libby said hugging his neck.

"So will I," David said bringing his mouth down to hers for a long kiss.

Chapter 31

After sunset the following day, another anonymous driver took Libby, David and Fr. Larry to the abbey. Located on a cliff overlooking the ocean, it looked like a medieval fortress. The abbot, Fr. Clement, met them in his stone-walled office. He graciously inclined his head to each of them. "You must be eager to meet Brother Alerick and the night is passing, so let us go," he said with a Germanic accent. He led them down long hallways to a large room. It was difficult to judge the size of the space in the dim light. Flickering candles in wall sconces showed the rock ribs and the curve of the walls, but the ceiling disappeared into darkness.

"Brother Alerick, should be joining us in a moment," the abbott said.

As if on cue, they heard footsteps on a stair case that entered into the main chamber from somewhere below. Brother Alerick ascended the stairs with quiet grace. His hands were hidden in the sleeves of his habit. The front of his hood extended beyond his forehead over his bowed head, shading his face. The closer he got, the larger he appeared. He was well over six feet tall, and must have been considered a giant in his day. As the Prior introduced him to David and Libby, he withdrew his hands and whipped back the black hood. In his mouth were red and white wax fangs. "Grrr," he bellowed.

Libby gasped in fright while Fr. Larry and David looked at him incredulously. The abbot rolled his eyes and shook his head. Alerick took the false teeth out of his mouth and let out a booming laugh. The abbot chortled. In a moment, they were all laughing, wiping tears from their eyes.

"I forgot to mention Brother Alerick is quite the practical joker," the abbot told them, and to Alerick, "Where did you get those things? Who got them for you?"

Solemnly Alerick replied, "I will never reveal my confederates."

Libby looked closely at the monk. His face was fair with rosy cheeks and lips. His eyes were the lightest blue she'd ever seen in real life. His hair was a thick blond fringe around a tonsure. He didn't have a beard, instead he had the golden down of a teenager. *He looks around the same age as Brendan*, Libby thought. Alerick turned to Libby and held his hand out to her, palm up. She placed her hand in his and he covered it with his other hand. His hands were warm and strong. He made a slight bow to her, "Signora, I am delighted to meet you," he said in peculiarly accented English. She cocked her head like a puppy trying to figure something out. "How fortunate for us you speak English, but I can't quite place your accent."

Alerick smiled, "When I first arrived, Latin was the common language of the abbey, and for that matter all of western Christendom. Coming from the mountains, my native language was what some would call Old High German. I first heard Old English from a brother from Britain. What a tortured sound. Have you ever heard *Beowulf* read in the original?" he asked shaking his head ruefully, "Then along came Chaucer's English and then Shakespeare's. Meanwhile Italian and German were also evolving. You can imagine how I love the Latin Mass. Its language has hardly changed at all. Over the last few centuries, Brits, Americans, and an Australian have helped me update my English. My accent is rather strange I am told."

Then Alerick held out his hand to Fr. Larry and said, "I'm glad they told me you were coming. I would not have recognized you."

Fr. Larry smiled, "It has been a long time."

Alerick pulled the priest in for a bear hug, "My instincts were good about you, yes?"

Turning to David, Alerick gazed intently at his face, "Forgive me for staring. I have not seen another like myself in centuries. On one hand, I am surprised that someone found you and brought you to me. On another hand, I wonder that it hasn't happened sooner."

David stared back at Alerick. "I see a red energy around you, but there is also a white glow that tells me you have goodness in you. I've never communicated with another vampire before. I suppose you could say that my maker was a negligent parent, he disappeared after he attacked me."

"That is a good thing," Alerick said. "He may have left you in the dark, but he didn't poison your heart and mind along with your body." Alerick turned to Libby, but addressed David, "I can see why you desire the company of Mrs. O'Malley. Charity, wisdom and strength flow from her. She has faced evil, struggled and been victorious. And," looking directly at Libby, "you will face great temptation, again."

A young monk entered the room quickly and bowed, "I am so sorry to interrupt, Father Abbott, but our guests' driver insists on seeing them." A moment later the limo driver came in carrying Victor yapping in his traveling case. The driver said something in Italian. The young monk interpreted, "The animal is not happy in the box."

Libby took the carrier, and said to the driver, "I'm so sorry. *Mi scusi, per favore.*"

"*Senza problema, Signora,*" he said with a shrug. He turned and left.

"Oh, poor Victor, we forgot about you," Libby said opening the carrier. Victor bounded out and ran in circles around her.

"*Madre di Dio,*" thundered Brother Alerick looking from the dog to David, "is that what I think it is?" He smacked his palm against his forehead, "Why did I never think of this?"

Victor trotted up to a potted plant and lifted his leg. "No, Victor!" Libby chided too late.   Alerick let out a great belly laugh, "He is a marvel." Victor ran over to the vampire monk and rolled over on to his back. Alerick crouched down to rub the dog's belly, and then picked Victor up in his big hands, gently scratching him behind the ears. Looking at David he asked, "Will Victor stay with us?"

"Yes," David replied, "he's Libby's dog, but I've been taking care of him since he was changed about six week ago."

"Was this your idea, Mrs. O'Malley?" Alerick asked.

"No, after Victor was hit by a car, David, umm, surprised me by turning him into a little vampire dog."

"How did you do it?" Alerick asked David with new found respect.

"I'll tell you later," David replied.

"With your permission, Father Abbot, I think David and I should continue our talk alone," said Brother Alerick.

The abbott nodded. David said to Libby, "I'll see you later tonight."

"Plan to meet tomorrow night," Alerick said.

"All right," said David. "Libby, I'll meet you here tomorrow night at eight."

"All right," said Libby.

Brother Alerick put Victor down and took Libby's hand in his, "Mrs. O'Malley, when I first came here and took the vows of poverty, chastity and obedience, I was seventeen. I thought I would serve God on Earth for forty, fifty or at most seventy years. Perhaps you could imagine better, how it would be to be married for hundreds of years, it would be a long time to love, honor and obey. That is why the vows say 'until Death do us part'. Man was never meant to live eight hundred years." He let go of her hand. "Good night, Fr. Larry," he said and bowed to both of them.

Chapter 32

The next night, Libby and Fr. Larry were driven back to the Abbey. Fr. Larry went to the abbot's office to visit with him, while Libby was taken by another monk to the place where she and David had parted. David was there alone. The monk said, "Please, pull the bell rope when you are ready to be led to the front door." As he left, they heard his robe flapping around his legs and his sandals slapping on the stone floor.

David and Libby moved toward each other without a word. They hugged quickly, but did not kiss. It seemed out of keeping with the sacred place.

"What happened?" Libby whispered eagerly. "I mean, tell me as much as you can or are willing to."

David was subdued. "There are certain things that Alerick says I must tell you." He took her by the hand. "Let's go up on the wall, so we won't feel we have to whisper."

In the moonlight, the surrounding countryside was visible only in shades of gray. "Also, I feel free to kiss you out here," David said embracing Libby. He kissed her tenderly. He stepped behind her and put his arms around her. They both looked out over the land while he told what transpired after she left the night before.

Chapter 33

Alerick led David up flights of stairs to the parapet and Victor trotted up after them. The moist evening air carried the scent of mown hay. Fireflies blinked in the trees and along the pastures.

"I can see why you stay here. It's serene." David said.

"I cannot imagine living in any other way, in any other place. It has been a blessing," Alerick said, "but it is not without its trials. Brother Terence from New York once taught me the expression, 'There is no such thing as a free lunch.' You are familiar with this, yes?"

David laughed and said, "Yes, it's one of those universal truths. So, let's get down to brass tacks. Have you heard that one before?"

"Yes, another fine American idiom."

David nodded and said, "I'm here because I love Libby. I want to live with her as husband and wife. Libby is Catholic and you are the only Catholic vampire we know. I want to know how I can live as I am or change what I am and share my life with her. I want you to tell me how I can do that while she retains the integrity of her faith. Let's start with how you survive without drinking human blood."

"That is not exactly true, I drink human blood every day," said Alerick. "I drink the blood of Christ each day at Mass."

"Fine, however you want to explain it," David said with a wave of his hand. "What do you experience when you drink the Communion wine?"

Alerick stared into the distance, "It is like water in the desert. It satisfies my burning need in what I can only describe as an ecstasy. I feel I am one with the Lord, though I do not see His mind. I imagine it would overwhelm me to madness. But, I feel His love for me to the full extent that I am able." Alerick swallowed a lump in his throat. "And like a woman, I sob with joy every time."

"How can watered-down wine do all that?" asked David.

Alerick returned his gaze to David's face. "I don't know. From the time I was a boy, I believed the dogma that consecrated Communion wine is truly the Blood of Jesus Christ. I took it on faith. Now, changed as I am, though it still looks and tastes like wine, by a gift of God's Goodness and Mercy it feeds and satisfies me like blood. I don't have to hunt or kill or seduce to get it. It is given to me freely with love."

"Where is this blood?" David asked. "I want to try it and see if I can live on it."

Alerick stiffened, "I can't promise that the same thing will happen for you. The gift is not mine to give. Even as you say, trying it, isn't that simple. If you drink the sacred blood unworthily, it will bring you condemnation instead of life."

"What do I have to do to be worthy?" asked David. "Be a monk like you? Is that the price? Is that why I was brought here, so they could have one more immortal priest? I can't do that and marry Libby!" By this time David was shouting.

"Peace," Brother Alerick said raising his hands to calm David. "To receive the blood worthily you must have a conversion of heart, repent of your sins and be baptized, and believe in the True Presence of Our Lord in the Blessed Sacrament. but we have gotten ahead of ourselves and on the wrong foot, yes?"

Alerick stopped walking and turned to David, "You are young, my son," he said kindly. "How have you fared in this new form?"

Alerick's kindness caught David off guard. For a moment he could not speak. Clearing his throat, he looked down at his feet and said, "I've been wandering aimlessly without understanding or purpose. I am afraid of the evil inside of me and I have been very lonely."

Without hesitation, Alerick embraced him like a long, lost brother. Then holding David far away enough to look into his eyes Alerick said, "I can't imagine my life without the fellowship of my brothers and the comfort of God. I am sorry you have had to suffer alone. What can I do for you?'

"I have many questions," David said.

"Ask," replied the monk.

"Do I have a soul?"

Alerick smiled and said. "What a fitting subject for All Souls' Day. It is a common misconception, my friend, that vampires are automatically damned and have no souls, especially among those who have read too many vampire stories. It is also a myth that the older vampires perpetuate to control their fledglings. If a man thinks he is damned, he has nowhere else to go, but along with this 'new master'. XXXLet me answer your question with more questions. Can you choose to do one thing and not another? Can you tell the difference between right and wrong? Do you experience beauty, goodness, ... love?"XXX

David hesitated, so Alerick answered for him, "Of course, you do. You may not be exactly human now, but you began life as a human being and were endowed by your Creator with a soul, a capacity to know and to love, and that cannot be damaged by anything or anyone, but you. So, yes, you have a soul. What else would you like to ask?"

"Will I be able to live on this consecrated wine?"

"I don't know," Alerick said stroking his chin. "I do wish the vampire who changed me had waited until I was old enough to grow a beard. Pulling at peach fuzz is nowhere near as efficacious as pulling at a beard. Follow me down to my cell and let me think while we walk."   "Is it all right if Victor comes along?" asked David.

"He is so quiet, I almost forgot about the wonder dog, certainly he can come." Alerick turned and led the way back down from the parapet and deeper into the abbey. When he got to his small room, furnished with a bed, desk and chair, he motioned David toward the chair. "Please sit down."

Alerick sat on his bed and called Victor over, "Come wonderful dog." He put the dog on his bed and petted his red, silky fur. "David, you are asking me is if you will become a Christian, a Catholic Christian, but I cannot say. The gift of faith isn't mine to give either. I can instruct you, and I can pray for you. Even better, you can pray for yourself and ask for the supernatural virtue of faith. I believe it will be given to you in time. As it says in the Good Book, *'Seek and you shall find. Knock and the door will be opened. Ask the Father in My name and it shall be given to you.'"*

"Do you read the Bible, David?" Alerick asked as he opened a drawer in the desk. When he pulled out a Bible, David stood up and stepped back so abruptly he knocked over his chair.

Alerick held the sacred book out to him. "Don't be afraid; you can touch it."

David reached out and cautiously touched it with one finger. Alerick took David's right hand, turned it up and placed the Holy Bible into his palm. David stared at it as if it were a scorpion. He looked up at Alerick open-mouthed.

"Are you disappointed?" Alerick asked smiling. "No lightening, no fire, not even a wisp of smoke."

"I'm astonished," David said. Gingerly, he opened the book to a random page.

"Read it, just start at the top of any page," said Alerick.

David read aloud. *"Whosoever believeth in him should not perish, but have eternal life. For ..."*

"Go on, you can say it," encouraged Alerick.

"For ... God ...," David whispered, paused awestruck and then continued, "s*o loved the world that He gave his only begotten son."*

"How glorious it is you landed on that particular verse." Alerick said. "What do you think of all this?"

"I've read in so many places that vampires can't go into a church or touch a Bible or say the name of ... you know, and I didn't want to chance it since the punishments seemed severe," said David still dazzled by these revelations."

"I have a theory that the Bible even hints at vampirism," Alerick said raising his eyebrows.

"And what's your theory?"

"In the Bible there a number of people who are reported to have lived 500 to 1000 years,

Methusaleh, Adam, Lecham, the father of Noah, Noah himself. There are various explanations about these numbers. They were miscalculated, mistranslated, not meant to be taken literally like much of the Old Testament. But let's look at Methusaleh as an example. His is the longest life span recorded. His name means "Sent Death" and he is not said to be a particularly holy or good man. He dies before the great flood. That's as far as I've gotten. I need to ask the abbott for permission to do some more research."
XXX

"That's interesting, but back to the nitty gritty. Why do so many sources state that the Bible, churches, and the name of ... of God are forbidden, if its not true?" David asked.

"It wouldn't make much of a horror story," said Alerick, " ' ... and then the big, bad vampire went to church and read his bible.' Putting sensational literature aside, are you familiar with the Word of God?" Alerick asked.

"I wasn't raised to be religious," replied David. "My mother did talk about the Golden Rule, *'Do onto others as you would have them do unto you.'* But it was more a social rule than a religious ideal, but when I was changed even that simple human decency was replaced with evil desires and the power to fulfill those desires."

Alerick told him, "But you are not evil by nature, though you are faced with greater temptations."

"You mean the temptation to use human beings for food," David said sarcastically.

"Yes," Alerick said, "that is part of it, however, you seem to have found ways to avoid that near occasion of that sin with your bagged blood. If you'll forgive my curiosity, what is that like?"

David shrugged and answered, "It's adequate for keeping me alive and my hunger at bay, but it isn't very satisfying otherwise. It's obviously not fresh. It has a plastic taste to it and it's cold."

"Blech," said Alerick with a shudder. "You are to be commended for consuming that for so long. I assume there is no emotional communication with the giver of the blood."

David shook his head. "No, nothing."

"So along with rarely being truly satisfied, you have agelessness, pride in your physical abilities, never seeing the light of day and immortality itself leading to profound isolation. Now comes what I consider the worst of it, you will tempted by despair. Man was not meant to dwell in this body for hundreds of years. He was meant to pass through this mortal life and use it as a means to reach the next world of spirit and light." Alerick sighed.

"Immortality doesn't seem so bad, if you have someone you love to share it with," said David.

"Perhaps you are right, but you are still very young. You have not reached the place where I am, but it will come and not eight hundred years from now. I felt it hundreds of years ago and I am supported by the holiness of the abbey."

"I believe Libby can help me attain serenity and perhaps holiness, too," David said.

"Ah, but for how long? Let us talk about your relationship with Mrs. O'Malley," Alerick said.

Chapter 34

David stopped his retelling, took a deep breath and turned Libby around so he could look at her, "Alerick said I must tell you about the significance of our sharing blood."

"Did you tell him about that?"

"No, he could see that we had."

"He could tell?" Libby said. "Oh, God, does everyone know?" She covered her face with her hands. Anything that made her feel so ashamed must be awful.

"There is more," David said weakly.

"More?" Libby said, shaking her head no.

"You asked me the other night if there was some middle option between staying together for now and staying together forever. We are already living a middle option," David said slowly. He pressed his lips together, took Libby's hands and looked at her squarely. "Those capsules I gave you, you take them every day don't you?"

"You mean the supplements? Yes, I've taken them ever since you gave them to me in the hospital."

"And they helped you, right? I mean, you feel better since you started taking them."

"Yes, I feel great. Since then some people even say that I look and act healthier, younger. What does that have to do with us?" Libby asked.

"Those capsules contain my blood," he said.

"Oh, God," Libby groaned pulling her hands away from him. "Last night, Fr. Larry asked me if I had drunk any of your blood." She gagged at the thought of it. She put one hand over her mouth and the other on her stomach. She took deep breaths through her nose to control the rising nausea. When Libby straightened up, "I said, no. Now, Brother Alerick is asking about it, too. It must be important and … you didn't tell me." Libby was crying. "Why, David?"

"You were hurt, badly. You might have had a concussion. You could have been bleeding internally or had a blood clot in your brain. I wanted to make sure you would get better. I knew it would help your body heal." David said desperately, "I hadn't told you what I was yet. If I had told you what was in those capsules, you would have thought I was insane. You wouldn't have taken them, and I couldn't take the chance of losing you."

"What about after I was better or after you told me about what you are, why didn't you tell me then?"

"Those pills, my blood, can reverse the aging process. You were so concerned about our age difference; I wanted you to feel younger and to believe how desirable you are."

"Is that what you meant when you said that wrinkles, grey hair, saddle bags and ... and varicose veins could be cured?" She asked touching her face and her hair.

"In a way, yes."

"You wanted to 'cure' me so I would be more physically attractive," Libby said coldly.

David balked at this. "No, that is not true," he insisted. "I love you as you are, as you were when I first met you, but you couldn't believe it. I wanted you to have the self-confidence to believe I loved you, and to accept my love, if you wanted to."

"Have you been trying to make me a vampire all along?" Libby asked suspiciously.

"No!" he said taking her by the shoulders. Libby pulled away, suddenly repelled by his touch. He stepped back giving her some space and said, "I would never do that against your will. I have always hated the one who did this to me without my consent. Believe me, I wouldn't do that to you."

"David, how can you ask me to believe you, when you have lied about things as serious as this?" She turned away from him. "Why should I believe anything you've said that I can't prove for myself?" Suddenly she whipped around and asked in a low voice, "What is the significance of sharing blood? You've had mine and I've had yours. What does it mean?"

David lowered his eyes, "Alerick asked if you knew what it meant to me, to vampires, to share blood. I told him that you experienced the oneness. He asked, 'Does she know that to know you is to love you, that this is the same as knowing you in the Biblical sense?'"

"What are you saying, David?"

"It is the most intimate thing a vampire can do, more intimate than making love," David continued quietly, looking into her angry, tearful eyes.

"We had intimate relations and I didn't even know it," she whispered. She thought for a moment and the color drained from her face, "That's ... it's almost like rape."

"That's not a reasonable comparison," said David. "Rape is a violent act meant to humiliate or hurt someone. I acted only in love. You can't apply the normal human rules of conduct here"

Libby's voice became hard, "Here is a rule of conduct you can apply. If you love someone, don't lie to her. You acted out of love ... for yourself. You did what you had to do to manipulate me to get what you wanted. No wonder you were willing to forego sex, you had already gotten what you wanted."

"Libby, I'm sorry. I wanted to explain ..." David entreated.

"You lied about burying Victor. You lied about needing dance lessons. You probably didn't need any help with computers either, did you?"

David shook his head almost imperceptibly.

"I bet you got a big laugh out of my scripted spiel for turning on the monitor?"

"I never did that. I was just happy to be with you."

"Then you lied about your blood. What an elaborate ruse that was with those labels. How did you even get your blood into those capsules? No, don't tell me, I couldn't believe you. Everything you ever said to me was a lie."

"No, not everything," David said coming toward her reaching for her.

She stepped back from him.

He stood still. "I was drawn to you the moment I saw you, and, yes, I looked for ways to get close to you."

"You, you ... stalked me," she sputtered.

"I courted you," he said, "the way any man, fascinated by a woman, would. I wanted to us get to know each other, and I fell in love with you. Everything I said about my admiration for you, my desire, need and my love for you was true. I swear it. Please believe me, I hated keeping secrets from you, but the situation was so strange I couldn't think of another way."

Libby turned and ran down the stairs, faster than she had run in years. David followed her. He opened his mouth to speak, but Libby raised her hand in front of her to stop him, and pulled the bell rope. "Leave me alone," she said, her voice breaking. "I'm leaving; I'm going home … now. I don't care where you go or what you do. Just don't be on that plane."

A monk came. He looked surprised to see Libby in tears, but he said nothing. David stood there and watched the two of them walk away.

Libby dried her face with the handkerchief David had given her yesterday. "I must see Father Larry immediately," she told the monk, who answered the bell. He led her to the door of the abbot's office and asked her to wait.

The little priest came out, took one look at Libby and asked, "What's wrong?"

"I have to go home, back to the United States, now." Libby said flatly.

"What happened? Are you all right? Is David all right?" Father sputtered.

"I can't, I don't want to talk about it," Libby whispered.

"All right, my dear," Fr. Larry said patting her hand. "I have to think. I can't leave Italy just yet. I can arrange it, if that's what you want, but you'll have to travel by yourself."

Libby nodded. Father Larry didn't question her further. He called for the driver and Libby went back to their lodgings to pack.

Alone in the cabin of the plane, Libby felt a cold emptiness growing in her stomach. It started on the limo ride to the hotel and continued to the airport. It moved north and south to all her vital organs. It was the feeling she got when something happened that should make her furious. It opened the void where anger used to be, the anger she did not allow herself to express with screaming, hitting or throwing things. There wasn't much left to do, so like many women she expressed her anger with tears. She thought about the deceptions David had confessed. She covered her face with her hands. There was no one there to see her; it was a primal reaction.

Libby had made a fool of herself with a younger man. What she feared would happen, had happened. Father Larry had told her that they were doing the work of the Holy Spirit.

"Was making an ass of myself part of your plan, Lord, or did I just do it wrong? 'Sure, David, you can drink my blood. It'll be just like making a donation to the blood bank. We're just cutting out the middle man.' That was brilliant. I really didn't think he would do it. I didn't think he could do it!" she argued with God and herself. "Was falling in love with him and believing in him completely necessary, too?"

She went into the plane's bathroom. As she washed her hands she stared at her reflection in the mirror. Her eyes were red, other than that, even with no makeup she looked good. Her double chin was nearly gone. The deep lines between her nose and mouth had softened. Looking closer she barely saw the crow's feet at the corners of her eyes. Her skin was almost flawless. She examined the roots of her hair. There was the new growth, a little darker than the dyed hair above it.

"No wonder Hepsi was so freaked out," Libby murmured. "How could you be so stupid?" she chastised herself. "Did you think that being in love could make you young? That a little romance would bring your waistline back, make your hair dark again, botox the wrinkles out of your face, ... improve your hearing and your vision, ... make your period start up again? Oh, dear God, what an idiot I am."

Walking back to her seat and sitting down Libby noticed there was no creaking in her knee, no pain or stiffness. *It's so strange,* she thought, *you don't notice when pain goes away gradually as much as you do when it starts to hurt. It's like I've been drinking from the Fountain of Youth. How could I not notice that?*

Libby walked to plane's galley and got a bottle of mineral water. It hissed as she unscrewed the cap, and she remembered David getting sprayed at the theater. She laughed and sobbed at the same time.

She was talking out loud and rapidly, "I've got vampire blood in me and I've had what amounts to vampire sex. Who would have thought that such bizarre things could happen to a nice Catholic girl like me? Really? Libby O'Malley?" She took a sip of water and then a big breath, tamping down her hysteria.

"Up to now, I've been innocent of wrongdoing, because I didn't know what was going on. At least I think so; I have to ask Father Larry." She blew out a breath that fluttered her bangs. "I'm not looking forward to telling him what I held back last time, but for the future, it's what I do, now that I know, that's important."

Finally, she gave in to the emotional and physical fatigue that had been building for the last several days and feel asleep. She was awakened by the pilot's announcement, "We're almost there, ma'am. We'll be landing in a few minutes."

Libby still had the keys to David's Lexus, so she drove herself home. When she got there the sun was rising, and she stood in the side yard watching. The clouds were like melting scoops of orange and raspberry sherbet. Between them, a slice of translucent sky shone a perfect robin's egg blue. It was like a window through the clouds showing what was going on behind them. The sun's rays, at that low angle, colored the dead grass and fallen leaves gold. Then the magic faded as the sky brightened to its normal autumn blue and the clouds whitened.

Libby went back to the car. For the first time on this whole trip, she carried her own suitcase. At her door she was shocked to see a large, white box tied with red ribbon. The box was nearly three feet high and two feet wide and deep. She put her suitcase down on the steps and opened the box. Inside were dozens of long-stemmed, yellow roses. She assumed they would have a sterile or faint-hearted scent as many florist roses did, but these were real roses. She buried her face in the soft petals, ferns and baby's breath and breathed in. The scent transported her back to that magic moment of the sunrise that had just disappeared. The card inside the arrangement had three words on it, "*Please forgive me.*"

"No, no and no," Libby said giving herself a verbal shake, "David, you are not going to make a sap out of me with a box of flowers." She dropped the note back in the box, closed it and left it on the step.

Libby made coffee to help her stay awake and get back on local time. The coffee machine gurgled and hissed. It was the kind that you could pause and grab a cup before the whole pot was finished. She pulled a cup out of the cabinet and poured.

"Mother Mary, pray for me!" she shouted as hot coffee spilled on her and the floor. The cup was upside down and she hadn't noticed. "Geez," she sighed, "I really need to pull

myself together."

She put the pot back under the coffee maker and cleaned up the mess. Minutes later she

carefully poured a second cup into a travel mug and screwed the lid on tightly. She carried the coffee and her suitcase to the laundry to empty her dirty clothes into the washer. However, after only one very romantic evening, one fascinating meeting and one terrible reunion, this disappointingly short trip, left her with mostly clean clothes. She brought her luggage upstairs and wistfully hung the unused outfits back in her closet. She emptied the rest of the suitcase and put it the closet, too. All that was left to put away were her toilet articles. She opened the medicine cabinet and there was David's blood, looking for all the world like vitamins, fish oil or some other innocuous thing. She took the bottle in her hand as she had so many times in the past weeks, turned the cap and poured a capsule into her hand. She shook it and felt more than heard the fluid move. She held it up to the light, but the maroon capsule was opaque.

Taking the bottle downstairs, she set it on the kitchen table with her laptop. How had David put his blood in these capsules? She did an online search for do-it-yourself filled capsules. There were many options for liquids or powders. Empty capsules of every color were for sale. You could fill them by hand with a dropper and attach the two parts of the capsule. There was a machine that cost five hundred dollars that filled and sealed capsules automatically.

"That would have been chump change for David," she said.

Libby examined the bottle's label. It looked so genuine, but it could be color copying,

cut-and-paste art work, or designed online, printed and cut to order. The bottle had even had a tamper proof seal.

"If anything was ever tampered with, this was it," she said shaking her head, looking up from the computer screen and out the window. She turned back to the computer and looked up the weather forecast. The first hard frost was predicted for later in the week.

The sunny, early November day lured Libby outside, where the cool, dry breeze invigorated her and helped clear her head. She went back in the kitchen, got the bottle of encapsulated blood and brought it outside. She grabbed a shovel and walked over to the cherry tree planted over what was supposed to be Victor's grave. Stomping her heel hard on the head of the shovel she pushed it into the soil. In minutes she had what she hoped was a deep enough hole. She opened the bottle and dumped in the capsules. After she threw the dirt back in the hole she whacked it with the back of the shovel a few times. Returning the shovel to the porch, she threw the bottle in the trash. "That's the end of that."

Libby went back out with a couple of buckets to tend the gardens she had neglected for almost a week. Last night's light frost was dripping off of the red veined leaves of beets and delicate fern-like leaves of the carrots. The Brussels sprouts looked like a row of crazy, little palm trees. She started pulling and picking. The bucket of beets and carrots she took to the back spigot and gave them a good rinsing. The Brussels sprouts she would wash when she was ready to use them, so they would keep longer.

She couldn't wait any longer to see the orchard. Putting a five-gallon bucket into a wagon   she pulled it into the stand of apple trees. The Golden Delicious apples were indeed golden and freckled with red spots. The Winesap were mottled green and red with faint white dots. Libby snapped one each off its tree. Each gave a crack and came away with the stem intact. Two bites told her the frost had made the Winesap firm, tart and winey and the Goldens optimally sweet and crisp.

"Oooh, you are good!" Libby said. Her stomach reminded her that she hadn't eaten yet, so she had apples for breakfast. Afterwards, she filled the bucket in the wagon with apples and pulled it back to the house. This would be the first of many trips she'd make in the next few weeks. During that same time she'd also be bringing bags of apples to give away everywhere she went.

After lunch, she weeded the flower beds, cut back spent perennials and removed dying annuals. When that chore was finished along the driveway, she could see more clearly the success of the fall garden design she planned and planted in the summer - purple and yellow pansies were the first tier low to the ground, behind them daisy shaped mums with bright pink petals and yellow centers grew, great mounds of taller pom pom mums created a backdrop of gold, while mature Purple Fountain grasses' cattails waved above everything from the back row.

It was time to tackle vines. Heavenly Blue morning glory vines, as well as white and red honeysuckle vines tended to get out of hand fast as did the pernicious grapevine weed that draped itself over the rose and hydrangea bushes and anything else that stood still long enough. She filled a ninety-five gallon trash can with the remains of these alone and carted it to the road for pickup. Her labor in the gardens made her feel pleasantly tired. The work that had kept her awake during the day would help her sleep tonight. It was one of the many therapeutic effects working outdoors always had on her. Another was serenity. God was in His heaven and Earth moved through space and time in His ordered fashion, even if men and women did not.

Since she decided to go back to counting carbs, she made a cheese omelet for dinner. She didn't know how long it would take for the effects of David's 'tonic' to wear off, but she knew she must reassert herself in the care of her own body, mind and soul.

When her eyesight and hearing returned to their own normal she would remedy the deficits with glasses, hearing aids, surgery or whatever the latest technology had to offer, just the way everybody else did. Wrinkles she could live with, and she had Hepsi for her grey hair until she was ready to go *au naturel*. She would go for physical therapy for her knee when it started to hurt again. As for love handles and double chins, she needed to kick her exercising and eating regime up a few notches. The price of drinking David's blood seemed to be the deterioration of her mental and emotional maturity, and it was a price she wasn't willing to pay any longer.

Libby got ready for bed early. She'd done the best she could to stay awake, and if she ended up waking before dawn, it wouldn't be the worst thing in the world. She knelt beside her bed and blessed herself.

"Dear Father in heaven, I don't know what to do about this disaster with David. It's no news to You that I am nursing deep wounds and feeling brokenhearted ... betrayed ... humiliated and things that I can't find mean enough words to name."

Libby took a breath and wiped away tears.

"Please, give me wisdom, grace or whatever it is You know I need to get through this. Thank you for the apples, beets, carrots and sprouts. You know how stuff from the garden soothes my soul. Thank you for bringing me home safely.

"Have mercy on the souls in Purgatory, especially Frank and his mother and father and my mom and dad. Bring them into heaven with You. Keep Matt, Will and Brendan safe and close to You. Bless Ray with healing and Callie with strength.

"Dear Mother Mary, spread your mantle of protection over Fr. Larry, the abbot and Brother Alerick ... and David. Amen."

Libby got up and went downstairs. Putting on a coat and clogs, she went outside to bring in the box of roses from the front porch. "There's no point in letting you poor little things freeze," she said putting the box on the kitchen table. She opened the box again and unwrapped the roses. She picked up the David's card and put it in her coat pocket.

After filling a vase with hot water and stirring in the packet of plant food, she cut off the bottoms of all twenty-four stems and arranged the flowers. She brought them upstairs and put them on her dresser, from there the bouquet perfumed her bedroom. She always was a sap for flowers. "But this time,"

She fell into a dreamless sleep.

Chapter 35

Libby woke early the next morning. She made a good breakfast and sorted her mail, and still had plenty of time to make morning Mass. As the congregation prayed, "Forgive us our trespasses as we forgive those who trespass against us," Libby fingered the card from the roses that was in her pocket.

She called Jesse's school and told them she was back from her trip and could tutor him on Friday. She met him at ten o'clock as usual.

"Hey, Mrs. O, how come you're back early from you trip?" Jesse asked by way of greeting.

"Hello, Jesse. My plans changed, that's all," Libby said.

"You don't look so good," he said. "You're not all bouncing around and happy like you were when you were leaving."

"I'm still a little jet-lagged, I guess."

"What's that?"

"I'm just really tired from traveling so far," Libby said not feeling up to a complete definition.

"Oh. Do you want me to read to you?" asked Jessie.

"Thanks, Jesse, I'd like that."

When Libby went home there was another delivery of flowers on the front steps with the same message.

Father Larry called a few days later. "Libby, I'm coming back tomorrow. Would you be willing to pick me up at the airfield?"

Libby panicked. "Is David coming with you?"

"No, my dear, I would have told you that before I asked you to come. David, Brother Alerick and the abbot think it is best for him to stay a while longer."

"I see, of course, I'll be happy to give you a ride home. I really need to talk to you about all this."

Libby met Father Larry's plane at eight p.m. She gave him her hand as he came down the steps. He seemed older and more frail. His original enthusiasm for the trip had been worn away.

"How are you feeling?" she asked.

"Discombobulated," he said. "Thank you for coming way out here at night. I originally planned the flight expecting to bring David and Victor home as well."

"How are those two getting along with Brother Alerick?" she asked.

"Oh, famously! They are always together; talking, walking and playing with Victor, even pulling pranks."

Libby had to laugh at that, but it also made her teary. Her emotions were raw.

Father Larry saw her van. "For some reason, I thought you'd be driving David's car."

"That wouldn't be very discreet," she said. "I feel awkward just having it at my house. I pulled it as far into the woods as I could so no one would see it."

They got in the van and left for Father Larry's place.

"I'm sorry I acted like a diva, demanding to leave immediately. Did David tell you why I left?" Libby asked.

"No, he said you would tell me what you wanted me to know," answered Father Larry. "I guess he was trying to be discreet, too."

"I guess I should tell you everything and get your guidance," she said and then told her spiritual director the whole story including the sharing of blood and its significance. She finished saying, "I should have told you about giving David my blood when I first talked to you about him. I only believed he was a vampire, after he took my blood."

Blowing out a long breath, Father Larry said, "We sure are in strange waters morally. You and I both know that the Church's teachings regarding sexual intimacy are based on the principle that sex must be linked to procreation, but there are many forms of intimacy, intimate talks, emotional intimacy, intimate friends. There is a deep human need to know and to be known, to understand and to be understood. That's what I think of when I read the quote from Genesis, *'It is not good for man to be alone.'*

"Now, take this sharing of blood, it is intimate but it has nothing to do with having children, so where does that leave us? I would say that your erred by putting yourself in a dangerous situation. If David had not been honorable, something terrible could have happened to you."

"Honorable?" Libby said harshly. "He lied to me about almost everything."

"Yes, David was wrong to deceive you by both what he said and what he didn't say, but someone evil in that situation might have killed you or turned you in a vampire," Father Larry said with a shudder, "and David didn't."

They drove in silence for a while, then Libby asked, "Do you think all that courting and infatuation was part of the Holy Spirit's plan, or was I just a patsy?"

"I believe you would have helped David without falling in love with him."

Libby blushed to hear Father Larry say it.

He continued, "But, I think it was necessary for David. He had a lot to lose, and he needed to be sure he could trust you. He hasn't had experience with many other kinds of love - familial, friendship and certainly not the love of God in a long time, but the love of a man for a woman he could understand.

"Imagine how desperate he must have been to break his cover and reveal himself. I imagine he looked at his life as a wasteland that could stretch out for hundreds of years, barren of significant human contact. With no relationship with God he must eventually have despaired over the meaninglessness of his never-ending life. You surely remember the loneliness and emptiness of your life after Frank died. I'm sure you can imagine the horror of that life going on and on with no hope, no lifelines to the boys, your friends or the Lord.

"Still he had to be careful and chose the right person. Maybe he sensed the depth of your empathy having been through heartache of your own so recently. He knew the kind of woman he was looking for - someone with courage and a strong spiritual life, someone with a great capacity for love and compassion and he found that in you. He was in love with you from the start, and I think you were ready to be loved again."

Father Larry let those thoughts sink in, then he added.

"Libby, you do know that David is very sorry for the wrongs he's done you, don't you?" he asked.

"I been getting lots of flowers with that message," she replied.

"He cares for you, and misses you a great deal," he told her.

"Are you suggesting that I resume our relationship?" she asked in surprise.

"I honestly don't know about that, but I do recommend that you work on forgiving him."

"Father, if I take down my wall of hurt pride and indignation, I could fall in love with David again, and that scares me."

They were both silent for a while. Finally, Father Larry said, "I can understand that. We're going to have to do a lot of praying about this." XXX

Chapter 36

The whole town was in pre-Thanksgiving mode. Libby's church, Jesse's school and even the library ran food drives. Libby threw herself into all three of them and worked some extra evenings at the food bank. Driving around to pick up food donations, asking for cash donations to buy turkeys and boxing up food gifts filled most of her spare time. She reverted to writing all the things she did on a calendar as she had as a teenager to prove to herself how full her life was. She did it even more conscientiously now to assure herself that she was too busy to think or feel. The busyness had the desired effect. At night, she slept like a log and time sped by. Still, the flowers kept coming.

Saturday evening before Thanksgiving, Matt surprised his mother. He came through the front door and grinned, "Hi, Ma, look what I brought." Behind him were his brothers.

"How is this even possible?" Libby asked between hugs and kisses.

"My boss said things would probably be quiet around the office this week," Matt explained, "and if he needs me, I can work from here on the computer."

"That's incredible!" Libby said.

"Yeah, but I think he's expecting at least one pumpkin pie," said Matt.

"I'll make him three," Libby said, "but how about you two?"

"My profs unofficially cancelled some classes," said Brendan, "and Matt bought me a ticket."

"Ditto," said Will.

"This is the most wonderful surprise ever. Thank you, Matt. Thank you all." Libby's eyes welled with tears.

"Aw, don't cry Mom," said Brendan. "Is there anything to eat? I'm starving."

Libby pulled out left over chicken and frozen peppers and onions and in minutes whipped up a dinner of chicken fajitas while the boys unpacked the car and washed up. Soon they were seated around the table eating and talking.

"How's your tackle football club team doin', Brendan?" Matt asked.

"Man, you should have seen our last game. I had Tennessee on my left and Double D on my left."

"Who?" asked Libby.

"They're nicknames, Mom, don't ask," Brendan said with a grin. "D heard they're defensive line was going to T-bone me, so D and Tennessee went low and I went high and I pancaked that little f-," he glanced at Libby, "fart."

"Excellent little brother," said Matt.

The older boys bumped fists with Brendan. The stories went on until midnight, and Libby couldn't stop smiling. Her dearest wish came true. Her boys were home.

The next morning as the boys slept in, Libby called FedEx and asked them to hold any flower deliveries that might come for her. She didn't want to have to explain. She still had arrangements in her bedroom, but the boys weren't likely to go in there. She wondered if they had heard anything through the grapevine. She cleaned the colossal mess in the kitchen, shaking her head. It took the boys only one meal to make enough dirty dishes to fill the dishwasher. She cooked bacon and made batter for pancakes. The best way to roust the boys out was the smell of breakfast.

Matt was on a working man's schedule, he came downstairs first. Libby greeted him with a kiss. "Good morning, sweetheart. Eggs and pancakes?"

"Yes, please."

"It's wonderful to have someone to eat breakfast with," Libby said.

"It's even better to wake up to someone making breakfast," Matt said.

"You're sounding like an adult," Libby teased. "Brendan seems more mature, too. Maybe it was better for him to go to California for school."

"I guess," said Matt. "He seems like a college freshman to me, swearing like a sailor and drinking coffee."

"Oh dear," said Libby, "sounds like you had quite a trip yesterday, but college freshman is a still step beyond high school senior. Not necessarily better, but it's a phase he has to pass through."

When all three boys were in the kitchen Libby announced, "We're going to the Blakely's house for Thanksgiving dinner and I promised that Matt and I would help out at the Thanksgiving lunch at the fire hall."

"Yeah, Matt told us," said Will around a mouthful of pancakes.

"They're all onboard, Mom, and I called Mrs. Blakely and asked if she could fit two more for dinner," Matt said.

"That's great Matt. You thought of everything, although I can't believe Mrs. Blakely knew and never spilled the beans."

"Yeah, well, I only told her a couple of days ago, so there was less opportunity for a slip up," replied Matt.

"Excellent! So, helping at the firehall and dinner with the Blakelys are the only things we have to do. Is there anything you boys want to or need to get done while you're home?"

"I'd like to visit some friends that are back," said Will.

"Me, too," said Matt, "and they're having a reunion for young alumni tomorrow night at St. Joe's. We're all invited to that."

"Me, three," said Brendan," and I have to pick up some Tastykakes to bring back to the dorm. They don't have them out there."

"You three are going to have to sort out rides and sharing the cars," said Libby.

Within a few hours Libby was alone again and without the van, but she was content. She turned on the oldies station and sang along. She had baking to do, including extra pumpkin pies for Matt's boss. Eventually, the boys would return with news from the four corners.

When Brendan returned the first words out of his mouth were, "Can we have some of the guys over on Friday night?"

"Sure," said Libby, "I'll make some chili or something, but you have to plan the rest - drinks, cups, plates, snacks, set up and clean up."

"Sweet, Mom, I knew you'd say yes," said Brendan giving Libby a high five.

"No alcohol, not even for Matt's friends," said Libby.

"That goes without saying," said Brendan.

Will came in soon after.

"Mom says we can have a party," Brendan said.

"Thanks, Mom, that's great," said Will.

The days flew by. Thanksgiving Day Libby was so proud of her sons as they served dinner at the firehall. They didn't just put food out on tables and plates. They talked and joked with the elderly and the less fortunate people in their community and made it a joyful time. At four o'clock, the whole family went over to the Blakely's house. The O'Malleys brought enough pie and brownies to feed an army and it was just enough for six boys and five regular people.

The boys' party was a success. The house was full of older teens and twenty somethings. Libby caught up with the young people she knew. Some parents joined her in the grown-ups' party in the kitchen. She realized she hadn't seen many of the parents of her sons' friends in quite a while. It was another side effect of the empty nest syndrome, that part of her social life had faded. It seemed that she wasn't the only one to miss the fellowship. Many of the parent partygoers made promises to get together again while their kids were away. When the last adults left, Libby went up to bed and left the boys to take care of the last of their guests.

The next morning it was all hands on deck for washing floors and dishes, taking out the trash and consolidating leftovers. When they were done, all four of them sat at the kitchen table. Will stuck his head in the refrigerator and came out with some pie. "Hey, Mom, somebody was telling me about you going to the emergency room," said Brendan.

"*Oh, boy here it comes,*" thought Libby. She continued washing pots and pans with her back to him.

"Right," she said, "I told you Zoe threw me and I had to go to the ER."

"Yeah, but you didn't say anything about the man that took you there," Brendan insisted.

"He was a library patron, who was there when Sue started worrying about me, because I was late for a computer class and I hadn't called or anything. So, Sue told him where to go to look for me, and it was good thing she did," explained Libby.

"I heard something about that, too," said Will. "He didn't just drop you off, he stayed there with you for hours."

"Yes, he was a regular Good Samaritan. He called Sue to tell her what happened and then made sure I was all right before he left," she explained.

"Are you talking about that strange guy that's been hanging around Mom?" asked Matt, "Carl's girlfriend's mom told her that she heard he was also in some dance class you were taking. Was he?"

"That's right, he was in that class," said Libby still with her back to the boys so they wouldn't see her turn pink.

"That was a strange coincidence," said Brendan.

"It was strange," Libby said.

"I thought you didn't believe in coincidences, Mom." Brendan added, "You always say, 'God works in mysterious ways', but maybe this time it was someone else working in strange ways."

"Of course, scientifically, I believe in random coincidences, but I also know, God can work His will any way He wants including through coincidences," Libby said as she dried her hands and turned around.

"Man, is your face red!" said Will.

"I've been working with very hot water," she said. She held up her hands. "See my hands are red, too, but while we 're on the subject..."

"Oh, no," Brendan said with foreboding.

"We should discuss how you would feel about me possibly dating someone," said Libby blotting perspiration the hot water had caused on her neck and brow.

"Depends on what you mean by dating," said Will. "Are we talking about going out to dinner or a lecture at the college, or are we talking about making out in public and getting married and replacing Dad?"

"No one will ever take the place of your father," she assured them.

"Notice Mom didn't say anything about not making out," teased Will.

"Very funny," said Libby snapping him with a dish towel.

"Yow!" he cried rubbing his backside.

"Nice shot, Mom!" Matt cheered holding his fist out, which Libby bumped with her own.

Brendan, however continued the line of questioning, "Would we have any say in who you marry? Would we have to call the guy 'Dad'?" asked Brendan.

"I don't want you to call anyone else 'Dad', but your father," said Libby, "except maybe your fathers-in-law when *you* get married." Over groans from the boys, she continued, "And I would take your opinions about any possible marriage very seriously."

"So, you're saying you still might marry someone we didn't like," said Brendan.

"Wait a minute, guys," said Matt, "we've all gone off to live our lives and left Mom here alone to hold down the fort. Now she doesn't even have Victor to keep her company."

"Yeah, poor old Victor," said Brendan, "maybe Mom could get another dog, a real dog this time like a Rottweiller or a German Shepherd for protection."

"Hey, old Victor was gutsy for his size, remember the time he chased that stray Boxer off of our porch? That was awesome," said Will.

"Victor was a great dog," said Libby, " and a wonderful companion, but we're getting off the subject of my dating."

"What I was trying to say, before we got off on the subject of dogs," Matt said looking pointedly at his brothers, "was that Mom let us go wherever we wanted, to do what we wanted to do, and didn't ask any of us to change our plans and stay nearby. I think we need to cut her some slack, too."

Libby smiled inwardly at Matt's maturity, but didn't say anything.

"Okay, I can see what you're saying, but there have to be some rules or, you know, standards just like there are for all of us," said Will.

"Yes" Libby agreed, "All the usual codes of morality would apply to me as they do to the three of you. There is also the issue of our family's reputation. I will be moderate in my public displays of affection. Is holding hands and a kiss on the cheek acceptable?"

"Yuk, yeah, I guess so," said Brendan.

"But don't take anyone to St. Joe football games or other stuff that's part of our social network," said Will.

"I can be discreet about where I go, but I don't want to sneak around like I have something to hide. If I get serious about somebody, and want to introduce him to people I know, I'll let you boys know in advance, so you don't end up hearing about it through the grapevine. Can you all live with that?" asked Libby.

"Sure, Mom," said Matt.

"Yes," said Will.

"Okay," said Brendan.

Libby blew out a big breath. "I'm glad we had this talk."

Sunday morning Libby and the boys went the early Mass, and then it was time for them to go back to work and school. Will's flight was at noon, so Matt dropped him off at the airport on the drive back to New York. Libby took Brendan to the airport for his five o'clock flight. She was happy to have time alone with Brendan, they conversed better in the car. Brendan talked more freely when he didn't have to make eye contact, and he talked the most when he was driving, so Libby let him drive.

"We've got plenty of time before your flight, so you don't have to speed," Libby said as her foot involuntarily stepped on a phantom break on the passenger side.

"Okay," said Brendan.

"I imagine you're glad to be getting back to school," Libby said.

"Are you kidding! I'm going back to papers, projects and final exams," Brendan said. "I'm kind of stressed out."

"Oh, of course, I forgot about that. Sorry," said Libby.

"I mean I'm happy to get back to my friends and California," Brendan said.

"Are you happy with your college choice?" Libby asked.

"Yeah, pretty much. It was hard at first. I didn't know anybody, I didn't know where anything was and some of the assignment were tough. There were times when I thought I should have gone someplace closer or less competitive. I wouldn't want to change now, though, I mean, I'd have to start all over again."

"Going further away was probably good for you," Libby admitted. "You've learned to take responsibility for yourself. No coming home on weekends with laundry to be done or taking leftovers or goodies back to dorm. I see a change in you already."

"I guess it's pretty boring for you with nobody home," Brendan said.

"It's very quiet," Libby said. "but I picked up a few extra hours of volunteer work, and I took that dance class." She watched Brendan's face for a reaction, but his expression remained neutral.

"You're not going to ballet or anything where you have to wear a leotard, are you?" Brendan asked.

"No," Libby laughed. "It was a social dance class."

"That's good," said Brendan, "because spandex is a privilege not a right."

Libby smacked his shoulder.

"Just kidding," he said, "but I'm glad you signed up and went, Mom, 'cause it must be lonely, especially without Victor. I was really bummed out that he got killed."

"Me, too," said Libby.

"I have to admit, I felt sorry about leaving you all by yourself," said Brendan.

That was a balm to Libby's ego. "No," she said, "this is your time to go out into the world and start the next stage of your life. By the way, what happened with Lainie?"

Brendan smiled. "She's still in the picture. She was disappointed that I couldn't go to her house for Thanksgiving, but she was happy that I got to go home."

When they arrived at the airport, Libby asked Brendan, "Would you like me to go in with you?"

"Nah, I'm okay, Ma. Let's just go to the passenger drop-off."

The airport was busy and traffic crept along the departing flights road. Brendan had to double-park in front of his airline. They both got out of the van, and exchanged the keys. Before Brendan opened the trunk to pull out his luggage, Libby gave him a bear hug and a kiss.

"Safe trip," she said. "I love you, Brendan."

"I love you, too, Mom," he hugged her back. "Before you know, it I'll be back for Christmas."

Brendan picked up his bag and walked through the revolving door, inside he turned back and waved. Libby threw him a kiss. After he turned away again, she pulled out a tissue. She had to dab her eyes before she could pull out into traffic and begin her ride home to an empty house. She felt blue over the next couple of days, so she forced herself to get up and out to daily Mass, and also did Christmas shopping for additional therapy of the retail variety.

She did take some comfort in realizing that what she cleaned up one day, would stay clean until she messed it up herself.

Chapter 37

The only word Libby received from Italy, came with flowers. Every few days an arrangement featuring shades of pink, red, purple, orange, gold or even green flowers arrived. The written messages were short, "Please forgive me." or "I love you." The flowers worked their magic along with Father Larry's guidance. Libby's heart softened and she wanted to tell David she forgave him.

Finally, he sent a telegram, telling her he planned to return in three days, two weeks before Christmas, and hoped she would meet him at the same rural airstrip they had departed from six weeks ago.

At about two-thirty in the morning, David came down the plane's steps to the tarmac, Libby walked quickly toward him with a smile that came from her whole body. Seeing her he put down his suitcase and reached out to her. She put her arms around his neck and laid her head on his chest.

David wrapped his arms around her and rested his cheek on her head. Libby couldn't say a word. First, there was a lump in her throat and then the tranquility of his embrace. He was silent, too. After a while he stepped back to take in her face. He looked at her as if comparing her reality to his memory of her. David brushed back a lock of Libby's hair from her face with his finger. He enfolded her into his arms again and sighed deeply. When they finally let go of each other, they walked hand in hand to the privacy of his car.

David opened the passenger door for Libby and closed her in firmly, but gently. He got into the driver's seat and put the keys down on the console. He leaned across the seat to take her face in his hands.

"I have missed you so," David said, then he kissed Libby long and passionately. They necked like teenagers, not wanting to stop. Libby tasted salt on her lips, but she didn't know when the tears had started. In dark she felt David's cheeks; they were wet, too. Libby's nose was got stuffy, and she had to break off from a kiss to breathe.

"Oh, David," she said, "I am sorry I left without accepting your apology. I've had all this time to think about it, about us. I think we can find a way to be together; I want to make this work."

David shook his head against hers, "No, no, Libby, you weren't at fault. You were right. I was not honest or fair with you."

"Let's put that behind us," she whispered in his ear, "we'll spend Christmas together. The boys are coming home. They'll get to meet you, and you can all get to know each other."

David smiled at that, but Libby had never seen a sadder smile. "You do believe that I love you, don't you?" he asked straightening up in the driver's seat.

"Yes," she answered. For the first time she noticed there was something different in his eyes, but she couldn't tell what it meant.

"You saved my soul, Libby. I will always love you for that," he said holding her hands in his, he kissed each hand. "There is so much more to say, but it's getting late and we should start for home," he said turning the ignition.

David doggedly kept his eyes on the road. They were both quiet until they got out onto the highway. David sighed deeply again and resumed talking. "Brother Alerick taught me many things in the last weeks. He taught me vampirism is a condition of the body, not of the soul. I can be redeemed like any other man, but it will be a long, tough battle. I need to go back to Alerick to learn more about disciplining my wants and desires, and how to satisfy my needs in ways that won't harm anyone. One of my desires is you, although it feels like a need to me." He smiled slightly and cutting his eyes toward Libby for a second, "Alerick says the two can be hard to sort out. He and I talked a lot about you, Libby. He asked where I saw my relationship with you going. He said, 'You want her to be your wife, your helpmate. How long do you think that will last? Thirty or forty years? Or do you intend to turn her?'

"I told him I thought I could make you happy sharing this life with me. He said, 'What happens if you are wrong? What happens if you cannot make her happy for a thousand years or even a hundred years? What will you do then? One of the greatest joys of marriage is children and you cannot give her any more. Her family will be gone. Marriages weren't meant to last for hundreds of years. In Heaven, there is no marriage. 'When they shall rise from the dead, they neither marry, nor are given in marriage; but are as the angels which are in heaven.' You must think carefully about this, David, for Libby's sake as well as your own.'

David placed his hand on Libby's, driving with one hand on the steering wheel.

"Alerick taught me that loving you means wanting what is best for you. I know with all my heart that I love you, and I'm just as sure that I am not good for you. If we stay together, I will always hope that you will change your mind and become vampire, but becoming a vampire is not what is best for you. Your spiritual life is attuned to your human timeline. I understand that now."

David glanced at her and asked, "Libby, do you understand what I'm saying?"

Libby said, "Yes, you're going to leave me. We will never get married and live together. We're going to part. Forever."

Libby wanted to be shocked at this declaration, but this possibility had always been there. Deep within her a small tendril of relief sprouted. She wouldn't have to present the boys with a new man in her life. She wouldn't have to make up lies to explain why David was never there in the daytime or why he didn't age. Still, the finality and sadness of losing David struck her like the rolling waves of months ago. Tears blurred her vision and added to the illusion. She felt like she was sinking, but this time she was resigned to it.

David drew her hand to his mouth and kissed her palm. "I can make it less painful for you, if you will let me. I can help you to forget me, to forget us. Alerick taught me a way."

"Couldn't we wait a little longer?" Libby asked.

"I wish we could, but I'm afraid I'll lose my courage. I've been steeling myself for this for the last eight hours," David said. "Losing you is breaking my heart, Libby," he gripped the steering wheel with both hands until his knuckles turned white. "I can help you forget, but I will remember for centuries."

"Abandoning you is the safe thing to do and probably the right thing to do," Libby said looking down at her empty hands in her lap. "I wish for once that what I wanted and the right thing were the same." She took a shaky breath and went on, "So, whatever joy I get from a few more days or weeks or months will be forgotten with all the rest, right?"

"Yes," said David.

"What's the point of joy, if you can't remember it? The past is only real because I can remember it, I can relive it." She looked up from her hands and focused again on David face. "If I forget you and our time together, what becomes of that happiness?"

David stared straight ahead. "Oh, Libby, I don't know where the joy goes, but Alerick says three things last – Faith, Hope and Love. I have hope and I am learning faith, because I love you and I will go on loving you."

They were silent for a while.

"If I ever die," David said, "and if my soul goes to heaven, and those are some big ifs, maybe you will recognize me and remember that you loved me. Isn't that the way you think heaven works? The way loved ones will be reunited?"

"I hope that's the way it works," Libby said. "That's the way I pray it works."

When they arrived at Libby's house, there were still several hours left before the late winter sunrise. "We could have a few more hours together," David said as they crossed the threshold. He took Libby up in his arms and carried her up the stairs and she pointed him toward her bedroom. He pushed open the door with his shoulder and placed her on the bed. He sat on the bed near her feet and took off each of her shoes. He ran his thumbs across the balls of her feet and down the soles.

"Mmmm," Libby sighed, "that feels wonderful."

David kissed her stockinged feet. He took her right hand which was lying on her chest and kissed each of her fingers. He held her hand to his chest and lay down on his side facing her. She reached up with her other hand and laid her palm on his cheek.

"I'm afraid this is making things worse for you," Libby said.

"No," David said soothingly. "I need this goodbye. I will cherish it."

Libby stroked David's face to comfort him. She wanted to do all she could for him, as he would bear this sorrow, and all for her sake. "There are things I want you to know," she whispered. "Early on I worried that I was infatuated with your good looks, your gallantry, your being happy to be near me, it was all so flattering, then your kindness and love brought a part of me, that was dead, back to life. Thank you so much for the joy you brought into my life," she said and kissed him.

"But you brought me more than joy" she continued," by bringing me on your spiritual journey. Your questions about the soul and eternal life made me really think about what I believed and forced me out of the spiritual complacency I'd fallen into. Some of the ideas I shared with you came together for me just as I was saying them. Revelations and mercies that God showed me over the last thirty years fell into place. I saw in new ways how much He loves me. It made me remember how much more important eternal life is than this fleeting one, it's so easy to forget. The kids have an expression they use the justify any crazy thing they want to do. They say, 'Yolo.' It stands for 'you only live once.' Dozens of times I told them, 'That's not true, you live twice and what you do here and now effects the much longer and more important next life.'

"They must have gotten sick of hear that," Libby said with a little laugh, "because they stopped saying, 'Yolo' in front of me."

"You only live once," said David, "I certainly believed that, but for an unlimited number of years."

"I can only imagine how hard it would be for you to think about life after death in your circumstances. Even with a normal life expectancy, it's hard enough for me to keep the long term goal in sight, instead I worry about mundane things like what's for dinner, when should I mow the lawn, which shoes should I wear. Your passion for finding your soul has helped me to concentrate on my priorities, even the hard parts, maybe especially the hard parts like learning to forgive you and now losing you, even the memory of you. I hope I won't lose the spiritual lessons you helped me learn. I wanted you to know how important you've been to me."

"Oh, Libby," he said.

She nestled her face into his neck.

After a long silence, David said, "I have something I want to ask you, but ..."

"Please, David, tell me what it is."

"Knowing what drinking your blood means to me, would you allow it one more time?"

Libby pulled back and looked into his eyes for a long moment. "Yes, I will."

"Would you permit me to keep some of your blood as a relic of our love?"

"How would you keep it?" she asked pushing up on her elbow. He took a stoppered glass vial out of his shirt pocket.

"You knew I would say yes?"

"I hoped," he said.

"Hope is a virtue," Libby said and she gave him a small smile.

David helped Libby to take off the cardigan of the red twin set she wore. In the dark, her bare arms looked like alabaster. Again, David was careful to leave no visible marks. He kissed her wrist and the inside of her elbow. His tongue rasped slowly across her underarm three times. Libby trembled.

"Are you ready?" he asked softly, his breath warm on her skin.

"Yes."

David bent his head. Libby better understood this means of communication now, and knew they would share both thoughts and emotions. She felt a charge surge through her as his teeth pierced her skin. A current of feelings flowed, chaotic at first - love, confusion, bittersweet joy and sorrow. Libby resolutely steadied her thoughts, and pictured David's face. Longing and love for him surged from her heart. She showed him how the Lord's

Prayer had moved her to forgiveness, and she felt his relief as any doubt about where he stood with her dissolved.

Libby felt the hurt in David's heart. He loved her and longed to stay with her, but because he loved her he would leave her life and return to Italy. David showed her his admiration and affection for dear Brother Alerick. David showed Libby his vision of her surrounded by the glow he saw. Her whole being was radiant.

They continued to tell each other the stories of the time they had spent apart and to show how much each loved the other. When David ended the connection, he opened the vial and slid the opening along Libby's skin collecting blood from the two rivulets running from the wounds he had made. He replaced the stopper and cleaned the outside of the vial with a handkerchief, then placed the vial in his breast pocket and buttoned it closed. He licked the remaining blood from Libby's skin and the wounds under her arm. She was left relaxed and sleepy.

"If you still give your permission for me to help you forget about ... us. This would be a good time to begin the memory altering techniques Alerick taught me," David said quietly.

When Libby nodded her consent, he got up and sat in the bedside chair. "Take a deep breath. Let it out slowly. Continue to breath slowly and deeply. Relax your neck, ... your shoulders, ... your chest, ... your back. There is no tension in your face.

"Concentrate on the slow breathing. Relax your chest. Feel it open with calm.
Your arms are heavy ... Your legs are heavy...

"With each breath your body grows heavier. You are falling onto a hundred featherbeds. You fall deeper and deeper. It is safe and dark and warm. ... Go deeper."

David's voice poured over Libby and enveloped her like a bath of warm, silky water. He lifted her wrist. She could feel her hand and fingers hanging from it limply.

He continued, "You are going to find a secret room. It is quiet and safe and only you know what it looks like and how to get there. Open the door. Go in and sit down. Around you are small glass cubes with memories of our time together and a wooden chest."

In her mind, Libby walked into a circular room. The floor was covered with thick oriental carpets. The walls were papered with an antique maroon and gold design. Also, on the wall were wine-colored velvet draperies and sconces with candles. In the middle was a large, gilded coffer with a domed top. Scattered round it were glass cubes of various sizes. Some were only one inch cubed. The largest had sides four inches in length. Each one held images of her and David.

"There is a key in your pocket. Unlock the chest and open it," Libby heard David say. "Now, look at each of the memories and think if there is someone else who knows about it besides you and me. You are going to lock away the memories of us that no one else knows about. If someone you know saw us together then you must keep it out of the box so they won't think you are deceitful or mad when you say, 'I was never there with David Baynard'. Look carefully for any memory in which you know I am a vampire. Those must all be locked away. Our trip to Italy must be stored away."

The first cube Libby picked up was David burying Victor. She must keep that one. Sue knew about it. Next David was carrying her into the car after her fall. Everybody in town knows about that. "Keep it to the side," she told herself.

Libby picked up a picture of David taking her to the play. They were careful not to let anyone know about that, but someone might have seen them somewhere along the way. She kept that one out. Scenes of them cooking the fish at the cabin, of her visits to his house, of Victor   alive again joined the others in the box.

"Libby, you need to create two new memories," David said.

Libby saw two empty cubes near the corner of the coffer. "All right," she replied.

"Remember that I told you I got a new job and had to move away. Then think about Halloween and a few days after. See yourself going to a spiritual retreat with Father Larry at the Carmelite monastery on the Chesapeake Bay. You read, you listened to talks, went to Confession and to Mass. You returned home with renewed peace and hope."

Libby thought about these things. The cubes glowed. She saw herself talking to David about his move in one and Fr. Larry and herself at the retreat in the other. She placed them on the floor. She sorted through the rest of the cubes. The gilded coffer was full. She kept memories from the library, dance class, the emergency room and other events known by others. All but the cube with the vision of herself as David saw her. This is the way she wanted to see herself, the way she wanted to know that she could be. She thought perhaps she should put it in the box, but it only had her image in the cube so she slipped that one into her pocket.

"I've finished," Libby said.

"Are you sure?"

Libby looked carefully around the room and then said, "Yes."

"Take the key," David directed, "when you lock the box, you will forget all the memories that you put away and everything that happened tonight. Lock the box, return to your bed and sleep well. You will wake up tomorrow morning rested and content."

Chapter 38

Libby awoke early to a beautiful new day. She felt like dressing up for daily Mass. She pulled a new bra out of her drawer and cut off the tags with her nail scissors. She put it on the way the sales woman in the lingerie shop had directed, and definitely felt more attractive wearing a new bra that fit properly. She paired a caramel mock turtleneck sweater with an olive and brown plaid tweed suit. The knee length skirt had kick pleats. She added brown opaque tights with the new 'sensible shoe' style of lace up shoes with chunky heels. She put on pearl earrings and a gold tone circle brooch with a pearl. The outfit had the look of vintage 1940s fashion.

Libby came out on the landing and stood before the full length mirror. She turned from side to side and threw her reflection a kiss saying, "You look mahvelous." She practically skipped down the stairs. She put an English muffin in the toaster and made tea. She said grace and her morning prayers. After eating, she went back upstairs to brush her teeth and take her vitamins, but when she looked in the medicine chest she couldn't find the bottle of pills that Mr. Baynard had given her.

"Oh, for heavens sake, they were in here yesterday," Libby said. She looked around the bathroom and her bedroom and even into the boys' bathroom, which she hardly ever used. *"They couldn't have just disappeared,"* she thought. *"I don't have time for this now. If I don't get out of here I'm going to be late for church."*

After nine o'clock Mass, Libby had an appointment with Derek to practice a solo for next Sunday.

"You are spot on today," he complimented.

"That's good news," Libby said. "I'll see you Sunday, then. I'm off to the library."

At the library, Sue gave Libby a hug and said, "Well, don't you look all spiffed up."

"Why, thank you!" Libby said with a little curtsy. They worked quietly at the desk for a moment, then Libby said, "You know, Sue, sometimes I wish I'd had Victor cremated. I could have him in a little urn on the mantle. It would be nice to talk to him. He always was a good listener."

"Would you consider digging him up and having it done?" Sue asked.

"I don't know, I guess I wouldn't want to see him all decomposed, besides I already planted a cherry tree over him. I wouldn't want to disturb either of them, but I'm surprised I didn't think of it at the time."

Sue shrugged sympathetically and asked,"So, what are your plans for Christmas?"

"Brendan finishes his exams on the twentieth and he and Will are both flying home on the twenty-first. I'll pick them both up in the same trip. If their flights arrive on time they'll only be an hour apart. Matt is driving down on the Saturday before Christmas."

"Are you going to invite that nice Mr. Baynard over for Christmas dinner?"

"Oh, didn't I tell you? He left town," said Libby.

"Where did he go?" asked Sue.

"I believe he went to Europe for a new job or something."

"That's too bad," Sue sighed."I thought you two had the beginnings of a lovely romance."

"Susan Blakely, any romance between me and Mr. Baynard was a fantasy in your head."

"Mmhmm, and so why are you blushing?"

"Well, maybe it was a bit of a fantasy in my head, too," Libby said with a smile and a wave as she walked back to the computers. She was blushing because she woke up this morning almost remembering a dream she had about David Baynard. There was plenty of kissing and other shenanigans. He also told her something, a secret, but she couldn't remember what he said.

Later that week, she went to confession with Fr. Larry. After they finished with the sacrament, they began chatting. Libby said, "You know that retreat I went on with you just after Halloween? I feel like it was really good spiritually," she looked up at Fr. Larry sheepishly, "but I can't really remember much of it exactly. Do you remember some of the important parts?"

Fr. Larry didn't answer the question, but said, "What I think you need spiritually now, is to make a more structured plan for what you are going to do with the time and talents God has given you, after the boys leave the house again, after Christmas."

"I know I've been drifting. There've been moments when I forget where I am in time. I wondered if I was going cuckoo. Recently, I've had memories of things I could swear really happened, but I can't place them in any real-time sequence. I try to focus on what happened before or after them, but I hit a wall and they dissolve like a dream. And the dreams I actually do have!" Libby shook her head with wonder. "Let's just say I've had some real lollapaloozas."

"What troubles you about them?" Father asked.

"They're very real, too. I'm shocked when I wake up that I'm not where I was in the dream. It's hard to explain," Libby said with frustration.

Fr. Larry looked concerned. "You must be gentle with yourself, my dear."

"I feel grand, better than I have in years. I don't know why. I don't see a big difference between then and now, but I'm not going to look a gift horse in the mouth," Libby said smiling.

Fr. Larry gave a sigh of relief, "Well, I'm happy to hear that. So just pray that you will be open to whatever God has in mind for you."

"I do that every morning, but God's been rather subtle."

"Yes, Einstein said that, too, 'God is subtle, but he is not malicious.'"

"I'm trying to get to daily Mass more often. I promise I'll pray more about what I should do next. By the way, did you ever meet a man named, David Baynard?"

Fr. Larry's face colored as he answered her. "Well, you know I don't get around too much anymore, Libby. Did you introduce him to me?"

"I can't remember," Libby said rubbing her forehead, "but I think I wanted to. I thought of it as I was walking through the monastery – I mean the retreat center this morning."

"When you're my age, you're always meeting new people, again and again," Fr. Larry laughed as he patted her hand.

"I'm sure it will come to me, probably in the middle of the night," she said.

Chapter 39

Libby went to her class with Jesse on Friday. "Good morning, Jesse."

"Boy, am I glad to see you Mrs. O. I'm having a hell of a time with math."

"Jesse!" Libby reprimanded.

"Sorry, I mean a heck of a time," he said.

"You seem to be getting it," Libby said to him after they went through his most recent chapter in math.

"Maybe we should go over some grammar stuff," Jesse said. He was antsy in his chair.

"Is something wrong, Jesse?" she asked.

"Mrs. O, I got news for you," he said.

"Is it good or bad?" she asked.

"It's both," Jesse said, "so I need you to concentrate. You seem spacey this morning and this is important."

"All right, Jesse," Libby said looking at him intently. "What is it?"

"My Grandma is moving to Florida and I'm going with her."

"When?"

"Next week."

"That's so soon!" Libby said trying not to sound too upset, after all, Jesse had said some of this was good news.

"Yeah, I know, Grandma said she been thinking about it for a while, and just this week all her ducks lined up."

"How do you feel about going to Florida?" Libby asked.

"We're going to stay with my Grandma's sister, so that'll be another woman telling me what to do," Jesse said blowing his bangs out of his eyes with an exasperated breath. He looked up at

Libby and continued. "And I'll be leaving my mother and my friends behind."

"What's the good part? You said it was good news, too."

"It'll be nicer in Florida, so I can go outside more and we're supposed to be living near some boy cousins around my age."

"That is good," agreed Libby.

"But my grandma is putting me into a all boys Catholic school. She says she doesn't like the public schools down there and my great-aunt got me a scholarship to St. Augustine School for boys. You know what they call them? Auggies. Isn't that the dumbest thing you ever heard?"

Libby shrugged. "Maybe not the dumbest, but ..."

"Now I'm gonna be the new kid and that sucks," he added.

"Being the new kid isn't so bad," she said."You get to start over where nobody knows you. You can be whoever you want to be."

"I guess, but I'll have to make new friends and learn to fit in. I heard those all boys schools can be tough. Your sons went to one, right? Was it bad?"

"My oldest boy gave the other two this advice, when they first got to St. Joe's: 'Keep your eyes open and your mouth shut for the first few weeks. Watch and see how things work. Don't show off or have a chip on your shoulder.' In your case, Jesse, I wouldn't introduce myself as either a pimp or a drug dealer."

Jesse laughed. "I was just yanking your chain, Mrs. O."

"Thank you very much," Libby said rolling her eyes, "but seriously, don't yank anybody's chain when you first get there, especially not the older boys. Be the real you, the boy who knows his way around fractions and percentages and nouns and verbs. Be you, the kid who likes sports and dogs. Is your dog going with you?"

"Oh yeah, he's coming," said Jesse.

"Good," Libby said and then added quietly, "So, I guess I won't be seeing you."

"I guess not," Jesse said. "Even though I yanked your chain Mrs. O, I knew you were on my side from the beginning."

"Thanks, I'm glad to hear that, because I always was," Libby said. "Thank you for being straight with me. I've been working through some issues since September and you helped me. And I can't forget the time at the beach. I'll miss you, Jesse."

"You, too, Mrs. O, and thanks for buying me the rest of the rest *Indian in the Cupboard* books. I'll be able to take them with me." He gave her a small wave as the school aide led him out of the room.

Libby didn't follow them out immediately, she needed a moment to herself. Tears she had held back while Jesse was there were stinging her eyes. She pulled a tissue from a box on the desk. She closed her eyes and the tears fell. She sopped them up with the tissue. "Dear Lord, please watch over Jesse and his grandmother and his dog," she said with a little laugh and sob. "He's such a smart kid and a good boy at heart. He and his grandma are working so hard to make it without his mother and father. Please protect him and send him good friends and teachers to help him along the way. Thank you for sending him to me, when I needed him."

She looked in the mirror on the wall to see if it looked like she had been crying, she looked normal. She took a deep breath, walked out of the room and closed the door behind her.

Chapter 40

The following week, Libby's parish priest, Fr. Daley waved her over when she came through the front doors of the church. "Libby, do you have time to join me for a cup of coffee after Mass today?"

"Make that tea and you're on," Libby answered.

"Tea it is," the priest said with a nod.

After Mass they walked over to Main Street to the diner. "This my treat," said Fr. Daley, "because I'm asking you for a favor."

"Oh goody," Libby said rubbing her hands together to warm them up.

Alice, the waitress arrived. "What can I get you, Father?"

"Ladies first," he said to Libby.

"Hi Libby, what'll you have this morning?"

"Hi, Alice, I'd like a pot of hot tea with cream and a … raisin bran muffin."

"And you, Father Daley?"

"A cup of coffee and an English muffin, please."

Alice turned away to place the order.

Fr. Daley looked at Libby and said, "I've got a problem. Well, it's not a bad thing it is a good thing that needs something done about it."

"What's up?" Libby asked.

"We've been blessed with several new babies in the parish over the last year or so," Fr. Daley said, "Some of the young mothers don't have family living nearby to help them and they seem overwhelmed and isolated."

"That has been a problem for years in society in general," Libby said nodding her head.

Alice showed up with their drinks and food laid out on her left arm. "Here we go, tea and a raisin muffin for you, Libby. Coffee and an English muffin for you, Father."

"Thank you, Alice," the two chorused.

"Your welcome, is there anything else I can get you?" Alice asked.

"No, everything is fine," said Fr. Daley.

Alice went off on her rounds.

Father continued, "So, some of these young women have come to me and asked if there is some way they can have a mothers' group at the church."

"That's a great idea," said Libby

"I'm glad you think so, because I'd like you to head it up."

"Why don't you want the young women to do it themselves?"

"They could do that, but I think they would get even more out of this if they could interact with some more experienced mothers. I want it to be more than a coffee klatch. The Church encourages families to accept children willing from God, and women are called to the vocation of marriage and motherhood along with all the other demands of the outside world. We need to provide some physical, emotional and spiritual support." Fr. Daley looked to Libby for a response.

Libby was speechless for a moment. Then she found her voice, "Wow, Father, I'm impressed that you thought of this. I've had fragments of those ideas floating around in my head for years."

"Would you be willing to take it on?" he asked earnestly.

"I have a few questions first. Will this only be for women from our church?"

"No, not necessarily. I would like the group to have a religious component, but it could be opened to any mothers and children who want to come."

"Will there be any money for this program?"

"Not much, but perhaps you could charge dues or look for grants or sponsors," he suggested.

"I like the idea of grants and sponsors. I'd also like to have a pantry of items mothers may need for their babies, but might not be able to afford." Libby had her chin in her hand. She was thinking about Jesse's family. "We could have free-will offerings for those who could afford it. I need to work out the details, but yes, I'd like to take it on. I won't be able to start right away. I'm going to Mexico on the Our Lady of Guadalupe pilgrimage for women that the Oblate Fathers are leading in a few weeks."

"That's fine. Thank you, so much Libby. My work here is done and yours is just beginning,"

"Not so fast, Father Daley. My first inclination is to have something like my friends and I had when we were young mothers. We called it the Mothers' Mass. Fr. Larry was our chaplain. This started twenty years ago, long before you came to St. Francis. The moms met twice a month on a weekday. Of course, they brought their children. We'd start in the nursery, where we'd say the Rosary and watch the children while each of us took turns going to Confession with Fr. Larry. Then we went into the church and Father said Mass for us. After Mass we'd go back to the nursery and have snacks or a potluck lunch. The mothers socialized and shared their troubles and their tricks of the trade. We became extended family for each other ..."

"You think that would be the best way to do this for the parish mothers?" Fr. Daley asked.

"Yes, I do. It really helped me, Sue Blakely and others," said Libby

"You'd need a priest for each meeting for about two hours," he said.

"Preferably the same priest, so the women can develop a relationship with their confessor, who could become their spiritual director if that is what they wanted."

"Give me some time slots to choose from and I'll be there," Fr. Daley promised.

On the way home in the van Libby had a conversation with God, "Well, that wasn't too subtle for me. Maybe this will help save the sanity of some of those new moms, and I could get my mothering or premature grandmothering fix." Thoughts scuttled through her mind. "This is gonna be great."

Looking out the window she started singing, *"Wait till the sun shines, Nellie, when the clouds go drifting by ..."*

Epilogue Six Months Later.

> *"Ride a cock horse to Banbury Cross.*
> *To see an old lady upon a white horse.*
> *Rings on her fingers and bells on her toes.*
> *She shall have music wherever she goes."*

Libby sang as she held three-year-old Robbie and bounced him on her knee. The little boy shrieked with delight. "Do again, Mom O. Do again!"

Libby gave him a hug. She breathed in the scent of baby shampoo in his hair and peanut butter and apples on his chubby hands. She beamed at him and held his hands for another horsey ride.

The door to the church nursery opened and two young women entered. Sandy, a short, very pregnant brunette told her companion, "My husband tried to force Robbie to eat peas, by actually putting them in his mouth and moving his jaws up and down. It was a mess! My husband ended up having an anxiety attack. I told him, 'That's it. We're never having peas again. They aren't worth it.'"

Sandy's willowy, blond companion, Beth laughed and said, "Sandy, what are you even doing here? You look like you're about pop any minute."

"Are you kidding!" Sandy said, "I would go to a ditch-digging party if it meant getting out of the house." She smiled and continued, "You know, this bunch helped me keep myself together through this pregnancy, and I'll need you all even more after the new baby comes."

"You've got me on speed dial for when you go into labor, right?" asked Beth.

"I've got you, Barb, Sheila and Mrs. O or 'Mom O' as Robbie likes to call her. I'll call the minute I know this baby is coming. Right Mrs. O?" Sandy said as she put her hand out to Robbie to help him down from Libby's knee.

"You betcha," said Libby. "Oh, and help yourselves to some cherries. I've had a bumper crop, which shocked me, since this is the tree's first year."

"Wow," said Beth, "are they ripe when they are so bright red? That is arterial blood red."

"Only Nurse Beth would make that comparison," said Sandy.

"Sorry," said Beth, "but I thought they were supposed to be really dark, almost black when they're ripe."

"They are an unusual color for Bing cherries," said Libby, "but they taste great. I don't ..."

Then Robbie wailed and pulled his hand away from his mother. "I don't want a baby," he shouted.

"It'll be fun," said Sandy, sounding like she was trying to convince herself as much as Robbie. She, too, was tired and getting teary.

"May I talk to Robbie for a minute?' Libby asked.

Sandy nodded. Robbie wiped his runny nose with the back of his hand and turned back to 'Mom O', "What?" he whimpered.

"I have a secret to tell you. Come here," she said putting her lips to his temple. "Do you remember when Brendan came in to play with you at church?"

"Yes, I like Brendan," Robbie said sniffling.

"He's like a big friend or a big brother, right?"

Robbie nodded. Libby continued whispering, "Your baby is going to like you the way you like Brendan. You'll be able to do things a baby can't do. That baby is going to think you are so smart and strong. He's going to like you more than you like Brendan. Your baby is going to love you, because you are the big brother."

Robbie had begun to smile, "Yeah," he said.

Sandy was amazed when Robbie walked over to her and took her hand. "What did you say to him, Mrs. O?"

Libby shook her head, "It's a secret that only Robbie can tell you, if he wants to. My lips are sealed." She mimed zipping her lips, locking them with a key and throwing the key away.

"Me, too." Robbie giggled as he zipped his lips, too.

"Okay, then," said Sandy with a smile and a nod of thanks to Libby, "let's have some lunch."

A woman named Sophia with curly black hair, a baby on her hip and a 4-year-old girl holding her hand came up to Libby. "Mama O, I got a question for you."

"Hello, Sophia," Libby said as she hugged her and kissed her cheek. "What's up?"

Sophia was the first in a queue of young women circling Libby to ask her questions or just to say hello. Libby was in her glory, loving and being loved.

Meanwhile, Fr. Larry received a surprising visit. A man in a pilot's uniform appeared at the door to Father's room and handed him a letter with an old-fashioned wax seal. The pilot bowed slightly and left. Fr. Larry's hands shook as he opened the letter.

Lawrence, dear Brother in Christ,

In the early morning darkness Brother Alerick was shot with a crossbow after he and his brothers received Communion at Mass. As the metal tip and wooden shaft of the arrow pierced his heart, he disintegrated into ashes. His habit remained.

An antique crossbow and four arrows were missing from the armory. The bow and three arrows were found in the vestibule of the chapel. David and the dog, Victor, are no longer at the Abbey. Our search for them this morning was in vain.

Attached to the arrow that killed Brother Alerick was a small piece of parchment. On it was written, Rom 7:24 ; Mt 5:7.

Keep a vigilant watch over Mrs. O'Malley.

Please burn this letter.

Prayerfully, Abbott Clement

Fr. Larry checked his Bible to verify the first verse exactly from the Letter of Paul to the Romans, Chapter 7 verse 24. Fr. Larry drew in a sharp breath as he read.

"What a wretched man I am. Who will save me from this body of death?"

Matthew's gospel Chapter 5 verse 7, Fr. Larry knew by heart.

"Blessed are the merciful, for they shall receive mercy."

Using the excuse that he had another appointment, Fr. Larry called Libby and asked her to move the date for her regular confession to the next day. He wanted to check on her right away.

After her confession Libby joined Fr. Larry in the retreat center's dining room for tea.

"So, I wanted to tell you, Fr. Larry," Libby said, "I have a date with a nice man I met."

Fr. Larry started and the color drained away from his face.

"You don't have to look so worried," Libby said with a laugh. "His mother introduced us before she died."

Fr. Larry raised his eyebrows.

"Mrs. Palmeri was one of my computer students at the library," Libby explained. "She finished her classes months ago, but before she left she introduced me to her son, Lucio. He's a stone mason. Anyway, last week Mrs. Palmeri passed away. I went to the funeral to pay my respects. I also sang in the choir at the funeral Mass. It was really old school. She was well into her eighties and an Italian immigrant. She had written out what she wanted at her funeral. She wanted the old Latin Mass. She even requested *Dies Irae*."

"I haven't heard that sung at a Mass in over fifty years," said Fr. Larry regaining some color, "sounds like she had good taste in music."

"The whole family seems to. After the burial, Lucio invited everyone back to his house for lunch. When I was leaving he asked me if I wanted to go to the Botanical Gardens next Saturday."

"I'm happy for you Libby, I hope you enjoy it."

"Oh, I'm sure I will. We're both big gardeners and morning people. We're going to leave early and try to be the first ones there when the gardens open. It's supposed to be a beautiful, sunny day."

Made in the USA
San Bernardino, CA
19 December 2018